Two Songs and Other Novellas

Stephen Verry

Contents

Two Songs

Chapter 1

When first setting out on my voyage from Nova Scotia to England, little did I know what new passion would soon so wholly consume me. The agreement with my father was clear: he wanted me to study economic theory and the practice of business. With that knowledge under my belt, I would return to assume my new post in his ceramic ware business. Yes, and what zeal my father had for his profession! Many a winter's evening we'd spent over our dining room table, discussing the pros and cons of this or that theory. Fondly, my father would use botanical analogies to show me how a business should expand. So, business—far from being dull—appeared to me the grandest of all life's pursuits. When spring at last rolled around, almost with a sense of mission, I set out for England.

Arriving in London, the city's greatness and pageantry appeared larger than life. All I had ever dreamed of greeted me round every street corner. The words of great luminaries echoed on, yet in the streets, I would dreamily stroll. The architecture matched these great thoughts—hard stone that tended upward, all built to last. Yes, days to remember, those few, with my head in the clouds... Soon enough, though, the industrial-age grit and discordant sounds—not part of my romanticized longings—began to eclipse these shining first impressions. For this, in fact, visible film coating stone and woodwork, represented London's present condition.

For not far from the business district, vast working-class boroughs sprawled out. Here lay a world of people determined to better their lot as London said no. This conflict appeared etched in the faces of both young and old as they trudged to their grimy mills for long days of toil. Then, too, London streets abounded with costermongers, as Londoners called them. They sold various small items quite cheaply, some even selling snails to the poor for food, of all things. As for those with no jobs, throngs of this underclass wandered about with no homes to return to. A few imaginative sorts turned to low-overhead enterprises for their daily bread. Called sewer hunters, they would pop up onto the streets with bits of scrap metal discovered below. How their faces would light up, both at the treasure in hand and the sight of the sun. I once saw one in the process of buying a fine top hat, apparently having saved for some time to do so. For the most part, though, this spectacle of human wretchedness existed far removed from the grand and genteel lives of a class set apart.

In this city within a city, I soon began my studies, my mind yet stirred by these vivid first impressions. At first, I immersed myself in books, relishing those evenings in our study hall where I burned the midnight oil, literally. For our library lamps used for fuel that emollient of the sea—whale oil. Then, one evening, while strolling home through still-bustling streets lit up with burning lamps, I paused to reflect. Yes, whales, through human agency, transmuted from life into light as their oil fueled welcome street lamps. At first, I pondered this in a positive sense, and, well, clearly, it represented a great good for our kind. But then I considered more deeply. Behind this basic act of providing light for lamps, a vast industry existed, although it had passed its heyday. From ports up England's eastern coast, ships would head out to sea in that age-old quest of man—a whaling voyage. This risky endeavor went back to the 10th century when sailors hunted these creatures first for food and second for baleen. Baleen was used to make various things, such as fishing rods, chairs, and corsets, among them. The oil was used for lamps back then as well.

Curiosity aroused in this way, on my first days off I decided to visit Hull, well north of London on the east coast, a major whaling center. Here I watched as ships hauled kills to dockside factories for dressing. A fascinating yet grisly sight, I will never forget seeing my first whale there. Dead, of course, it hardly impressed as a live one would. Yet even in death, this grey whale had a certain natural majesty—huge, slick corpse with a skyward-aimed eye still open, looking sad.

Later, I visited several shops which displayed and sold scrimshaw, a type of folk art made from whale bone or teeth. One immediately drew my attention. A curved whale tooth, light orange in color, it bore an intricate engraving of a three-masted ship. I began to envision the sailor-artist first fetching the tooth from the carcass, lovingly cleaning and maybe aging it for a time before beginning his project. Funny, it transformed the predator/prey relationship into something near transcendent. I considered at once my first thoughts of the whale being transformed into light for modern man, yet here the bond was intimate and personal rather than abstract.

I bought the piece and studied it on my way home. As the train clickity-clacked over the countryside, my imagination propelled me across the sea in the vessel the tooth portrayed. Ah yes, there's our whale, alive and at one with the waves rather than artificially mated to this handiwork. This image faded as the scrimshaw once again filled my eyes, representing something of the life of both its components—hunted and hunter.

Immersed again in my studies, I would occasionally look up from my book as images of my visit came to mind. At such moments, imagination swept me into a whole new life, one with no boundaries on the open sea. Together with my mates, we scoured the high seas for whales. Yes, what could be a more fitting prey to slake man's ancient hunting instinct on? What other creature approximated the design and speed of this summit of our craft and knowledge—a grand sailing ship? A whale hunt was no ordinary hunt as two behemoths clashed—first creature of the seas and subduer of continents. In this life-and-death struggle, they challenged each other for supremacy of the globe.

Clearly, these flights of fancy bore an extravagance tinged with violence, with not much empathy for the object of the hunt. Perhaps this reflected in part the era I lived in. For in the year 1848, revolution swept the continent. The downtrodden classes, having reached their limit of endurance, simply exploded. Governments struck back with predictable fury, crushing this short-lived upheaval. At this time, many a gentleman in London looked over his shoulder while out for a stroll. England, they mused, must never succumb to this pox.

Torn then, as I was, between the role my father wanted me to assume and the gulf that accepting it would create between me and the bulk of humanity, more and more I turned to thoughts of the limitless sea. Here, as ships left port and the moorings of culture behind, lay the most primary symbol of the freedom humanity longs for. Here, distinctions between classes blur as sea and sky soak into our very fiber.

So off I would go to Hull during breaks in my studies, talking to seamen to get a sense of their world. Wary at first, they soon smiled while relating seafaring adventures. No easy task awaits the men who hunt down whales, one assured me. These creatures wander the sea at will, as free as free, while we men force thoughts and emotions through channels of habit. To succeed, he confided while leaning forward, a man must throw off such shackles and think as a whale. When we succeed in doing so, we find what we seek.

Back in London, these and other words began to sink in. During strolls along the Thames, a new thought world took root. Ordinary barges began to appear as floating worlds, at least temporarily cut off from the mass of contradictions men on dry land live in. As I sat down to watch, images and sensations of my voyage to England returned. Experienced anew in the light of perspective, I processed them more fully. At the time, it had seemed a mere ride of sorts, one that a doting parent places a child on. But now, that world of rolling, endless horizon spoke of hopes unbound.

This feeling later drove me back to Hull. Once there, for some obscure reason, I decided to actually tour the processing plant. The thought of cutting up an animal troubled me not, having, with my father, dressed deer numerous times. And yet, as I watched a magnificent specimen savagely reduced to consumables, at last it registered: these creatures themselves draw forth my heart and imagination. How does one comprehend their presence off our settled coasts, these creatures of the fore-world? The sea, much more than a vast stretch of water, is in reality another world entirely. As such, laws govern it, too. True, these creatures roam the sea in a freedom unknown to us, and yet, as residents of a world apart, they too must conform to certain laws.

On my next outing, I made a clean break from Hull and its whalers and processing plant. Instead, I went to Cornwall for the first time. A classmate had recommended Porthcurno Beach at the tip of the Penwith Peninsula. In summer, the weather proved clear and bright. As I walked down the steps leading to the sheltered beach, a hillside to my right abutted a calm, open sea capped with a sky stretched out to create a horizon. Beauty of this magnitude nourishes the soul. So, as I sat down in the sand and intently took in the horizon, this thought hit home: I love the sea and how it interacts with those who live by it or on it. The most cherished of my childhood memories mingled with this sight of sky and sea. How this had always been the dominant theme of my life, without my full awareness, now seemed as unfathomable a mystery as the wonder beheld. I knew just then that pursuing my ends in an office would no longer do—the sea my proper world.

Back in London, I confided my new feelings with a trusted classmate, John Austin. At first, he laughed and thought my change of heart a symptom of some malady. Yet as he listened to my new narration, he turned misty-eyed and confessed: he too longed to somehow escape from the world of his parents and strive for new horizons. An avid reader, he mentioned Matthew Fontaine Maury, an American gaining acclaim for his exploration of the world's oceans. Beginning as a naval officer, with ambition and insight, he turned his love of the sea into the practical and emerging science of oceanography. Through an ingenious study of ship's logs, he was able to tentatively establish the fact that vast currents move the earth's oceans so as to make them resemble immense interconnected rivers rather than huge static lakes. Not only that, he added, by using ship's logs from whaling ships, he had established the fact that these creatures too move about their vast world in predictable ways, contradicting age-old beliefs. He also told me of England's own Edward Forbes and his explorations in marine biology. Gradually growing, according to him, was a need for the modern world to more scientifically approach the study of the ocean and its manifold life forms. He told me too that the University of Cornwall now sought to organize study of this nature into a formal department. My latest trip connected with this comment in an almost organic way. Instantly, I faced the horizon of a new future, or at least the possibility of one.

From that day on, I began to actively resist the currents that carried me to a preordained future. At first, only in symbolic ways, like sketching ocean scenes on lecture notes, later my rebellion would become overt with the skipping of classes. Not long able to endure the strain and self-destruction of this state, I resolved to approach my Uncle Theodore with the issue. A practical man of business, he would likely try and convince me of the error of my ways. Even so, I had sensed in his beaming smile and genial nature a man who would at least listen.

So then, after a fine Sunday supper, at first haltingly, I began to relate my change of heart. When he raised no objections and actually listened, it all came out in an inspired torrent: my visits to

Hull, my reflections, and finally my Porthcurno Beach revelation. Upon summing up my case, I awaited his harsh judgment. Instead, he poured me another glass of sherry and took out a cigar. Strangely, though, he eyed it with disgust and put it back in his pocket. Curiosity overcame fear as I tactfully asked him about what he had just done. With a sigh, he said that in fact, he had never really enjoyed smoking cigars, the habit rather taken up as one would a ritual. In business, he said, the smoking of cigars symbolizes fellow feeling and success. With this remarkable confession out of the way, he went on to say that passion trumped convention and wholeheartedly endorsed my proposed new plan of action.

Near ecstatic, my blood cooled at the sobering realization that I must still convince my father that marine biology had a future—no easy task this, considering his ironclad attachment to business. A father so inspired would naturally wish with all his heart to pass the torch on to his son. Yet fate had favored me in one small way, as I did have a younger brother. Could it be that Carl might make just as fine a first mate as I might have? He did have talent and a desire to succeed. Through default, then, by my falling into another sphere of the universe altogether, his star might rise to a new height. Yes, first of all, I must confide my change of heart to him and so perhaps have a Trojan horse of sorts in the fortress when I attacked in earnest.

Unfortunately, it helped little when I at last broke the news to my father in a long and impassioned letter. The reply I received, while written on mere paper, contained words more suitable for granite tablets. In no uncertain terms, he related his abiding concern for my welfare and went on to say that no man with a taste for his own survival would make an experimental vocation his life's goal. In the end, it took Uncle Theodore's intervention to break this logjam. As a fellow businessman, my father had to listen. He assured him then that this new science was no trifle but rather the wave of the future. Science of all stripes now and in generations to come would transform human life, he added. Not only that, he summed it up, those who got on board early would be assured of high positions in the future. This apparently did the trick.

So began my own experience of reformation and renewal— no easy task at first, this raising up of a new thought world. Even so, my studies at the University of Cornwall acted wonderfully to clarify my new goals, here at last a subject to pour my whole heart into. My classmates as well helped me greatly. They proved to be intensely individual in nature. In fact, visionaries of sorts, they had dedicated themselves to a deepened understanding of the world in the face of daunting obstacles. These new friendships drew me into a whole new society of sorts, as with great animation we discussed our perceptions and goals after hours over beer. This quaffing and backslapping proved almost as needful as lectures, here where the abstract turned face to face real. Moments of solitude also helped reinforce my new sense of self. Often, I walked the beaches of Cornwall alone, especially in autumn. On one such occasion, while looking out to sea, it hit me with force: Somewhere, somewhere over that vast horizon, where sea met sea and sky capped all, I would find what I ardently sought.

Chapter 2

The next several years blended into one integrated unit of learning. Imperceptibly, yet perceptibly, my mind and mode of expression took on new forms. As my classmates and I walked on the beaches of Cornwall, we viewed them in a new light, understanding something of their hidden life. And yet, as ever, the unitary face of the deep held us spellbound—the whole greater than the sum of its parts. The species the sea contained, like actors on a stage, together told one compelling story—the main actors, for me, the sea's great whales. They most perfectly embodied the sea's essence, giving it form, thought, and voice. To understand the whale was, in my estimation, to understand its world.

All of these impressions together prepared me for the day I unexpectedly received a fellowship that funded one full year of independent research. My work, it appeared, had come to the attention of our Dean and the review panel. When Dean Ruskin then asked me what the subject of my study would be, I unhesitatingly said *whales*. When he asked for specifics, my answer proved less clear. I did mention Maury's work on ocean currents in relation to what we knew of whale migration. His face lit up as he saw possibilities. Even so, fine details evaded me at the moment. These would occur to me only later, as I grappled with the concrete rather than the theoretical. Yet for then, the keenest of pleasures carried me off into various fanciful scenes—the grant representing a great personal triumph.

At last, I decided the Pacific Ocean would be my goal, and the grey whale my object of study, thus combining two fascinating variables: the now imperfectly understood concept of ocean currents, and whale migration. I theorized that whales, on some level aware of these currents, in fact made use of them in their migrations. As preparation for my study, I pored over all the information available to me, relying greatly on Maury's research. And so, with many a fond farewell, I once again found myself seaward bound aboard a renowned Yankee clipper. Those sturdy modern ships made such travel safer and faster. Even so, my voyage would prove an adventure.

I begin my journal en route. Observations mostly routine, I try to note prevailing wind patterns—doubly so when we round Cape Horn and enter the Pacific. I had theorized on our Atlantic crossing that its twin on the other side of South America would not be notably different in appearance and feel. This theory proves inaccurate, as in fact, each face of the sea reflects its own hemisphere, latitude, and atmospheric conditions. Strikingly, horizons expand as weather conditions improve and waves smooth out—making the Pacific look vaster, at least in my mind. As well, it appears more translucent than its cousin, at least in particular stretches. But then, looking straight ahead and envisioning my goal of coastal Alaska, my thoughts surge towards their goal.

And yet, an unforeseen event occurs as we sail off the coast of Vancouver Island, me having transferred to a fur trading ship. Our captain announces we will be dropping anchor at Nootka Sound for provisions. The name sets off several associations. Nootka Sound and its Friendly Cove is where Captain Cook dropped anchor in 1778. Yet first, as he had headed for a cove opposite Friendly Cove, the natives, in their language, told him to go around and drop anchor in their cove. And so the name *Friendly Cove,* as the friendly natives guided them in—*Nootka* in their tongue meaning *go around...* or so the story has it. The name stuck—to the inhabitants as well as the sound—with most now referring to them as the Nootka. They are, among other things, whaling folk.

It then hit me like a thunderclap. Just possibly, I might enhance my study by including the observations and impressions of this obscure people. In fact, likely an elaborate lore exists relating to their whaling culture. Not only that, but here also is a chance to observe my object of study up close. Lastly, I recall what John had said before I left England—something to the effect that improvisation forms the core of field studies. That clinches it. I will stop here for a time and see what happens.

Next morning, I step ashore and first get my bearings as our captain heads for the village. Friendly Cove is on the southern tip of Nootka Island. The inlet proceeds northeasterly into Vancouver Island proper, while branching into sub-inlets. I sight Bligh Island in the sheltered waters near me. Off in the distance, on the island proper, as rain clouds rise snow-capped peaks appear. The inlet waters—calm and expansive, hint at a profusion of life concealed in their depths. I next sight a long hoped for event. About two hundred yards off, the water begins to churn as a glistening arc appears, plume of vapor following. An arced back proceeds downward as a large curved tail vanishes with a flap and a ripple, my first whale sighting. Breathlessly I smile while my heart pounds away. I have made the right decision.

Not knowing the species just sighted, I resolve to find out. Likewise, I must learn as much as possible about its population. Whaling in this Western Pacific region is not nearly as intense as on the Atlantic coast, and yet still represents a force to be reckoned with. Right whales have almost vanished, while humpback, blue, and finback populations are known to be declining. Much of this stems from the shoddy methods of hunting and retrieval. Between 50 and 80 percent of whales killed end up on the ocean floor rather than in processing plants.

Having no real information on native whaling methods, I am unsure what to think. Still, likely enough their take is low compared to white whalers. I wonder, though, at their success rate and how many whales may be wasted. Then too, while non-native whalers still hunt whales more or less haphazardly—Maury's study and information still largely unknown to them—maybe the natives have a store of customary knowledge that helps them in their hunts.

All now begins to percolate in my mind. Lacking the time and resources to deal with all these variables, my newly conceived study must nevertheless include man in relation to the species just sighted—our effect on whales much too great to ignore. And, with whaling an age-old tradition, this effect has become ingrained over time. Then too, what other types of human/whale interaction might exist? While not much has ever been said of this, a well-known folklore of sorts surrounds its cousin the dolphin. Even in tales related to me at Hull this came out, with colorful accounts of men rescued by these creatures. Might there be an ever-so-tenuous affinity between man and whale that has been blunted by the hunt?

Almost trembling with excitement, striving for calm, I turn my attention to the land. Streaming clouds break as sun illuminates rain-drenched vegetation. All around looms primeval forest—some of the species familiar. Here cedar, hemlock, alder, and spruce, among others, thrive. And yet this forest is denser, and the trees larger, thick moss coating their trunks. Stepping into its fastness, moist, spongy ground gives way to footfall. I touch various ferns and note mushrooms growing nearby—huge slugs on a few. Evidently, a type of rainforest, only its northerly locale limits the tree and animal species to familiar ones.

"Is your name Daniel Evans?"

I practically jump upon hearing this unexpected voice from behind. Turning to face the man, I see he is one of the natives. Tallish and stocky, he wears a fibrous type of shawl around his upper torso and a garment with designs on it that reaches below his knees. Broad-faced, his curved and well-formed nose bears a ring. He wears his long dark hair in many small braids with beads at their ends and has a thin mustache. Most striking are his deep brown eyes and expressive brow. I begin to frame the man in his natural setting—lush forest and rich sea. Something clicks. He returns my look with a calm and intelligent regard.

"Yes. How did you know my name?"

"Your captain told me. He said you need a Nuu-chah-nulth who speaks English."

"Um, a Nuu-chah-nulth?"

"Yes, the name of my tribe—a name your people made shorter by calling us Nootka."

"Ah yes, I see. But um, your nickname—the Nootka—it is more widely known by my people. May I use your nickname in my writings?"

"In your writings?"

"Yes, all part of my study of whales."

"So… you came here to study… our whales."

I note the emphasis on *our*. His formerly placid expression now shows a tinge of suspicion. Perhaps they have had past problems related to whaling.

"Yes, I did come here to study, ah, your whales."

"Why do you want to study our whales? Are you a white whale hunter?"

"No, I am not. But to be honest, I once knew men in England who did hunt whales."

This answer does little to ease his suspicions. I will somehow have to make my real mission clear to him.

"Did they hunt many whales?"

"Um, well, yes, actually they did—and still do. In fact, they have hunted so many that whales are disappearing from English coasts."

His scowl informs me I'm on the wrong track.

"Ah, but you see, my mission is to learn about whales for their own good. Those in my science know that we humans cannot continue to hunt whales the way we do now. We must allow the whales freedom to multiply again."

"So, you want the Nuu-chah-nulth to stop our whale hunts…"

"I didn't quite say that… But look, try to understand—um, what is your name?"

"Makanta."

"Yes, try and understand, Makanta, that I did not come here to interfere with the lives of your people. I came only to study whales."

He audibly sighs and looks to the ground. After a minute or so, he looks up. The expression on his face almost hurts me to look at.

"You are too late, Daniel Evans, to not interfere in the lives of my people. You are too late. Go at once. I do not want to talk to you. I do you a favor. You would not like what you hear. I think you are a good man. No, you would not like what you hear…"

Taken aback by the darkness of the emotion expressed, I almost prepare to leave. But no—I am here for a valid reason: the study of whales, mainly, but also to learn about the people connected with them.

"I would like to hear your story, Makanta. Will you tell me your story?"

He looks at me long and hard, at last deciding to unburden himself.

"The downfall of my people, Daniel Evans, began with Captain Cook's discovery of us. The Nuu-chah-nulth thought it was a great event and a time to make discoveries of our own. Your Captain Cook treated us kindly—often he laughed and told stories with hand movements. And so we liked him and showed him our ways. Later, the Spanish would come and claim our land. The Spanish did not treat us well. Once, when our great chief Callicum boarded one of their ships with a gift of salmon for its captain, he was insulted and shot through the heart."

"Ah, but Makanta, the Spanish are notorious for their cruelty. They treat many people badly, even people in Europe."

Makanta listens in silence, sensing rivalry in my comment. Then he continues.

"The English challenged the Spanish and claimed this land. Our lives and our presence were ignored by both nations as they fought over rights to our island. The English won this struggle. We believed the English would treat us more fairly, but they did not. Once, the captain of a trading ship accused the Nuu-chah-nulth of stealing some nails from his ship. As the visitors got into their boat and left for home, he ordered his men to shoot. Nineteen men were killed. Other English captains treated the Nuu-chah-nulth badly. Reaching the limit of our endurance, our great chief Maquinna attacked an English ship and fought with the crew. He took two prisoners who lived with us for two years. One of them wrote a story that brought us more unwanted attention."

"Your account of that captain's conduct overwhelms me, Makanta."

"That was only the beginning, Daniel Evans. In the next thirty years, the English brought unknown diseases to my people. These diseases killed a great many of us. Yes, Daniel Evans, many died beyond counting. The full fifteen nations of the Nuu-chah-nulth at the time of Captain Cook are no more. Our settlement here at Friendly Cove is a shadow of what it was in the years of our glory. So now you come here to study our whales. I will tell you a truth: as whales became less numerous off our lands, the Nuu-chah-nulth dwindled in numbers. So, tell me now with truth, Daniel Evans— why do you want to study *our* whales?"

Taken aback by his tale, I look to the sea. Almost, I want to board my ship and never return, while at the same time knowing myself somehow bound to this region—at least for a time. Makanta embodies his land and much more. I am honor-bound to come to a fuller understanding of him, his people, and the creatures that connect to their lives, the whale primary amongst these. And so, a new thought hits me. Reaching into my shoulder bag, I take out my most cherished possession.

"Makanta, I want to give you a gift. It is the tooth of a great whale. The etching on it was made by a man in England who hunts them."

Eyeing the scrimshaw, Makanta extends a hand to accept it. He examines it closely, fingertips tracing the ship. Then he jabs the point into his palm and smiles, instantly grasping the essence of design and raw nature. Finally, he nods appreciatively and gestures to a canoe by the water.

"Come, Daniel Evans. Let me show you my world. Oh, and to answer your question—yes, you may use our nickname, the Nootka, in your writings."

Taking me to a canoe on the beach, we both get in. He asks me if I have ever been in such a craft. I say no, but that I can manage.

We begin to paddle across the inlet entrance. Broken clouds stream by, crash into distant mountains, and flow over them like a wave. Calm water reflects the sun in a pleasing way. We reach the opposite shore. Makanta points out Resolution Cove, where Captain Cook landed in 1778. A lovely but otherwise unremarkable sight, I try to picture the HMS *Resolution* anchored there. Amazingly, my imagination—for a moment—fills the scene with a majestic vessel. Perhaps a trace of the man lingers on in the enclaves he once keenly surveyed.

We then paddle up the narrows between the shore and Bligh Island. Something about easing over water between two shores creates an expectant mood. Gulls circle overhead. I spot two eagles perched in an island tree. Fearlessly they watch us as we paddle. One takes off, its circular flight over the water a wonder to behold. Back on its perch next to the other, I'm left to wonder at the meaning of its flight.

As we reach the far tip of Bligh Island, a vast inlet opens to our east. Makanta, though, turns north. We round the island only, not entering those mysterious waters. As we now head in a southerly direction and face the open sea on our right, the mood changes. Beyond the inlet's mouth, the Pacific Ocean surges into these sheltered waters. I almost get the sense of a gargantuan natural engine generating its own movement—and the weather to a large extent. It feels as if we paddle near a huge and invisible wave. At first, this unsettles me as I consider what prevailing winds brought ashore for these people. But then its elemental aspect hits home. The spirit of this world depends on that endless and ultimately refreshing influx of airs from vast Pacific stretches. These mild airs ensure a mild coastal climate in winter—and copious rain.

At last, Makanta takes me to his village, a small and rather forlorn settlement of cedar log houses. He takes me into his own. Appearing at first small and drab, his wife's welcoming smile warms the air and expands its dimensions somewhat. As we eat, Makanta tells me of the village in its glory days, and what it once meant to visit his great chief Maquinna.

The guest would be taken into a huge cedar log lodge. The vast interior space had racks above on which salmon dried. On the far wall were skins filled with whale oil—a symbol of power and wealth. In the center was a carved wooden likeness of a deity: human-faced, dragon-like at the neck, and with eagle claws. Other guests sat on log benches along the side walls. The Chief and his circle would enter. A robust man, Maquinna walked with calm purpose. He wore a robe of skins over his shoulders and a fibrous hat on his head, cone-shaped with a domed top. It depicted a whaling scene. Men gathered around him, those of high rank closest. He would next beckon for the feast to begin. Guests would dine on whale meat and other dainties, too. All wore fibrous clothing—a type of dress down to the knees, with beautiful geometric patterns. They would sing as a man in a dark fur robe began to dance—the village shaman. No ordinary dance, it told a story in gestures. In its intricacies, whales would emerge.

Later, lying alone in a dim guest room, sleep evades me— images of the day in my mind still so lively. As well, my bed of ferns, while comfortable enough, still feels a bit rough. But then, as I adjust, one thought takes over—that of vast new horizon.

Chapter 3

The next day dawns with falling rain. Only half-awake, the sound smooths my edge. Makanta, touching my shoulder, says breakfast is ready—this wakes me up. His gentle and attractive wife graciously serves me first. I thank her and eat. Makanta and I have a chat, but then fall silent. Here, I note they both appear the right age for children, and yet have none. I wonder at this but say nothing. Maybe children will come later, as the village once again prospers.

Prosperity of old had meant whales. I venture to ask about their ancient whaling customs. Roused from his silence, Makanta tells me that before a whale hunt, Chief Maquinna would seclude himself on a mountaintop all day, singing and praying to the spirits for a successful hunt. He would fast for the next two days, appearing gloomy and hardly speaking to anyone. He wore a large red token made of bark around his neck, and a branch on his head as a sign of abasement, all while shaking a rattle.

His crew, as well, would observe a one-week fast before the hunt. They bathed several times a day, sang, and rubbed their bodies with broken shells to the point of bleeding. They also abstained from relations with their wives—this was all considered a prerequisite for success. I thoughtfully digest his account and wonder what it all means. He tells me spirits inhabit all things. He further states that particular spirits befriend particular men—these spirit allies help them succeed in the hunt. When I ask for clarification, he briefly says they will invoke a whale spirit.

Here, several things click. Like my friends at Hull, these men identify with their quarry. Yet they carry this identification several steps further—as it transposes into spirit. In a sense, the Nootka become the animal they hunt. Killing their prey wouldn't produce the same feeling for them as, say, an Englishman shooting a stag on his estate. Some kind of near-mystical union must take place.

At this point, qualms arise. I had come here to study whales scientifically, and yet I'm now drawn into something else altogether. How might I successfully relate the human factor to the natural one? In what sense might a whale identify with a human? And even if they do feel some affinity for humans, what would that prove about their life in the wild? Yet another thought occurs: just what is the nature of the wilds they inhabit today? Yes, various species compete with one another—but what about the bigger picture? Might not humans, through the simple act of observation, somehow alter or mingle with a whale's natural rhythms and mode of life? And this aside from issues of the hunt. Might not this principle include all of the natural world humans inhabit? A far-fetched notion at first—it sinks in and begins to gain credence.

The next morning, Makanta proudly informs me that a whale hunt will take place in seven days. He further tells me I've been invited to be one of the seven men to man a beautiful cedar boat—a great honor. This catches me off guard. Yes, I did have a strong affinity for whale hunters. The tales they told me at Hull combine with the mystique of Makanta's tribe to awaken this faded attraction. Even so, by profession and true temperament, I now want only to observe these creatures and learn as much as possible about them. The thought of actually going out in a boat to harpoon a whale repels me. Instantly, I mask my true feelings and thoughtfully observe him. Excited to include me in this great honor, Makanta cannot conceive of a negative answer. So, I assume a more detached mode and begin asking him questions about the nature of the hunt.

Makanta first tells me that naturally, their chief will lead it. As we speak, he says, the chief begins his ritual purification. The hunt, while a hugely physical effort, ultimately depends on the strict observance of ritual and the spiritual forces it will elicit. The chief must be especially careful here—success or failure of the hunt affects his reputation. His is both a spiritual and a social role. He must show that the whale spirit works for him in order to remain a strong leader. Makanta goes on to say that the crew too must be scrupulous in their preparations. He urges me to begin my fast and points to the spot reserved for our daily purification rituals. Seeing that refusal would crush him, I manage a smile and say yes. With a satisfied grunt and a slap on my back, he leads me to the stream. We strip down and enter, at first repeatedly pouring water over ourselves.

Next, the painful shell-scraping begins. This will take time to get used to. My white skin shows the scrapes and abrasions much more than my companions'. They find this somewhat amusing, and one makes a remark in his tongue. I ask Makanta what he says. He hesitates, then tells me he said that I am as white as a dead fish. I frown, then smile, and continue my scraping.

Later, we douse ourselves with water again and make imitation whale movements. Makanta tells me this is very important, and to focus my mind on whales as I do. I think then of the whale first sighted here, over and over. This has an unusual effect. I begin to imagine myself as that same whale swimming out to sea. Out on the open ocean, I rise to the surface again to massively exhale before plunging into the depths. At first, the sea, suffused with light, orients me—but then the depths darken. How do I see? How do I know what is around me? How do I communicate with my fellows? Do we proceed blindly, or does some mysterious mechanism guide us on? Later, having my fill of the dim vastness, I surface again for air and light.

Our scraping at last concluded, our fast proves more painful than that. Longingly, we watch as others dig into their evening meal, while we eat only greens. After this spare meal, we rest for the evening. This austere routine repeated for six more days, we then prepare for the hunt.

The massive cedar boat—about twenty-seven feet long—its carved prow grinning, looks out to sea as we board it and shove off. Each man has a specific task to fulfill: one in charge of lines and floats, one diver, one lance man, several rowers, and of course the chief-harpooner. All wear conical hats, save for the chief, his being domed. The boat is laden with rope and floats made from seal air-bladders. Paddling arduously, we make our way to the open sea. Spring sky radiant, we rise and fall with the waves. My companions glisten with sweat as they pour their all into this work. A forceful, rhythmic song breaks out as, in their minds, they picture the sought-after whale.

Fortune favors us greatly that day as the cry goes out: a whale spout appears on the western horizon. Intuiting the direction of our submerged quarry, the chase begins. Unaware—or unconcerned—by our presence, the whale rises again for breath as our chief, with an effort that twists him from head to toe, throws his harpoon. Finding its mark, I almost hear a cry of pain as downward the whale plunges. Rope hisses while the coil unravels, taking it and a string of floats out to sea. And so it begins.

Despite its wound, the whale harnesses all of its primeval strength for this fateful struggle. With force, it dives and emerges for air, striving to dislodge the harpoon. With an enormous splash and swirls of water, again it plunges into the depths. Our crew responds by likewise mustering strength. The chief, energized and animated, shouts directives and encouragement. Oarmen paddle valiantly to keep us on an even keel. Our diver helps with various tasks as the moment demands. Our line man makes adjustments, taut line with floats acting as a telegraph wire that transmits the whale's strength and spirit to us. Our boat foams at the prow as the whale hauls us seaward.

Hours pass in this way. The whale must begin to tire, I think, and yet our forward speed remains constant. Our profusion of sweat and emotion flows on, but something else struggles to surface. I look first at the fighting Nootka—muscles contour bodies as faces show a mix of strain and determination. The whale hauls not only our boat but the men's emotional state as well. I begin to sense how they must continue to struggle in order to succeed. If the whale slowed its efforts at this point, the effect would actually be negative on the crew. The whale could take advantage of this laxity and possibly slip away.

At the same time, if the whale mustered some great burst of force, it might shake the tenuous stability of our current mood and succeed in losing the harpoon. As it is, while our boat rides swells, our spirits likewise ride a wave—our object now to maintain our position on that interior or spirit wave, so to speak. If we lose our balance, we lose the whale.

My astonishment only grows as night descends. Our fight continues unabated as clouds blow in and it begins to rain. We welcome this rain as it refreshes while trickling down strained and overheated muscles. The sound of falling drops combines with the swish of our prow, punctuated by the splashes of a lunging whale.

Next day, as the sun rises, our mood begins to change. Strain and sleeplessness combine to gradually draw us into some other type of consciousness. The men begin to sing. I wonder at the words and want to ask Makanta what they mean. But no—this is no time to play the researcher. To do that now might shatter the mood and adversely affect our hunt. Rather, I begin to imagine what the words might mean and conclude it's an invocation of the whale spirit. Yes, that must be so, as listening, I picture in my mind the whale swimming below.

And so my focus shifts from men to whale. As I imagine the loneliest time in my life, that feeling multiplies by a factor of ten and transfers to the whale. In truth, what more desolating experience can there be than to struggle for one's life alone at sea? For while social creatures, we cannot see or sense other whales around. It could be that a whale engaged in a life-and-death struggle instinctively acts to draw off the threat from the herd by heading off alone. While only speculation, it nevertheless makes sense to me. At this point, my heart goes out to this magnificent, suffering creature. I brush away tears and hope that none have observed them.

Late at night, the rain stops and welcome stars come out. Combined with song and swish of waves, the effect mesmerizes. A massive contradiction emerges. This creature is in pain and yet is not, as collectively we induce a rare form of consciousness where raw physicality recedes into the background. The sea, reflecting dim starlight, bears ours and the whale's spirit in its medium. The sea itself has become a conduit for our vicarious experience of *whaleness*.

Next day, the mood shifts yet again as our prey starts to tire. The Nootka continue to sing, the force of the song taking over. At first dismissed as an unnecessary cultural appendage to the hunt, I now begin to understand otherwise. The song becomes the hunt and flows from men to whale. In my imagination, I see the whale actually listening—and somehow taking comfort in it. This interchange goes on throughout the whole day and then on into the night. At this point, I begin to lose my own sense of self, as starlit night and wind become my own boundaries.

Then, on the third day, something has changed. The speed of our boat has grown slower, while stronger grows our song. And so I sense, beneath the whale's flesh and bone, its quivering spirit turning neutral in its disposition toward life and death. I think here of one of my first impressions in England. The whale transmutes from life to light as men consume its oil—part of the chain of being that firmly binds all. Perhaps, then, this suffering creature dimly grasps its impending transformation.

By the end of this third day, we draw close enough to the exhausted whale for our lancer to spring into action. With a long, sharp lance, he slashes the whale's most vulnerable parts. Bleeding profusely now, the sea for a time turns to blood—and then it is over. Our diver enters the sea and sews the whale's mouth shut to keep it air-filled and buoyant. With great relief, we begin the long trip back to Nootka Sound.

The trip back, while anticlimactic, yet has drama of its own, as in fact we have been hauled much farther out to sea than the Nootka normally paddle. Not only that—the free ride is over. Instead of being towed, we must now tow our whale behind us. Drained bodies must somehow muster the force to paddle like never before. So, not only is the right spiritual disposition necessary for success, but also the very heartiest of men. While no slouch in this regard, it becomes clear to me that my more sheltered life has not produced a dynamo of a body. Makanta notes my sweat and strain with a smile. At least he appears pleased by it all—but then, I smile too.

Our rowing continues under a mixed night sky of cloud and stars. This time, though, the rain chills bodies and adds to our strain. With great relief, all eyes turn to the stars when they appear.

Turning to our whale, I note, as at Hull, the skyward-turned eye. Open still, much to my amazement, it catches starlight. I had imagined that in death the eye dims. But no—this eye shines on yet, the effect sad and touching.

Next day, we haul the whale up on the beach at Friendly Cove. Late afternoon—our arrival is timely. All in the village turn out to welcome us back. The chief, proud as a peacock, stands at the head of the whale and gives a speech. Done, the villagers set about the task of cutting up our haul. A grey whale—much of its blubber will be rendered into oil, the remainder to be eaten. The chief doles out the choicest slabs to those highest in the tribal hierarchy. All, however, receive a portion. Lastly, with song and prayer, they thank the spirits for bringing them success.

As we join all in a festive supper, I cannot help but get caught up in the joyous mood. True, a whale has died. And, while absolutely unable to prove it, I imagine this whale's fellows in some way know of its death and grieve its passing. The sea too feels just a fraction less full as I gaze out on it. Even so, this whale's death means life to these seafaring folk—and more than mere life. The very fabric of their social and spiritual being is interwoven with the life of the whale. Life, in fact, transmutes to light—the light in Nootka eyes.

Chapter 4

Only the next day does the extent of our ordeal begin to hit home. Aching from head to toe, I realize now the sheer physicality of what we had done. Our four-day struggle had us exerting ourselves without relent—though I must confess to taking breaks. How had we managed this feat?

White whalers, too, endure sea and storm and hardship, but nothing like this. With a relatively spacious craft and ample food, I see English whalers now as several layers removed from both sea and quarry. Meanwhile, the Nootka man a long boat that, face to face, exposes them to the sea and the action of whales.

In fact, I wonder now how many Nootka might have perished in pursuit of their livelihood. Fishermen and whalers from my parts face considerable risk in this regard—how much more for men mere inches from the sea's ragged edge? And yet, in the end, the hardships of our crew pale in comparison to what our whale had endured.

Here I think again of the whale that had greeted me upon my arrival. Was it a permanent resident of the sound? Did it pause in the midst of migration? Or had it arrived from some other point to take up temporary residence here?

After breakfast, Makanta listens intently as I explain my next goal. When I tell him of the whale I'd sighted, his eyes flash with emotion. Perhaps it has never occurred to him to look for a whale merely to watch, but clearly, he finds the idea intriguing. Perhaps, as well, he hopes to learn more about them. So, we board his canoe and head out.

All morning we paddle about, staying close to Bligh Island. The spring sun shines brightly. I see and sense much life below the surface of the water. As we approach the mouth of that deep and mysterious inlet to the east, we spot it—a swirling mass in the sea punctuated with rising and falling dorsal fins.

I gaze in excitement and ask Makanta about this. Without undue emotion, he names them orcas and says they go about in seaborne packs. He goes on to depict them as dolphin-like in appearance and says they will attack and eat a variety of creatures, both large and small.

Holding our position steady, I watch in fascination as that mass of seaborne carnivores mills about the entrance of the inlet for some time. No random movement, I conclude—something we cannot observe explains their behavior. Perhaps some creature or other has drawn their attention. I conclude, too, that I must get a closer look to determine just what it might be.

The next day, we return to the inlet. From a distance, with binoculars, I watch its entrance for signs of life. Water reflecting sunlight smooths out my mood. When a frenzy of activity erupts, I am almost unprepared. The orcas reappear and energetically move towards a small beach.

Then I spot it—a whale, in the midst of a desperate struggle, actually beaches itself. The orcas continue to mill about but then seek deeper water. Collecting our wits, we swiftly paddle for the small beach.

How astonishing to land right next to a beached whale. Labored breaths it takes, while its eyes madly rotate. About thirty feet long, black-skinned and white-bellied, with a small dorsal fin and two large, pointed flippers, it appears to be a female minke whale.

In wonder, we just take it in. Makanta moves close and gently strokes its side. Strangely enough, this calms the whale in the midst of its struggle. At first fixated on its large and animated eye, I do likewise—and the whale calms down even more. The odd sounds it makes gradually fade.

For several more minutes, we continue thus, completely absorbed in our efforts. But then it occurs to me: time runs out for this creature. The longer it remains beached, the less likely it is to survive. I tell Makanta we must return to the village and tell everyone what has happened. It will take many men to get this whale back into the water.

We next man our canoe and paddle off in all due haste.

The villagers quickly respond when Makanta speaks. Some grab knives, and others lances. With great emotion, I wave my arms and shout "No!"—but am ignored. Makanta intervenes, telling them we must not kill the whale and that I want to save it.

At first appearing puzzled, Makanta adds that it will be good to help the whale back into the sea, as all will thus drink of its spirit. Grasping his message, they drop their knives and man canoes for the trip over.

One last thing occurs to me before we shove off—I ask Makanta to tell all to bring improvised shovels with them. Again puzzled, he complies when I say I'll explain all when we arrive. Shrugging, they comply and we set out.

Arriving at the beach, all encircle the whale with glee, some stroking it gently. One youth, both hands pressed against its side, begins to sing. Others, imitating his pose, join in.

This appears to have a tranquilizing effect on the whale—or its condition worsens. Jarred out of the ritual, I point to the digging tools and then walk to the whale's seaward-facing tail. I begin to dig, the idea being that with the tide out, pulling the whale down a trench will be easier for us and safer for the whale.

The villagers, grasping the plan, join in my effort.

Soon we have paved a way out for the whale. Aided now by the rising tide, we begin the massive task of hauling our whale back out to sea. Waves washing up higher, plus our united force, have their effect. As the whale moves back towards the water, it makes another funny sound—like surprise or relief.

As waves begin to wash over its aching body, with a flap of its great tail, it returns to life.

Wholly immersed now, for some reason, our whale lingers close to shore and its audience. This delights the Nootka, who interpret it as gratitude. They could be right—but then, too, perhaps our whale simply fears heading back out of the inlet to possibly face its foes once more.

Whatever the reason, the villagers row out to stroke its reappearing head. For all the world, our whale appears appreciative of their gentle attention—swimming in slow circles, raising its head as it does.

Villagers sing and dance, interacting until sunset. I watch on, rapt, while taking copious notes.

That evening, I have several mysteries to fathom.

First: was this whale a resident or a migrant? Makanta tells me that whales show up in spring after a winter's absence. Some stay here, as others continue on north.

Ah, so that is fact one—this whale is a migrant. Where it winters must remain a mystery for now. Yet the fact is it does migrate, as Maury indicated in his study.

A deeper mystery surrounds the orcas. With care, I reconstruct the sequence of events involved. By all appearances, these hunters will not venture into the inlet proper, but rather mill about its entrance.

What might explain this? Might it have to do with an adverse change in sea temperature?

For Makanta informs me that an extensive river empties into the inlet at its inland end. I consider this notion but then find it wanting.

Ah, but could underwater currents deter the hunting orcas? Possibly—but this explanation too lacks force.

Makanta then informs me that it has to do with spirits. When I ask him for clarification, he says that a certain type of spirit in the inlet repels the spirit of the intruders. I muse on this for a moment and leave it at that.

Considering now my main object—the whale—a dazzling array of impressions almost confuses me with its richness.

First, our whale had chosen to beach itself rather than face encircling foes. Had it, in some sense, understood its fateful choice? Or did it merely reflect disorientation and panic?

If the former, that would indicate it capable of making a rudimentary judgment—that is, better to die on the relative peace of the beach than to face fierce hunters, although there might be the possibility of escape in so doing.

It had also emitted curious sounds. Were these merely the result of panic? Or do these creatures have a customary array of sounds they use for various reasons?

Again Makanta casually informs me that whales sing in a manner analogous to the Nootka. Naturally, I tie this in with their spiritual beliefs and again leave it at that.

Yet another mystery is the isolation of this individual whale. Normally social creatures—where were its fellows? Had she broken off from them to draw off the danger? Or had she entered the inlet alone?

It occurs to me now that I had seen no others when sighting my first whale here. Could it, in fact, be the whale of our previous encounter? If so, why had it entered the inlet alone?

More crucially, had this whale shown an actual affinity for humans, analogous to dolphins? Or was its behavior an instinctive response we had all misinterpreted?

Lastly, could we hope for future encounters with this specimen? Would it remain in that inlet for safety—or would it head back out to the open sea?

I mull these questions while salmon cooks over an open fire Makanta has made. We had decided to camp on the spot, hoping the whale still lingered close by. The clear sky, now starry, hums with crickets chirping nearby as moths flutter close to our fire. Splashing sounds in the water tell us fish still hunt, and perhaps our whale also swims about. So, as nature returns to fill the void left by the animated and vocal Nootka, Makanta listens intently, as if to another language. At length, he speaks.

"Are you happy, Daniel Evans, to have found your whale?"

"Yes, Makanta, I am very happy to have found a whale to study. I only hope it will be here tomorrow."

"It will be here tomorrow. I feel it near right now."

"Really? And why do you think it stays close by?"

"It is young and lost. Somehow it has separated itself from its companions—maybe two or three of them. It is afraid of the orcas and thinks we will protect it."

"It thinks, Makanta?"

"Yes, it thinks. It thinks like a whale, and our song has charmed it."

"Have you and your people had many similar encounters with whales?"

"No, not many. But we understand the whale and what it feels."

"I see. And what does this whale feel?"

"It longs with might to be a whale, and so joyously complete its dance in our world."

Quietly, I digest his thought. It might well be that Makanta projects his own feelings onto the whale. This would be natural. And so, put in the whale's place, what would he yearn for most?

"Tell me, Makanta, what do you know of these orcas?"

Falling silent, he looks skyward for a moment before replying.

"Some believe that our great chief, Maquinna, said while dying he wanted to return here as an orca. My people believe they are powerful and the freest of creatures."

"Yes, it makes sense that he would express a wish like that. They do appear to be kings of the sea in a way—and whalers, too. I suppose that Maquinna would want to continue his passion to hunt whales."

"You believe what I say?"

"I believe that human aspirations can take many forms."

Not sure how to respond to this last thought, Makanta reflects for a moment.

"What you say is partly true, Daniel Evans. Maquinna's greatest moments in life were standing up in a boat with a harpoon in his hand. He lived for those moments. We all live for those moments. At these times, we feel most alive and in contact with our most loved spirit."

"Ah yes, the whale spirit. I sense a paradox here, Makanta. If the whale spirit is the greatest, why not long to come back as a whale?"

"Because a whale's greatness becomes known only when other creatures look upon it. The whale cannot look upon its own greatness."

A rich thought—I tuck it away for future reflection. For now, other questions press.

"Your people must have found it hard to check their desire to kill and eat the whale."

"Yes and no, Daniel Evans. These days our whale hunts often end in failure. The whale is our main food. So, if we do not kill enough, we sometimes go hungry. But the sight of this great whale alone filled my people with delight. It was food for them this way. It was food for their spirits."

"I see. Yet the desire to hunt them is strong. Your chief wanted to return as an orca to hunt great whales."

Here, Makanta falls silent and ponders secret thoughts. Sensing it rude to inquire further at this point, I let the matter go.

"What is your secret desire, Makanta?"

"My secret desire? The thing I love most in life?"

"Yes."

"A hard question, Daniel Evans. I cannot tell you in words. You must watch my actions. Then you will see the answer. Can you tell me your secret desire, or must I watch your actions too?"

"My secret desire? My fondest hope? Hmm, that is a difficult question. At this point though, I think my fondest hope is to not only understand whales scientifically but to understand them in a more intimate sense as well. And it seems to me that in order to do so, I must understand how people closely linked to them interpret their lives and come to understand them. Does that make sense to you?"

"Yes, it makes sense to me. But is there nothing else you have to tell me?"

Considering this a full answer, I am somewhat taken aback by this further probing.

"Well, I—ah—I suppose that you will learn more about this through my actions too."

"Then I will watch you in the days to come."

"And I will watch you, Makanta."

We talk a while longer about our unique and stunning experience. Almost as amazing is the way we connect, in spite of diverging temperaments and cultures. Tiring at last, we prepare to sleep under the stars. Soon, Makanta snores while I lie awake. Bits of the day float through my imagination like the glitter my mother used to toss on festive occasions. This day for me has been the most festive of occasions—a veritable feast for mind and senses: whale and Nootka, dance and lapping sea, and now a cap of stars to crown it all. Too soon to draw hard and fast conclusions, I savor this sense of unknowing—in its tantalizing possibilities, almost more delicious than knowledge itself.

Chapter 5

Rising at dawn, mist hovers above the inlet waters. Makanta, stomping his feet, moves his arms about, energizing himself for the new day. First looking at each other, we then turn to the water, hoping for a sign that our whale lingers on. Then, as the parting mists reveal the sun on the inlet waters, with a *Pfffpp* sound and a *splosh*, an exhaling whale dives down again. Happily relieved, we smile and prepare breakfast.

As we finish eating and the morning mists part, we must now decide on a plan of action. Referring to my notes, I show Makanta item number one on my agenda: to prove or disprove the notion that whale and man share a certain bond. While the continued presence of our whale now strongly suggests this, we must probe the theory further. The most obvious way to do so is to paddle farther up the inlet and see if our whale follows.

A fine day for an excursion, we man our canoe. Out into the inlet we paddle, eastward toward its source. Mists still part in the far distance as the splash and drip of our paddles count off time. A mass of swirls to my right instantly draws my eyes. A blowhole sounds off as a face appears. For a moment, a huge sparkling eye holds my own, then vanishes under the waves. So far, so good—with more evidence of a dolphin-like attachment our whale exhibits. As well, when we go ashore for lunch, our whale lingers nearby. Then, as we sit back after eating and take a rest, with a swirl of water and a slap of her tail, our whale appears to signal for our attention. Still, we delay our return as we savor the moment. When we finally man our boat, our whale pops up her head. Casting an eye on us both—with an indignant huff, it seems—she dives out of sight for a moment. It would appear that our whale does not like waiting.

Later at camp, I complete my journal entry while Makanta cooks our dinner and makes tea—something he has acquired quite the taste for. As we sip and discuss the day, I note him gazing over the water, looking beyond our whale at something else. I almost ask him what, but change my mind. He will show me through his actions what he looks for, I conclude with a smile.

Next day, we prepare to perform my new experiment. Makanta and I get in the canoe and begin paddling up the inlet. Our companion follows. But then, I order our course reversed. We now head toward Bligh Island and away from this deeper branch of the inlet. As we pass over the inlet mouth, our whale surfaces, blows a great blast of air, and energetically churns the surface before turning around. We stop our rowing to observe as I scribble down notes. Our friend rises again and repeats her performance—with the addition of making rude noises. These appear to indicate alarm or displeasure. When it becomes apparent our whale will no longer follow us, we turn back and, as yesterday, paddle up the inlet. Our escort returns, this time making harmonious sounds. Makanta, no longer able to contain himself, laughs out loud at the wonder of it all. His whole life, he has hunted whales—never once befriending one. But now that he has, all of his instincts and beliefs find a natural object of affection in our young minke whale.

That night, as we discuss the day's events, the next phase of my study comes into focus. Our whale had refused to enter more open waters, as if she sensed or understood that feared orcas lingered on. So the question is: why does our whale equate one stretch of the inlet as the source of danger, and not others? After all, with no natural barriers to prohibit entrance, the orcas appear at liberty to hunt where they will. Clearly, our whale makes yet another judgment—but a judgment based on what? There must be a logical explanation here for us to impute intelligence to her actions.

Next day after breakfast, this issue still disturbs me. I sit by the water with binoculars and notebook, as if awaiting a stroke of inspiration. Finally, I decide this will call for a day of close onshore observation. I need to discover what other species inhabit our whale's safe nook. When I explain my plan to Makanta, he says it's a one-man job that will give him more time for fishing. A little miffed by his lack of interest, I nevertheless agree. As he walks off, he looks over his shoulder at me and smiles a secret half-smile. I wonder at this. Does he know something I don't? At any rate, the day is perfect for studying the open water. The sky is bright and sunny, the inlet calm. Ripples of surging fish show on its shining surface as I scan it with care. At this point, our whale— who just this morning Makanta had named *C'awa' Nuu*, Nootka for *Two Songs*—surfaces and greets me with squeals of delight. Yes, truly, she has two distinct songs: one expressing satisfaction and the other displeasure. While at first sounding unmusical to me, Makanta calls them songs at once and convinces me likewise.

I rise and move about to attract our whale's attention. Closer to shore she moves, slowly raising her head and looking at me. I get my first really good look at her in the water. What a marvel of design—smooth, pointed nose with a curling mouth, large eyes even with her curved mouth's end. A fold of flesh above her eyes resembles eyebrows. Her round eyes flit about as she, in her turn, observes me.

Towards noon, I spot a most unwelcome sight—a group of orcas up the inlet heading my way. Two Songs, close by but not in view, appears unaware of their presence. They might well catch her off guard as they approach. Panicking, I dash for our canoe and madly paddle toward Two Songs. As she surfaces, I actually shout out a warning. Calmly, she assays my antics and dives down again, seeking out krill and small fish. Alone, it seems, I must do what I can to thwart orca aggression.

The feared moment draws near. Orcas close in as Two Songs surfaces. The sight of her enemies will momentarily send her into a frenzy. But then—they swim peacefully by, as Two Songs sings a short but pleasant refrain. What goes on here? Was my first observation of orca attack somehow wrong? But no—Makanta said this happens on occasion. Relaxing, I sit back down in the canoe. Our favorite whale again appears, completely undaunted. Here is yet another enigma to probe.

Back on shore, furiously jotting down notes, I pause as something occurs to me. My first whale sighting had been near the entrance to Nootka Sound. Supposing that whale had been Two Songs, then it appeared as if she had just entered from the open sea. If so, perhaps the hunting pack had followed her in. Then, through speed and guile, she had evaded them and made for the deep east branch of the inlet. This must have been a random choice—supposing her just passing by in the open sea. Or might there have been an instinct at work? Or had she visited the inlet before and remembered it? Whatever the case, once there, her pursuers would not go beyond the inlet's entrance. What might explain this? And now, knowing other orcas in fact inhabit her sanctuary, all my work and observations are now thrown into question. What might be the answer here?

Needing a break, I rise for a stroll on the beach. Seashells in abundance litter the sand. I pick up a fragment and look at it closely. While formerly uniform in appearance, when the shell of shellfish breaks up, each fragment is shaped into a unique form by the sea's action. Looking intently at one such piece, this impression sinks in… That could be it! Different locations in the sea just might act to shape the same species into two or more distinct forms. The hunting orcas, living in stretches of turbulent seas and strong currents, are thus shaped into fierce carnivores. Their cousins, in more placid and salmon-filled inlets, on the other hand, themselves become more placid. And so, they feed on its abundant fish rather than mammals. While all speculation just now, I nevertheless scribble it down.

Done with my writing, Makanta's remarks bubble up in my mind. He had said that the action of unlike spirits explained why the hunting orcas avoided this inlet branch. While finding this colorful, at the time I had dismissed it. Yet now, nature just might have borne it out—at least in a sense. If we take *spirit* to mean *temperament*, then yes, two separate forces might be at work here.

But another problem occurs to me. How did Two Songs understand this distinction? Through instinct? Past experience? Makanta would likely explain it as an equivalence of spirits, as both our whale and the inlet orcas sought similar prey—although Two Songs hunted smaller fish than the orcas.

When Makanta returns with a beautiful salmon for supper, I recount the day's events with great animation. Account concluded, I await his response.

"I think, Daniel Evans, that you want to fly like a bird, the way you flap your arms about."

"Oh really? How can you joke at a time like this, Makanta? And this morning you just take off to fish when I might have needed your help."

"You have seen much today. So think, Daniel Evans, if I had stayed and watched with you, your notes and reflections would be different."

"What exactly do you mean, Makanta?"

"I mean that the river of events would have been different for you. And so your thinking would have been different. You learned much alone as you thought about what you saw. You are right. The orcas are different. Some eat salmon. Others hunt large animals. The hunters roam in the open sea. The fish-eaters live in calm waters. Yes, you have learned much. Now you must agree with what I told you about spirit forces."

"I, ah, well, I do agree that an analogous natural principle works here…"

"Why do you see things from the outside in? That only makes it hard to reach the heart of things."

"Could you make that clearer to me?"

"I understand things from the inside out. You understand things from the outside in. That is what I mean. Why do you look at things in so distant a way? Do all people in England and Nova Scotia think the same way?"

"Well, no, not all. My way of looking at things is not really mine, Makanta. It's the scientific way of looking at things. When we look at things scientifically, in time we will come to understand more perfectly what we look at."

"Maybe you will understand what you look at that way, but you will not feel what a creature is that way. Let me tell you something. I believe when a whale enters our inlet, its huge body leaves an invisible spirit tunnel underwater. Through this tunnel, salmon from the open sea find a way into this inlet. That is why inlet orcas like whales."

Concluding his remark, Makanta gravely folds his arms over his chest.

"Really? And just how did you arrive at such a conclusion?"

Makanta just looks at me sternly, but then starts to smirk.

"I don't believe it. You're joking! Why would you joke about something like that?"

"Why would I not joke? You sometimes joke. And maybe I am right. Like you, I sometimes like to speculate."

"Alright, so you speculate that this might be the case. Well, who knows? But that raises an interesting point. Why do the inlet orcas and Two Songs get along so well?"

"The true question, Daniel Evans, is why would they not get along? They share the same beautiful world. The orcas hunt big fish and the whales hunt small fish. So why would they not get along?"

"You believe there is some other reason they get along, don't you?"

Makanta huffs indignantly at my presumption of understanding him. But then he fetches cooked salmon and bids me be seated with him next to our fire. We eat in silence.

Finished, Makanta pours two cups of tea and hands me one. Here it comes.

"Yes, I do believe another force explains the peace between inlet orcas and whales. It is not Nootka lore. It is my own belief."

"Please, tell me about this belief."

"I told you before that Chief Maquinna spoke of a wish before dying. He said that he wanted to return to life as an orca."

"Yes, I recall something like that. Do you believe that he actually has?"

"I believe it could happen, but even if he was not born into a new life as an orca, his speaking of the wish had spirit power."

"I sense here two possible beliefs."

"Yes. If our great chief made it into the world of the orcas, it would be well. If he did not, the force of his wish might have had a… a similar effect? Is that the right expression?"

"Yes, the right expression. But now, we know that orcas differ. Some hunt mammals, and some hunt fish. One would think then that the great whale hunter Maquinna would want to come back as a whale-hunting orca. Do you agree?"

"No."

"Why not?"

"Because we speak of the spirit world, not the world of our eyes. In the spirit world, our chief would desire to defend what he loved in life. He hunted whales, but only to live. They gave him life. He owes whales something of his own life. So he would want to come back as an orca that did not eat whales. He would want to act as a whale protector."

"Fascinating. Well, thank you for sharing your thoughts with me, Makanta."

I exhale with delight, having had my plate laden to the brim with food for thought. Sensing me a little overwhelmed, Makanta smiles and returns to his tea.

Yes, tomorrow, we both sense, will be a rare day.

Chapter 6

The next day dawns with fine weather—no wind or clouds. Through parting mists, the inlet waters appear glassy and calm. A flock of cranes flies by; fish swirl and jump near the shore. Makanta, cooking breakfast, looks my way. Then, with a beckoning hand swish, he invites me to eat.

Breakfast down, we map out another day of observations. Again, we'll paddle up the inlet—only this time, hoping to encounter orcas. I need to observe more closely how these two species mix. As we paddle off, though, the obvious flaw in my plan becomes clear. Two Songs is not of a mind to cooperate today. Instead of following like before, she stays near the inlet mouth. We circle back again and again to try and draw her off. Again and again, she refuses. At length, we throw up our hands and head for shore, there to probe the issue.

While filling a page with confused observations, I notice Makanta observing me. When I turn and ask if he has anything to say, he merely nods a no and says it's time to go fishing. Off he walks, leaving me alone to figure a way out of our impasse.

Sitting in the grass by the water, notebook in hand, I turn my attention to Two Songs. For a while, she appears calm, diving now and then to hunt for breakfast. In about an hour, her odd behavior resumes. She swims towards the mouth of the inlet, then turns back once more. Again and again she repeats this, adding to it an unpleasant sound.

With binoculars, I scan the waters and see nothing. With no visible source of her agitation, I must somehow figure out the unseen one. Setting down the binoculars and simply taking in the vistas, something occurs to me. While I've been looking for local causes, maybe the answer lies in the vistas themselves.

As the impact and extent of it all sinks in, a focal point emerges: the open sea. Of course. As whales migrate up these coastal waters, maybe they seek the same nook they left in the previous season. A story begins to take shape. Two Songs migrates up the coast with her companions. They encounter seaborne orcas. She gets cut off and speeds into the inlet, with pursuers behind her. Finally, she makes it to this far end of the inlet. Her pursuers relent—possibly because the inlet orcas behave territorially and drive them off.

But now, after a long confinement, she longs for the open sea. She hopes to find her proper inlet and rejoin her group. When Makanta returns, I can't wait to tell him.

"Makanta, I think I understand why Two Songs won't follow us."

"Tell me the reason."

"She longs for her freedom. I suspect this isn't the inlet of her birth. I also suspect whales long to return to such places at the end of their migrations."

Again, Makanta smiles a knowing smile.

"You already knew this, didn't you? You knew she wanted to return to the open sea."

"Yes, I knew. As for her family home being far off—I agree. But even if it's not true, Two Songs still needs the freedom of the open sea. We must help her get there."

"I'm pleased you see it that way. But what about the prowling orcas? You think they might still be lying in wait for her? Do you think animals might have something like personal grudges to settle?"

"I will tell you a story, Daniel Evans. It happened when I was a boy. The father of a friend of mine returned from a fishing trip. He had caught three beautiful salmon. As he got close to his home, crows in a tree saw the salmon. They flew down, cawing, and tried to steal his catch. Angry, the fisherman began to shout. Finally, he threw a stone at the flock. The crows were angry, but they backed off. My friend's father went inside and, with his family, ate the salmon.

The next day, as he walked out of his home, many crows flew from the trees and cawed with hatred, threatening attack. He had to swish a few away before going about his business. But the crows stayed angry for a long time. They'd caw at him often. The lesson, Daniel Evans, is that some animals remember insults or injuries—and they want to get even. Just like humans."

"Ah yes. So, maybe Two Songs injured one of her pursuers?"

"Maybe. I do not know. But she surely injured their pride by escaping."

"And the inlet orcas somehow help by keeping the hunting orcas out. I think instinct drives them to defend their territory."

"That might be true."

"Yes, but your look says something else. Tell me what you really think, Makanta."

"Watch my actions, Daniel Evans, for the answer to your question."

"Your actions? But what actions might we take here? You think if we paddled for the open sea, Two Songs would follow? She wouldn't before."

"I think Two Songs would truly desire to follow if we paddled for the open sea. She thinks of us as great protectors. Even so, she still fears the orcas."

"Yes... But if she did follow us this time, do you think we could protect her if there was an attack? Could several manned canoes keep her safe?"

"No. Hunting orcas are masters of movement. They would drive Two Songs away from us before attacking. We could not help her."

"Then, is it possible for us to get her safely to the open sea?"

"You are a clever man, Daniel Evans. You always think of solutions. I am certain you will think of one for this too."

"You're much more certain than I am, Makanta. Right now, this problem feels like it has no solution."

"I will leave you with your thoughts. Meanwhile, I'll go catch our supper."

Nothing has occurred to either of us by the time we sit down to eat. Talking here and there, we punctuate the mood with silence. For this, in the end, is what it all boils down to: creature eating creature.

Yes, on nature's face we see supernal beauty. As I look out on the sea now, all appears calm and light. Yet just beneath the surface, a pack of flesh-eating orcas mills about. They're only doing nature's bidding—and still I feel pangs of regret. Talking again with Makanta, he feels the same. So we pause to reflect on the nature of life. Yes, how do we humans reconcile the razor-toothed depths of it all with what we sense as high and far beyond us? Each of us drawing partial conclusions, we finish our supper.

The next morning, while peering into growing light, something feels off. Getting up to investigate, another rare sight greets my eyes. There, on our little beach, lies a grounded orca. Running up, without a second thought, I touch it—to register wonder with my senses. As smooth as it is shiny, my gentle strokes seem to calm it. In truth, this orca doesn't appear unduly alarmed to be stranded. Maybe it imagines a way out is still within reach. Possibly these creatures have some instinct for freeing themselves from such hazards. In fact, other orcas swim nearby, seemingly unwilling to abandon their cohort.

While I try to imagine the cause of this odd event, Makanta rises—and out of the blue says he must leave for his village. When I ask why, he says, "Just watch my actions." Pressing him for a real reason, he finally adds that he's going to get help. Puzzled, I say it'll take just two men to free the orca. He repeats what he said, mans the canoe, and sets out. And so, I sit by our fire alone to tend to our new guest.

As the light grows, the orca's size and shape become more apparent. About nine feet long, its body bulges with blubber and muscle. Its huge dorsal fin is its most striking feature. Next, its jet-black and pure-white coloring catches the eye. Its head—rounder and blunter than our minke's—looks almost designed for ramming. The eyes, though, show no sign of alarm.

This moment of quiet fades as daylight brightens. Our new guest starts showing signs of discomfort. Of course—the sun must irritate skin meant to stay underwater. Fetching Makanta's teapot, I fill it and pour water over the orca, again and again. It grunts with something like satisfaction at the cooling touch. Still, I know it must be back in the water soon to avoid injury—or death.

My relief is great when Makanta comes into view, escorted by several canoes. The Nootka fleet lands. The men disembark and quickly begin a well-planned action. Two of them attach an improvised harness to the orca. Then several others lift it and walk backward toward the sea. Into the water it goes, harness still attached. The assembled Nootka then man their canoes. Makanta beckons me to join him—and so we set out.

At the mouth of the inlet now, a most curious spectacle begins to unfold. A clutch of Nootka-laden canoes assembles around the harnessed orca. Amazingly, it shows no fear or signs of discomfort as other orcas gather around it. Then, we all proceed into the inlet passage that leads to the open sea. Most astounding of all, Two Songs follows just as naturally as a sheep follows a shepherd.

Somehow, this assemblage of Nootka and orca reassures her as she enters predator-infested waters. Still, with great trepidation, I scan the waters as we proceed, expecting to see, at any moment, a roiling mass of tall dorsal fins.

In fact, as we proceed past Bligh Island, the dreaded event comes about. A pack of frenzied orcas carves their signature on the placid sea surface. Closer now, they sight our royal retinue of orca escorts. Then, just as swiftly as they had materialized, they melt back into the depths, leaving not a trace behind.

Blinking in disbelief, I try to surmise just what has happened. Well, alright—the sight of the inlet orcas might have signaled that this would be no quick and easy kill. Our orcas might have shown, in signs understood by this species, that they would fight them if they drew closer. I think here of a sight witnessed in London. A knot of toughs had followed a man out of a grog shop, poised to trounce him for some offense. But when nine of this man's chums stepped out of the shadows—realizing they had a fight on their hands—the would-be assailants meekly retreated back into the shop. Could the effect here have been much the same?

Then too, as Makanta's crow story suggested, certain animals, at least on the surface, mimic human emotions. Or is it the other way round? Or might there be some kind of continuum here?

Again, Makanta observes me immersed in thought and smiles. Looking around, I see all the Nootka smiling and laughing in triumph. With great emotion, they now gush out their whale song—this marvelous reversal of events bringing about the same close bond with the whale as the hunt does. I revel in this rare jewel of a moment, a piece of raw nature with a shining spark of human spirit in it. Boundaries that I once imagined could never be crossed have just been.

As we approach the open sea, like a great symphony of nature, we reach the moment that consummates the whole work. The Nootka now toss spruce boughs in the water as their song peaks and they upraise their arms. Here, our harnessed orca is gently released, yet it and its fellows—who have followed its lead out of the inlet—linger by our canoes. Two Songs rises up majestically to take a deep breath, turns sideways, and plunges back down into the depths.

Free at last, with energy and purpose, she swims north. The Nootka erupt into applause so natural that it must be a universal human response—a spontaneous outburst of approval. Mission accomplished, we linger over the spot some moments before heading back into the inlet. Oddly enough, the orcas appear to proceed back in with us, where they speed off into their sheltered inlet. While nature and ritual had been one living thing, it all quickly fades into memory. Almost, it all seems unreal to me—and yet wholly real at the same time. At this point, I am aware of how closely my feelings have interwoven with the Nootka's. For several breathtaking moments, we had transcended barriers of culture and become one.

Back in the village, I furiously scribble down impressions while they're still fresh. They will have to be sorted out later from the mishmash I now record. Where does nature begin and man end in these observations? Perhaps I have become too caught up in this event to objectively assess it. Still, realizing that my study follows its corollary path of including human impressions, I relax.

Yes, it does appear to be true: the simple act of human observation, in some way, alters what we observe. Physical intervention acts to deepen this effect. Pausing to take this all in, I see that Makanta has been watching me while I wrote. Putting down my pen, I know it is time to talk.

"Makanta, have you ever seen anything as beautiful in your whole life?"

"No, Daniel Evans, I have not."

"What do you think of it all?"

"It does not matter what I think. What matters is what I feel."

"Just what did you feel then?"

"My actions should have shown you what I felt."

"Yes, of course. Your actions have shown me what you cherish most in life."

"What do I cherish most in life?"

"Life itself."

"You have learned your lesson well. I hope in your writings you will save this day for other people to read. I hope they learn that the Nootka and the whale are one."

"And you are one with your world here."

"Yes."

The feast that night, while splendid, is marred by the knowledge that I must soon depart. And yet, I know in my heart that a part of me will persist here. Makanta, for one, will never forget our encounter. He will tell the story to his children, and they, in turn, to theirs. And in some mysterious way, I feel as though the land itself will remember—yet how could it not? For the Nootka, too, change the nature they inhabit in subtle ways. Creatures connect to their presence like ornaments on a Christmas tree. And so, a tribe defines the nature around it—wears it on their patterned robes, in fact. Then too, somewhere out at sea, traces of our presence meld into animal thought.

Late at night now, the revelers have all returned home. Makanta sleeps under furs with his wife. In his dreaming mind, images of this great day must flit about. Yes, here is the greatest gift of all: While we consider it a trifle to communicate with another human being, by doing so truly—with meaning—we mingle with each other at our cores, a type of communion. Yes, most of all, I will miss my new friend, Makanta.

A Bend in the Sky

Chapter 1

Our most singular quest began on the 26th of August, 1768, with the sailing of the HMS *Endeavour* from Plymouth, England. Our main objective: to observe and document the transit of Venus over the Sun. British scientists hoped, by so doing, to gain new insight into the distance of our Earth from the Sun and the size of the Solar System.

Our own comparatively modest Atlantic transit would take us past the Madeira Islands, the Canary Islands, and the Cape Verde Islands. We would then round South America's Cape Horn and set our course across the vast Pacific for Tahiti. From there, we would commence our vital astronomical venture.

But now, and to more properly begin my account of our voyage—my name is Benjamin Peale, graduate assistant to the renowned botanist Joseph Banks. And while admittedly our botanical observations represent an earthier goal than the astronomical charting behind our voyage, to my mind at least, our observations will prove no less vital in the fullness of time. For surely the grandness of creation at large is reflected in the humblest of all living things—plants included. Yet our astronomers take an entirely different view on this matter, unshakably convinced theirs is the summit and crown jewel of all the sciences.

As one may clearly see then, our crew evidenced no shortage of—how shall I say this—overinflated heads, myself amongst them. We may be forgiven this, I believe, as we represented the supreme self-assurance of our own society, at least in its higher moments. Yes, our England... and what a marvel to behold as we set sail from Plymouth that day. Beyond her rocky shores rise cities—cities that reflect a new order of humanity. Yes, freed at last from the stultifying shackles of the past, our devout and inspired nation surges into the future, just as the prow of the HMS *Endeavour* surges into the choppy Atlantic.

But enough of this preamble. I must now begin to relate the rather dry tracts of my journal into more lively English. So yes, we leave Plymouth that fine spring morning. The weather, blustery at first, sanguinely turns calm as we head seaward. Captain Cook stands at the helm, shouting orders. He wields an invisible baton that seaman-musicians quickly respond to with harmonious actions. Ah yes, his is an exalted role and I almost envy him for it... almost. For with command, of course, comes grave responsibility. My decisions merely affect me and a small circle of intimates. His, on the other hand, involve not only the well-being of our entire crew but that of our nation as well. With the consequences of his success or failure affecting our entire national destiny, the weight of his command is no light one, indeed.

Even so, here stands a man who bears up under this weight. A veritable Atlas, arrayed in His Majesty's Navy's trimmest attire—buttoned trousers, blue coat, and fine hat together bring out the natural sculpture of the man. Robust of body, his face shows bluntness and fineness at once. Those piercing brown eyes, while somewhat fearsome, more naturally elicit an attentive taking-in of the man. This, in turn, proves a delight as his visage inspires confidence. Other captains are noted for commanding respect through the severity of their rule; ours, through the benign strength of the self-assured. He need not humiliate another to elevate himself—he a quite naturally high-minded man.

It goes without saying that our ship's astronomer, Charles Green, reflects his sterling intellect with natural ease. He has much to be proud of. Preeminent in his field, he is a pioneer in the truest sense of the word. For how might man arrive at a true estimation of his nature without taking the movements of the cosmos itself into consideration? Such rarefied knowledge almost frightens me. And yet, he too is a mere human, subject to the most mundane of afflictions. As I observe him now, he leans over the rail, vomiting. Yes, well—sea legs do come with time. This humbling spectacle also hints at the all-too-human qualities that would later obscure his brilliance with occasional fits of pique.

Our ship's clerk, Richard Orton, presents a striking contrast to these notables. I do not mean to suggest that his role is in any way less vital than theirs. Each man on board plays an important part in this functioning whole of a ship. Still, he would appear more at home in an obscure government office than on a royal barque. The hat of adventurer slips down somewhat over his eyes. Even so, as our voyage progressed, he would surprise me.

And then there is my own Joseph Banks to size up. Yes, it is true—on the surface, at least—our science is more humble than astronomy. No mental brass band announces our presence when we enter a room. And yet, as I previously noted, a plant bears the marks of the cosmic as much as any distant star or moon or planet. And so, my mentor too is a man of keen intellect and razor-sharp eyes, the latter being developed to a high degree. In fact, he once told me the well-trained eye transmits an object's essence to the brain, where our reason dissects it.

Sidney Parkinson comes next, one of our ship's artists. A private man, he mostly keeps a low profile, immersing himself in his work. I suppose this comes with being a man of his temperament. He tends to avoid excessive excitement, as if too much commotion is a difficult thing for him to endure. Yes, rather he prefers those quiet moments alone with the subjects he lovingly commits to paper. His is a world primarily of the eye, an interesting adjunct to my Joseph's observations in this regard. And so, in time, his insights would help to solidify my own impressions of the novelties we encountered.

Of course, many other engaging crew members come to mind, but for the purposes of my account they must unfortunately be glossed over. Suffice it to say at this point that aside from mission specialists, the crew taken as a whole had a life of its own. How well I recall seeing all in action—especially when the weather proved unfavorable. At such moments, Captain Cook took center stage to give his great performance of seamanship. He orchestrated his crew like a master, each man sounding his own particular notes at the swish of the maestro's hand. Ah yes, and how the *Endeavour* responded to our efforts—how she responded to our touch. How odd that wood and canvas turn alive at the transmission of human effort, and yet that is the overall effect. It is true, then, that men at sea bond with their ship in a most profound and mysterious fashion.

On the other hand, being composed of individuals with their own particular outlooks and affections, an undercurrent of tension also flows through this sea of fellow feeling. Yes, we firstly cooperate for survival and the furthering of our mission's ends while at the same time pursuing individual goals. For with the collective success of our mission, each man stands to gain personally—from the highest ranking to the lowest—renown, after all, a factor to be reckoned with. With this in mind, friction is inevitable, as each man's perceptions vary as to how best to advance collective interests.

Yet, for the time being, we make good progress in fairly unitary fashion. Personalities and the conflicts thereof tend to abate as great natural events awe us with their power, danger, and beauty. Our first encounter with high seas is one such episode. As a novice seaman, I must say the experience quite bowled me over. I have seen high surf at my home in Cornwall from the comfort and security of a beach. Yet even there, the thunder of large waves may cause unease as well as wonder. On the ocean at large, these emotions multiply by a factor of ten. Living mountains of water they appeared to me, and our grand vessel—a mere cork—as she rose onto peaks and fell into ever-shifting valleys. Time almost stands still while this marvel of nature unravels. For once such a tempest begins, it must run its course—us along with it. In the midst of our first such trial, I became as white as a sheet, convinced that these fulminations of nature would engulf our small vessel. Our stouthearted captain only laughed, slapping me on the back as he strode by.

The mystique of adventure thus begins to take over our lives. Gone are the pleasant moorings of my green and orderly England. Day by day, as we cross the Atlantic, only in my mind may I place our homeland. Horizon after horizon has hidden it from everyday experience. Well—not quite. For a strange thing happens. The men about me become more than men; they become a living connection to my own living reality as an Englishman. How could it be otherwise? About us now stretches vastness beyond our wildest reckoning. This is no scenic coastal sea that we float on. This is the sea which has existed for eons, almost immune to the passage of time. We could just as well be two thousand years in the past as we are two thousand miles from England.

This fanciful-sounding notion takes on dimension as we round Cape Horn. Its dismal starkness engulfs us with desolation. We gaze about and see nothing but the most rugged coast imaginable. The atmospherics astound. Wind-driven clouds collide with stony peaks before flowing over, the dark grey sky alive with electric potential. I ponder in silence this peculiar weather and begin to picture it in my mind. Yes, of course—the ragged end of this continent thrusts a stony finger at the South Pole. That ice-capped land of astonishing extremes of light and dark acts as a gigantic storm generator. It thus propels waves of cold air northward, their impact with warmer air masses engendering storms. Tragically, we lose five men while rounding Cape Horn. The strident god of storms, it seems, must claim our sacrificial victims.

At last free from that treacherous region, we surge across uncharted waters towards our goal, Tahiti. In reality a tiny speck in a vast expanse, we only hope through our navigator's skill to arrive intact. Yet a wilderness of waves stands between us and our tantalizing goal. Storms still stalk us, even though we have made it through one of their prime spawning grounds. Yet when we emerge from the latest of these eruptions, a wonder greets our eyes. For as the storm recedes behind us, upward-billowing clouds glow crimson, as the deepest dark beneath lends preternatural contrast—almost, it seems to me, a hallowed event, hinting at worlds beyond ours.

Yet even with these welcome moments of relief, the strain of our voyage takes its toll. One man, no longer able to endure it, throws himself overboard and is lost to the waves. Wonder-struck, we grieve—he, normally a genial sort. Many ponder in their hearts the meaning here. On the one hand, this event terrifies. On the other hand, some cannot help but feel a morbid fascination at the thought of the eternal sea absorbing, at last, one's life.

Our captain takes note of this grim mood and seeks to jar us back to something like reality. So he renews with vigor his experimental diet program—the eating of sauerkraut in an attempt to thwart that scourge of sailors: scurvy. Oddly enough, even the thought of a gruesome death is not enough to get some to eat this smelly dish. Our captain's advisers recommend the lash for balking sailors. Captain Cook, however, has other thoughts on the matter. So, in plain sight of the crew, he and his officers eat with relish their own sauerkraut. Stubborn sailors take note. Well now, they conclude, if our captain and his officers eat theirs with nary a qualm, so can we. And wonder of wonders—the plague of scurvy passes us over, we children of Israel marked with the sign of that vegetable.

Our transit continues more or less smoothly, until at last the great day arrives. On the morning of the 16th of April, 1769, Joseph and I stand at the prow, watching with fascination as our ship falls and rises in moderate waves. A shout goes out from the watchman up on the middle mast: "Land ho!" How this galvanizes us into action, like an anthill stirred by an unexpected presence. Ah, but this is a most joyful arousal. It has been a long and dangerous voyage. And so, the mere thought of stepping onto dry land again fills us with tender emotion. Tantalizing images of a lush green paradise come to mind. Only one other European expedition has ever made it to Tahiti, and yet this island's rumored paradisaical glories have already become legendary.

The actual event proves these rumors one-dimensional, as here our Earth lives on in its original state of divine perfection—at least on the face of it. The lush vegetation veritably drips with delicious things to eat. Pristine beaches enchant, as a sea of liquid topaz beyond coats the eye like a living jewel. Soft trade winds waft in, neither too hot nor too cool. In the background, perfectly shaped and magnificent tropical mountains arise.

The women here prove hardly less alluring. Of a creamy-chocolate complexion, they exhibit all the qualities of a fine confection turned to life. Lively dark eyes sparkle as they laugh with delight at the least of our gestures or utterances. Evidently, they consider our otherworldly appearance immensely desirable. The homeliest of men now find themselves adored as Olympian heroes—and so begin to believe they are.

But enough of this. The purpose of my account has more gravity than this experience suggests. And even with this and other distractions, Captain Cook and Charles Green carry out their crucial observations on what they name Point Venus. How sad, too, after so much grief and travail, the readings are compromised due to intense celestial light that blurs the edge of Venus's disk. Their separate readings do not agree temporally, either.

Yet surprisingly few of us dwell on these disappointing results—the true event, for most, is the island itself. Ha, yes, in the end Venus herself, personified in the flesh of the native women, more wholly captures popular imagination. This annoys our esteemed astronomer no end. At times he rails on about the two poles of human existence—the spiritual and the carnal. How sad, he laments, that men choose a fleeting moment of pleasure over the imperishable beauty of contemplating the cosmos. Some few crewmen listen on ruefully, while most smile and sigh at the mere thought of recent romantic encounters. Still, our astronomer and a few others continue to maintain that this island is more a snare and a delusion than a true paradise.

Even so, with the weaknesses of the flesh man must ever contend with, many a crewman's heart throbs away in pain as our time of departure approaches. With one of our mission's objectives imperfectly completed, Captain Cook is still tasked with a thorough exploration of the South Seas. And while none dare imagine what lies before us, more than a few dream of another earthly paradise.

Chapter 2

Onward into a blue void we surge, Captain Cook's task now to either prove or disprove the theory that a giant continent lies somewhere in the vastness beyond. The Venus project behind us, this goal now wholly consumes him. For our captain shares something of astronomer Charles Green's rarefied nature in that he truly loves the thrill of discovery. Back on Tahiti, even as crewmen freely cavorted with the natives, he would retire to his ship's cabin to pore over various charts and graphs. Then too, as a married man, with honor he cleaved to his vows. Yet he did not condemn the men for their behavior, understanding well human needs and weaknesses—although he would expound at length on the need for temperance and devotion to our ultimate cause.

With his manly comportment a model for all, we adapt again to the circumscribed life aboard ship. Even so, most look forward to daily rations of grog. Under the influence of rum, we retrieve Tahitian memories. These we snuggle up to at night. Yet this is the most ephemeral of consolations. The rigors of life at sea again begin to take their toll. Some grumble with disgust at the poor fare we eat. One crewman tosses his knife repeatedly into a beam, this giving us pause—him no genial sort. And so our moods rise and fall, as do the ocean swells, tedium and high hopes in a shaky alliance.

In spite of this, we make forward progress. At last, the anticipated day arrives. On the 6th of October, 1769, Nicholas Young, son of the ship's surgeon, lets out a "Land ho!" from the masthead. How appropriate it is to make a discovery in the southern hemisphere spring, as everywhere a season of hope. For as we squint and gawk, a never-before-seen land takes form before us. As we draw closer, mists move across the water. The coast to our east, a hilly point juts from the north out to sea. All espy a beach as we approach a bay. We note plumes of smoke and suspect the land inhabited. So, even with no natives in sight, we sense eyes peering out from hidden posts.

Captain Cook, having sized the land up, next orders two boats ashore, he manning the first. At anchor now, we on board breathlessly watch as the boats hit the beach and men debark. Ah, what is this? We see dark-skinned men approaching. From this distance, it is hard to judge their emotions. I imagine them curious and friendly, as the Tahitians. Most of our crewmen feel the same way and dare now to imagine a romp. Oh, but then, in stunned wonder, we draw back from the rail as shots ring out. For one of the natives had approached the landing party in a threatening way. As he crumples to the sand, the men's sweet dreams do likewise. Most decidedly, we have not discovered another lost paradise. Captain Cook and his men soon man their boats and return to the ship. Their stricken faces say it all. This will be no pleasant entry in our ship's log.

As the day wears on and evening approaches, the sun arches majestically over this undiscovered country. The air is warm and the breeze gentle. How odd—flies apparently have picked up our scent and now buzz about. Most often annoying, for sailors months at sea, this commonplace terrestrial sound strikes us near pleasant. A flock of unknown seabirds fly overhead as a crescent moon rises. In the distance, we hear the crash of the surf. Benign nature softens the cruel blow of our day.

Yet we dare imagine this episode is a fluke, the unfortunate result of too much newness at once. We put ourselves in the natives' places. Our ship, with its tall masts and billowy sails, must have looked threatening. Our appearance likewise took them aback. We recall how they placidly watched the landing, conceivably in benign anticipation. Something had simply gone awry. We had gotten off on the wrong foot. For beneath his warlike exterior, man longs for concord with fellow beings—or so some suppose.

In this hopeful mood, next morning Captain Cook and his coterie row for shore. Surely, they reason, their measured pace and calm appearance would not arouse fear. Indeed, as they beach their boat and step ashore, the natives reappear. This time I use a spyglass to get a closer look. Ah, one of them instantly draws my attention—he rather tall and of a light brown complexion. His long black hair tied back, muscular upper arms are covered with intricate tattoos resembling intertwining plants. His face is painted with a geometric design, not merely daubed with color. On his bare chest he wears some kind of beaded vest. His eyes then narrow with intensity as he watches our men land.

I scan his fellows. They all appear similarly bold and focused. I watch for a sign of peaceful intention. One native strokes hair from his face as he looks on. Our men approach. Captain Cook extends his hands, bearing tokens of peace. For a frozen moment, the outcome of this encounter hangs in the balance. Then, out of thin air, a spirit of malevolence infiltrates the scene. One of the natives rushes forward and grabs a crewman's cutlass. Instantly, he is shot as his fellows jump up and down in an agitated and threatening manner. Without showing fear, slowly our landing party back-steps to its boat. They launch into the waves as the tribesmen become even more aroused. A second tragic scene in so short a time has a profound effect upon us. We turn to each other and chatter away to break the tension. Some mutter darkly; others speak sadly of a lost opportunity for contact.

As a second evening descends, the same luscious sights and sounds as before engulf us. Almost, some are tempted to succumb to the mood. Yes, here is smooth flowing water to wear down the sharp edges of our day. We observe an added delight as a flock of colorful tropical birds for some reason passes over the waves. They are green, have red heads and long tails—parrots of a sort, we surmise, as some crewmen smile. Yes, we had all dreamed of the exotic and found it in Tahiti. Yet this gentle mood quickly fades. These natives are no eaters of fruits and greens, our reluctant conclusion.

Undeterred by these initial setbacks, our captain confers with his advisers. They perform a post-mortem, as it were, on those two unfortunate incidents. They consider first the possibility that another party of explorers had landed here and treated the natives badly. This would naturally predispose them to behave aggressively towards subsequent Europeans. Unfortunately, they simply lack the evidence to reach any such conclusion, and so in the end must assume some other cause.

So they next, with care, reconstruct both encounters. Might these natives simply be by nature a warlike people? Clearly, the tattoos had offended the sensibilities of some. Such designs, a few venture to say, signal a primitive and aggressive state of mind. Emboldened, another adds that the painted faces buttressed this impression. When one crewman of a more objective persuasion notes that uniforms, guns, and cutlasses may similarly signal a warlike state of mind, the others merely scoff and think him naïve. His fellows reiterate that to arm oneself in unknown regions is simply prudence and not aggression. He rejoins the consensus. At the end of the day, the only thing they decide on is to leave the matter undecided. We simply must, for the sake of England and mission, continue to explore and chart this new land.

Next day our captain decrees that we will continue our exploration. We will chart the coast about us to determine what manner of land has been discovered—island or continent. With this pronouncement, we weigh anchor. Then, with the gravitas of Cicero, Captain Cook turns to one last time look at our landing spot. Solemnly, he names it **Poverty Bay**, commemorating the fact that we received no provisions here.

Our mission continues without further mishap, as for the most part we limit encounters with natives. So the task of charting proceeds marvelously well, as in subsequent weeks we round a prominent point and proceed on south. Here we begin to surmise this land is an island—and no giant continent.

And so it comes about that on this eastern coast of the island, we attempt yet another commingling of peoples. Captain Cook orders two boats to row out and greet two native boats as they approach. On board ours is Tayeto, son of Tupia, our Tahitian translator. The four boats converge as the mood appears even enough. For how might men in small boats reasonably be expected to fight? And yet, as two opposing boats touch, the natives strike with lightning speed. They abduct Tayeto and madly paddle for shore. Captain Cook orders our men to open fire. The native boat buckles under the ensuing fusillade. Tayeto jumps overboard and swims towards us, the natives beating a hasty retreat. So, scooping our grateful man from the sea, we return to our ship.

At this point, we practically throw our hands in the air. For while, in fact, we have had some peaceful encounters with the natives on other parts of the island, on the whole our record in this regard has been dismal. Static sparks seem to quite naturally arise whenever our two peoples attempt to rub shoulders. On the one hand, it may be true that opposites attract. After all, we and the Tahitians were opposites in culture and temperament and yet had gotten on famously. These islanders, on the other hand, prove that opposites more often repel. I think here of the science of chemistry. Some compounds blend to form other beneficial compounds. Some combinations, however, can be toxic or even explosive. Our chemistries must simply be at variance, we conclude. And yet for a split second, a contrary thought occurs to me. Had the Normans first stepped ashore in England with gifts and smiles, no Englishman in his right mind would have concluded a peaceful intention. Swiftly though, this analogy strikes me as an improvised one and loses its impact.

With great disappointment, on the 31st of March, 1770, we leave the island behind us. The weather has changed. It is now more often overcast and showery. As the summer sun recedes, one can almost feel the cold air masses to our south edging ever closer. Of course, at this latitude, winter would be fairly mild.

Our captain now zigzags over vast tracts of ocean in an attempt to find the hypothetical monster-sized continent many of our geographers believe exists in this region. They reason mathematically. The southern hemisphere must, by laws that point to both aesthetic and geometric balance, act as a counterweight to the northern, and so, of necessity, would have a similar landmass.

When weary months of this quest prove fruitless, Captain Cook decides—over loud objections by certain advisers—to return to England via Africa's Cape of Good Hope. Next day though, and quite inexplicably, he orders a change of course. He now wants to explore the little-known tract of land named New Holland. Discovered by the Dutch, of course, they did little more than step ashore on its western edge and claim it. As almost nothing is known of this land, our captain evidently still considers it fair game.

So, as we continue our voyage into the deep unknown, a curious sense of expectation grows within me. No man knows what lies ahead and yet my mind's eye is tantalized by vague intimations of a sunlit beach and plains beyond. In this frame of mind, I join those crewmen I have become most familiar with—my own Joseph Banks, astronomer Charles Green, and ship's clerk Richard Orton. It is a bit odd that we have formed a close association, men of such differing professions and natures. And yet in the tiny, compressed world of a ship, unexpected mergers do occur.

So here we sit in the ship's mess, lingering on as others have left. Joseph listlessly pokes through a largely uneaten serving of sauerkraut. Charles dreamily peers into his mug of grog as if it were a crystal ball. Richard taps the table with his fingers. Clearly, clerical duties are the last thing on his mind. The tendency now is to look back with nostalgia on Tahiti, our latest experience such a punishing one. I find this disconcerting, as clearly the future must be grappled with in a straightforward fashion.

"So tell me, Charles," I begin, "what in your estimation is the most important task remaining for our mission?"

At first annoyed to be pried from his own thoughts, he looks up from his grog mug.

"The most important task remaining," he repeats, while squeezing the words for their essence. "The most important task remaining… The most important task remaining, young Ben, is one that a generation not our own will carry out."

At that, Joseph sets down his sauerkraut and picks up his mug.

"Oh come now, Charles, you're not going to carry on again about the Venus Project, are you? You gave it your best go, gathered useful enough information. Let the matter rest in peace, I say."

"Yes, rest in peace indeed, as all too many of the living in our times are wont to do. As for this crew, to what might we, with purpose and drive, aspire to here below when planetary movements, which make our own voyage contemptible by comparison, have not been properly charted and so accommodated to human reason? How might men of such incompleteness hope to accomplish anything of significance?"

"A trifle overstated, wouldn't you say?"

"Ha, yes, a trifle... You and a rum and a trifle – a portrait of Joseph."

"Oh come now, Charles. What are you drinking there, rum or sour wine?"

At first amused by this exchange, I give the matter renewed thought. Yes, the Venus Project was a once-in-a-lifetime event. Having botched the reading must have been deeply painful and frustrating for our astronomers. Joseph though will not let up.

"I think the cure for your malady, Charles, is perspective. You think big, but consider this: The vast and endless cosmos you seek to explain can all be compressed into a single human noggin… granting, of course, it's as brilliant a noggin as yours."

"And just what is your point, Joseph?"

"My point is that vastness is an illusion of sorts, if in fact its comprehension takes place in so tiny a place as a human skull— that, or our minds are expansive, like an oak growing out of an acorn."

"Been whiffing the daffodils again, eh?"

"Oh yes, mock if you must my earthly science. But be honest now. What is more precious to man—the movements of planets and stars, or the shade of a tree on a hot summer's day?"

"Ha! The great Heraclitus summed this matter up best, in my estimation."

"Oh really? And what did the worthy philosopher observe? Please, do regal us with his profound quote."

"Donkeys prefer straw to gold."

"Oh, so now I am a donkey for preferring plants to planets. Is that the implication?"

"Interpret it as you will, Joseph. It is merely an observation. I certainly did not mean to label anyone present with it…"

"I forgive you your arrogance, Charles, seeing as how you eye with such evident passion your third mug of grog."

"Huh! So now you accuse me of being a sot, eh? You, you who lose track of your mugs after four."

"Oh please, gentlemen," Richard puts in, smiling, "not another verbal duel, as sporting as it appears. Yet neither of you has answered Ben's question. Tahiti is forever behind us, and with it that entwining jungle of allures. And Venus will be back in due time, movement of the planets, at least, predictable enough. But what of the movement of our ship? Do none here dare speculate on what lies ahead?"

Amazingly, all fall silent. Charles and Joseph appear to have no opinion on this serious matter. Richard almost speaks but stops. This leaves me to imagine for us all. So I think again of the premonition I'd had that morning. Yes, something had stretched out in my mind, another unknown land—but more than that. Now, granted, we had encountered truly novel and exotic locales. Tahiti had been quite out of our reckoning, and yet we had quickly adapted to it. The large island, which our Captain had christened New Zealand, had been a rude awakening. Still, its geography at least bore a more or less familiar stamp. But now I imagine something so beyond our reckoning as to defy categorization. Was this merely fanciful thinking on my part? We would soon find out.

Chapter 3

Onward we plunge, over vast blue tracts of uncharted waters. The weather appears to be holding as summer slowly recedes. With shortening days, conditions become more variable. We experience an odd sense of equipoise, as nature cannot at this point decide which prevailing winds she will favor—cold or warm.

Our crew, as well, appears neither here nor there in mood. We have seen both masks of human nature—the kindliest and the most severe. Many of the men muse on the meaning of it all in relation to their own lives. Some feel apprehension about our future, noting that the natural progression of our experience of human contact has been from good to bad. *It stands to reason*, they assert, *that worse follows bad.* Others scoff and call them fainthearted. Even so, few dare to dream of another Tahiti—the consensus being there is no consensus on what to expect.

That is why, on the 23rd of April, when the cry of *"Land ho!"* goes out, only slowly do many move to the rail for a look. At first, we put hands to foreheads and squint, attempting to pierce the haze of distance. Ah, at last—there it is... a band of solid horizon. As we approach, it takes on definite form—and what a form! For it is broad and relatively flat, even as mountains add contours to the horizon. Yes, this is curious. For with a closer look, it appears mountainous and yet flat and expansive at the same time...

What might explain this perceptual contradiction? I take a closer look and get the vague impression of a cosmic hand placing itself over this land and pushing down. Hand withdrawn, the formerly mountainous terrain bears this handprint. It has evened things out so that plain and peak share a similar horizontal dimension.

Closer to the shore, this puzzling mood takes hold. Prevailing winds carry scents of land to us—oddly pungent in a not unpleasant way. We see, too, that thick forests clothe both flat stretches and smoothed-out peaks. Oh, how doubly odd. The land appears to give off a faint blue haze, like a woodland mist—only not so. Quite a contradictory impression. With bright sun and warm air, we begin to imagine various unusual species of tropical birds and animals dwelling in this wild fastness.

Ah, and then the next impression hits full force. Yes, Joseph and I had had a field day in both Tahiti and New Zealand with our discovery of manifold new species of plants. We had spent many a joyful hour describing them in journals and carefully preserving specimens. Yet here, I now sense a veritable new universe of plant species. Oddly too, having only just sighted this land, we sense at once it is far vaster than previously conceived. Something in the form and stretch of the coastline suggests a considerable landmass filling extensive tracts of ocean. Yes, here may well lie an entirely new world with indigenous species unknown in other mapped continents.

Next, of course, thoughts of possible human inhabitants occur. Surely, we reason, a land this vast will be inhabited by some permutation of humanity. And it rests with stouthearted Englishmen to discover something of their nature. So I ask our Sidney Parkinson again about his pet theory on lands and peoples. Smiling, he says that he had developed it while out on various sketching expeditions in Tahiti and New Zealand. He lightheartedly claims that the land shapes the man, so to speak.

He first asked me to consider our own England, with its moist temperate climate, once extensive forests, grand sweeping meadows, and various highlands. This land, he says, while generally benign, yet poses challenges of geography and climate that our human ingenuity had to overcome. Our often overcast skies, rather than making us dour, had forced us to turn inward in a quest for that light within—his own expression. In other words, our land and climate had shaped us into intellectual beings. We needed to develop our minds in order to subdue our surroundings, which, unfortunately, at times included war.

"Consider Tahiti," he goes on dreamily. "Here, man has all his wants at his fingertips—fruit, fish, objects of beauty, and tenderhearted women. A tropical island," he says, "being cut off from foreign human contact, blunts the need for developing ingenious methods of warfare to fend off invasion. Bright sun and blue sky act to promote tender emotion rather than flinty intellectual prowess. So it stands to reason," he concludes, "that the Tahitians are what they are."

Ah, I counter, what about the natives of New Zealand? For like Tahiti, part of its North Island is near-tropical in nature, and yet its people are as bellicose as the least refined of the Irish. "How do you explain this?" I ask. He counters that while part of that land is near-tropical, it yet has numerous tribes likely contending for the choicest locales. Then too, its geography intimidates more than that of Tahiti. The natives have to fight nature at times for their daily bread. It does not fall out of trees in the morning for them.

I smile and say that while interesting, his theory may lack scientific merit. Even so, I ask him to predict what we will encounter in this stark and extraordinary land. Here he goes misty-eyed and says that the most impenetrable of all human mysteries awaits us. I shrug and must partly agree with his assessment.

Our attention then turns to the land again as we sail closer. The sun arcs to the west as the day ripens. In the distance, we see billowy white thunderheads forming. Soon, rain will fall in torrents, drenching this alien landscape. In my imagination, I almost smell the scents the rain enlivens. I picture the sun reappearing and a myriad of brightly colored birds chattering happily away... hmm, and the natives reappearing after the rain...

Just then, a cry goes out as we round a point. We venture fairly close to land for a good look. Out of the forest, men appear—but no ordinary men. Shaking with excitement, I grab my spyglass. There stands a robust male without a stitch on him. He appears not tall, black-complexioned, and has short curly hair and a beard.

He had daubed chalky white paint all over his upper torso, forming patterns. In an upraised right hand, he holds a curved instrument.

And his face... His face does not appear African, despite his black skin. His eyes, as far as can be discerned, look deep-set and intense—something like the land itself. I then scan the entire group. How they eye us with curiosity... and fear. I wonder which emotion is strongest—and then they vanish.

We break out in excited chatter, speculating on what to expect upon landing. Some predict a fierce onslaught, worse than in New Zealand. *It stands to reason,* they assert, *based on their raw and unadorned forms.* So now we speculate: First, the Tahitians had appeared rather gentle, despite their brownish complexions. Second, the New Zealanders appeared more angular, reflecting a more warlike disposition. Some swear their complexions looked darker, although this was in fact not the case. And lastly, these natives appear the most primitive of all—unclad and almost black, they went on. Others disagree, noting their curious looks and lack of aggressive postures. Then too, they had quickly vanished from sight, possibly overwhelmed or even frightened by the encounter.

At this point, an odd notion strikes me—a thought of Sidney Parkinson's. Perhaps the natives will evince qualities of the land's geography and lifeforms. After all, even we in England identify with certain creatures—the stag, the bear, the hawk, and so on. As well, clans might incorporate a certain creature or plant into their family coat of arms. Though a rather shallow analogy, it yet captures my fancy. I will not let it rest until experiencing both this land's creatures and these long-lost cousins of ours.

I take one last look at the vastness about me while inhaling deeply. Sights and scents combine to form an entirely new template of experience. Yes, that is what it will take for this land, I surmise, as so far nothing of the familiar finds a matching slot within. We then watch as the coast begins to glow orange under the arc of the westbound sun. While perhaps no garden of delights awaits us, a unique garden of sorts assuredly does.

So that evening, I huddle in the mess again with my circle of intimates, prepared to pose the same question as before. This time, however, all appear lively.

"So tell me, Charles, given that we have more information to go on now, what do you think the future holds for our mission?"

"What does the future hold for our mission… What does the future hold? Well, young Ben, let us hope that it *holds* and does not *drop* the HMS *Endeavour* as we prepare to chart yet another Godforsaken corner of the globe with the floor sweepings of creation tucked into it."

I chuckle a bit at his answer.

"Oh, so you think my remark amusing, do you, young man? Have you no idea of the hierarchy of creation? Is that what you are saying?"

"The hierarchy of creation?"

"Yes indeed, the hierarchy of creation—as even the most elementary of philosophers has laid out for us. The lower were created for the sake of the higher, and the higher for each other. If memory serves, Marcus Aurelius wrote of that in his memoir. Have you not heard this or similar quotes before?"

"Of course he has," Joseph cuts in, "as have we all. And we all understand how this principle works in nature. The robin eats the worm, and the hawk eats the robin. But surely as an astronomer, a man who strives to grasp the whole, you take a more comprehensive perspective than this?"

"Indeed I do. Simply refer to *Genesis* for the Divine blueprint of creation. As you will plainly see, the natural order proceeds from the simplest organisms to the most complex—man. And so, as this logic decrees, creatures of the sea came first, then plants on land, then birds, mammals, and so on."

"Yes, interesting… but all in six days?" Richard asks.

His observation catches us off guard.

"Well," Charles retorts, "that is how it is stated, is it not?"

Silently, each man forms his own thoughts.

"Well," Sidney pipes in, "we do have Saint Peter stating that one day with the Lord is as a thousand years, a thousand years as one day—meaning to me, at least, that the cosmic timeline differs from our own."

"At any rate," my Joseph goes on, ignoring Sidney's remark, "something else occurs to me, Charles. You put man at the summit of creation. You further state that the lower serves the needs of the higher—the higher, I assume, being man. But tell me now: Does our own exalted kind submit itself to this principle?"

"What do you mean by that?"

"I mean that humanity is clearly not at the same stage of development worldwide. We all know this from our studies and have here confronted the reality face to face. So, do less developed orders of man exist to serve the needs of the higher? If you say yes, you must then defend the institution of slavery. While not clothing itself with noble premises, it nevertheless assumes this the case. This frees certain orders of man to enslave others without undue qualms of conscience. If, on the other hand, you say no, then you must join the ranks of our abolitionists and defend the Rights of Man universally."

Joseph smiles with smugness, thinking he has laid a trap for his friend.

"The Rights of Man," Charles echoes with a faraway look in his eyes. "The Rights of Man... All right, Joseph, granted, that notion has a certain appeal to it—the Universal Rights of Man... But really, it is one of those nebulous abstractions we utter for effect without giving it much rational consideration. You cannot get away with painting me a slave trader if I do not buy those frilly and right-sounding declamations. As a man of reason, I clearly perceive that in any progressive society, a division of labor is needful. Come now, be honest, would you want your village blacksmith at the king's right hand, advising him on grave matters of state? It is self-evident that not all men have the temperament and aptitude to rise to high office."

"So you would censure the smithy for his lack of statecraft?"

"Oh, stop your foolish jesting. You know very well I mean nothing of the sort. The smithy has his place in our society—none question that. And truly, a smithy's son may have a gift that bears a second look... But you use inappropriate examples if, as is clearly evident, you apply this Universal Rights of Man to the unenlightened races of the world."

"The unenlightened races of the world," Richard echoes. "Now there is perhaps one of the slipperiest concepts known to man. Is it not a fact, Charles, that some of our own countrymen consider the French to be a subspecies of humanity? Do you deny this?"

"Oh please, Richard, let's not drag the French into this. What would be the point? That issue more properly illustrates national rivalry than my principle at work."

"But you don't deny such denigration, do you?"

"I am beginning to question your loyalty as an Englishman, Richard. Perhaps you had best use a more balanced example."

"I have no more balanced examples to use."

Here Richard falls silent.

"Gentlemen, gentlemen," Joseph chimes in, "while interesting, of course, neither of you has answered Ben's simple question. It was not vague and philosophical, but a simple and direct one pertaining to our own immediate circumstances. We all sense something unique about this newfound land. We have seen with our own eyes the natives on its shores. So, the question is, what do you think awaits us upon further exploration? And just how will we deal with this situation in the near future?"

No easy question here. A curtain of silence descends.

"Well," Charles begins, "we will most assuredly find something. Likely, you and young Ben will find a veritable universe of new plant species. As well—and as has been borne out by our own eyes—we will find some new order of man… or, rather, perhaps some very ancient order of man, by all appearances."

"Do you think they will have anything to reveal to us?"

"Reveal? Reveal to us? I think it the other way round, Richard. Yes, I do think that. What we have to reveal is something that will be quite foreign to them. Yes, while the sun shines intensely in this land—much more so than in England—I suspect the interior light of this undiscovered race will not burn nearly as bright."

"Ah," I put in, "our artist Sidney Parkinson has alluded to that notion, although he states it as a positive and you a negative. He seems to believe that particular landscapes shape the interior life of man."

"Such twaddle," Charles counters. "What shapes the interior life of man is that Divine Reason which we acquired firstly at Athens and secondly at Jerusalem. Together the two blend into one inextinguishable light."

"An exalted notion," Richard notes, "and one in which the concept of the Rights of Man had its birth. One need only consider how the ancient Stoics and Old Testament prophets railed against mankind's oppressors and enslavers."

"You lack the wit to trap me in that way, Richard," Charles sniffs. "At any rate, I speak here of sound morality and the pure sciences."

Here he only smiles and again falls silent. We all do as well, each digesting what the other has said. So we decide to call it a night and go to bed.

Alone in my tight quarters, sleep evades me. Creaking timbers—at best an ambiguous sound—now hint at the true precariousness of our situation. We may debate and discuss, as gentlemen are given to doing, and yet ours is the most unstable of worlds, as the sea longs to master all that floats upon her. Yes, and so the sea may be interpreted benignly and not so benignly, and applied to our personal lives.

I think also of the new world that awaits our exploration. How we now fear a misstep, after our last unfortunate human encounter. We are so very alone, so very far from our beloved home—mistakes made here far more dangerous than there. Even so, even with fearful disaster always our possible companion, most still yearn intensely to carry out our mission. It has become an object of endless fascination. It has become our very lives.

Chapter 4

The next day, our probing continues. We now sail northward under favorable winds. Captain Cook seeks to chart this stretch of coast, as well as to find a more commodious place to drop anchor. We proceed on our way, many an eye glued to the languid progression of scenery on our port side. It captivates me still, as I gaze intently for hours, noting its changing contours and lights. Clouds of gulls and other birds follow us. While we sense a lush and hidden life ashore, we see no other signs of the natives. Here, I begin to suspect them shy to the point of reticence. On the one hand, this would mean our crew would not be put at risk when we landed. On the other, it would make contact and meaningful communication that much more difficult. For while not our mission's primary goal, it nevertheless is a priority for various reasons.

And so, the days pass uneventfully, yet eventfully—the tedium of our slow transit north latent with meaning. We see, hear, and smell never-before-experienced impressions. Even so, some of the men weary of this distant study of our objective and throw lines into the sea, hoping to snag a fish or two for supper. Our daily fare never having inspired acclaim for its savor, the thought of a fresh meal inspires the crew.

Six days pass in this fashion. At length, a cry goes out—it looks as if we approach the entrance to an enclave or bay. Curiosity piqued, we round a point—and what a most welcome delight. It proves to be a bay—a placid and expansive one, at that. In the late afternoon, Captain Cook decides to drop anchor. He prudently decrees, however, that we will spend the rest of the day making observations from the ship, with a landing set for tomorrow.

And so, excited men clamber to the rails—but not to gawk at the shoreline. Rather, in fevered pitch, they drop lines, knowing that these sheltered waters must teem with life. No sooner does a baited hook sink to the bottom than an ecstatic sailor begins a scrap to haul in his line. Others gather around, eager to see what he has caught. After several more minutes of excited talk and exclamations, the catch is gaffed and hauled on board. All gasp in wonder at what they see: a huge, flat, and still-undulating stingray struggles in vain to again find the sea. It pauses to rest. We note now its odd, flat shape, pinkish-grey color, well-developed eyes, and of course, the stinging tail. I peer more closely at its otherworldly form with a twinge of disgust—but then, of course, it was made for a vastly different world: the sea bottom. So, I begin to admire how well-adapted its design is for its peculiar mission in life, feeding off the seabed. Its eyes especially captivate—those reddish eyes that look at us almost with intelligence. Oddly then, I feel a twinge of pity for our prey. For while it once fearlessly fed on smaller species, now it peers about with apprehension at an array of alien predators. Most, however, quite naturally see a meal other than slop.

By suppertime, we have caught several large stingrays. They are hauled below to be cooked and unceremoniously incorporated into "higher being," as Charles laughingly puts it. After much poor fare, the taste is quite delicious. In a festive mood now, with relish we clang our grog cups, as Captain Cook has allotted us extra rations. The talk is almost as intense as the throbbing land around us.

With this in mind, I go to the deck alone for one more look at land and sea. Ah yes, and how they so naturally interact here—like a firm hand slipping into a liquid glove. I note a small beach on the cove to our south, a sandy "U" surrounded by rocky shore. Brush-covered slopes rise around it. Not quite inured to regional scents, I savor them again: subtle, yet pungent and raw. My God, what is this? A troop of fairly large creatures file onto the beach, likely looking for food. Grabbing my spyglass, I take a closer look. For all the world, they resemble huge rats—perhaps thirty pounds each. They look alien, and yet not wholly so. Before I can further evaluate, they quickly scoot off.

I next look north over the bay at large. What a natural marvel any good harbour is—this one doubly so. It is one of those rare natural formations our nation knows full well how to make the best use of. Oh, and what a thought. Could it possibly be? But yes—in time, possibly it could be so: a bustling city arising around this harbour. Yet for now, the shore appears but the boundary of the primal lands which surround it.

The next morning, we arise with the highest of expectations. Awareness of the historic nature of this moment overtakes us. Captain Cook's coterie, highly conscious of what is about to transpire, array themselves in fine attire and groom to perfection. The Captain appears in most splendid form, his uniform bringing out the natural majesty of his manly physique and finely chiseled features. Ah, what good fortune—I will accompany my Joseph in this first landing party, an honor of which I am keenly aware.

As we row our boat to shore, the moment absorbs me completely—a moment curiously made up of two components at once. On the one hand, we are England. Our vestments and bearing transmit this loud and clear. In fact, we all assume natives are watching from concealment. And so, the hiding natives and history itself combine to form our audience. Aware of this, we step ashore with a curious sense of theatricality. Heads held high, hands go to cutlass hilts as our flag bearer, with great deliberation, plants the Union Jack in this alien soil. Captain Cook pauses, one leg upraised as he rests his right foot on a rock. For a moment, he appears a living sculpture of sorts while gazing into this land. Then, with a surprising look of unstudied awe, he grapples with what he sees. Yes, for while keenly aware of this moment's historic nature, what Captain Cook sees fills his curiosity cup to the brim.

But next, the second stream of this experience hits full force. While we walk now as only men in the midst of authentic discovery may, nature flows in like a great gushing wind, blowing back our carefully barbered hair and lace finery. Two realities collide: that of our England, and that of an elemental force not in the least impressed by our strutting. *Yes, act on, gentlemen,* it seems to say, *but have a care. Your nation and your noble goals form the flimsiest of tightropes which you must with the greatest of daring and skill now cross over. One slip, and your day is done. I am primeval nature. With me, there is no forgiveness, no second chance.*

Oh, but gentlemen, she goes on more soothingly, *take heart. For whether you succeed or not, in the end I will treat you—if not kindly, at least justly. Yes, it is true that failure may cost you your lives. But think, gentlemen. You will have died in the midst of actions your ancient heroes only dreamed of. To die while so engaged is no disgrace. You would live on forever in your people's loving memory. Of course, humans that you are, success would be much more to your liking. And so, if you do succeed, I will show you aspects of myself unknown to your kind. Yes, I will show you aspects of myself that will help you and your far-off countrymen arrive at a more complete and satisfying estimation of my order.*

Our poses break as time swallows the moment. Even so, it will somehow live on. In any event, this one moment has forever transformed our lives.

I spend the rest of the day with my Joseph as we begin our assessment of this new world's flora. Our first day proves too overwhelming to actually begin systematic study. Rather, we wander about as children in a garden for the very first time. With more sensual delight than analysis, we look at and touch a multitude of alien species. And just when I imagine I have found one that will absorb me forever with its novelty and beauty, lo and behold— another, even more wondrous specimen draws my eye. I actually become intoxicated in a way never before experienced. How might I describe the feeling of standing before a pine tree with curved branches and symmetric fans of foliage? Almost it appears to have been deliberately shaped so as to make it worthy of appearing in a sultan's garden. I take a closer look. Dense and compact needles arise on menorah-like branches. This design clearly speaks of the mathematical symmetry at the heart of nature. Yes, Charles touts stars and planets as symbols of cosmic order, and yet now—I touch and smell this very principle.

Joseph, hardly less excited, exclaims with delight and calls me over to examine some fantastical new discovery. Face ruddy with excitement, he beams like a child opening presents on Christmas morn. This feeling sums it up for us both. All the pain and hardship we have endured—for one cherished moment—appear the most insignificant of trifles. This is the reason we came here. Yes, the one true reason. Thought and the life of the mind are vital to mankind, yes. Passion too plays a most vital role. And yet, in the final analysis, our lives congeal around such moments of childlike wonder.

With our day's exploration concluded, we board our boat and row back to the ship. Those who remained behind listen to our accounts while at the same time fishing for stingrays. They have caught more than a few and consider their haul a type of discovery as well. The evening meal is festive—we toast our success and heartily pat each other on the back. And while this day marks the beginning of a new era of exploration, the small and the personal now take hold of us. The hugeness of this event must be shut out, as more needful emotions nudge us to connect with one another. We must share our feelings on this matter and so make it real to us.

Next day, we resume our exploration. Our spirit of analysis returns as we set about the massive task of categorizing a new universe of plants. Of course, we still curiously touch and sniff. I again examine a type of tree that sheds bark, with no apparent leaves on the ground. Crushing a leaf, its pungent scent reminds me of the more subtle scent of the air we breathed upon arrival. I surmise that it gives off minute traces of its essence and so flavors the air. *A hallmark of this new land,* I think with a smile. Variants of this one species festoon the land.

Then I come across a fairly huge tree with enormous gnarly roots, a variegated trunk, and a truly impressive crown of branches that bear large waxen leaves. *What a specimen,* I muse, while stroking smooth bark. Its sheer mass suggests it is quite ancient. And then a most curious thought strikes me: is there something ancient about this land as a whole? Just what might be the mechanism behind such a phenomenon?

Later that day, while preparing to head back to the ship, we spot a most unusual-looking creature. Almost as tall as a man, it stands up on its hind legs to observe us. It has what appear to be almost two arms, which it holds against its body. The face is vaguely possum-like; long ears and a thick, muscular tail set it apart. A mesmerizing sight—we watch until it hops off. Clearly, we have landed in a place where the laws of nature do not follow our own in linear fashion, creatures here unlike any in the known world. How geographic isolation has brought about this distinction will be a lively topic of future scientific discussions—especially if we have discovered a lost continent and not a large island, as I now suspect. And so it occurs to me too that the intense isolation here cannot help but affect its human inhabitants as well. For lands connected to others by history and trade, a natural cross-fertilization of ideas occurs. This promotes, to a certain extent, the idea of novelty. Yes, we take for granted those elements of language, philosophy, and religion that often in the past impinged upon us from unexpected sources. These successive waves of innovation established both the concept and the appetite for newness.

The natives here, on the other hand, by the look of it, have lived cut off from the rest of the world. We think of Africa in this way too, but with an important distinction. The early Christians first, and next the Saracens, have a long history of spreading ideas on that continent—or at least to large parts of the north and east. Perhaps North and South America come closest to matching this land for isolation. Yet there, we find quite populous regions where advanced civilizations took root. This too appears a prerequisite for development as we understand it. For without a concentration of human energy, incentives for development would be lacking.

Here, on the other hand, I suspect the concentration of human settlements is quite low. This would have a twofold effect. First, it would suggest the energy and incentive to construct and develop was simply not there. Second, it would mean that the land itself would be vastly more potent as a shaper of who they are. Ah, again the notions of our artist occur to me. Perhaps they are mere whimsy, as Sidney really only half believes them himself. Still, it cannot be denied that our kind forms deep and abiding attachments to the lands we inhabit. Limited cross-cultural interaction and low population density could multiply the power of this factor many times over for the natives here. And so, the spirit of the land would find less obstructed human channels here for a fuller expression of it. In any event, I find my improvised theory an intriguing notion, and will use it as a measuring rod while assessing the natives.

These ruminations cling to me as I awaken the next day to continue our exploration. By day's end, I have amassed another impressive array of specimens. But something else occurs that day as well. My Joseph had gone out with another exploration party. They return now with a startling account of our first substantial encounter with the natives.

Joseph begins the narration. While exploring the harbour a ways up, they came across a village. The natives live in little more than low-lying huts made of branches. Several of them loll about a campfire, a mother with her small child off in the distance. Evidently, she gives the child a lesson of sorts. All are naked.

One of the men becomes agitated when he sees the explorers. He approaches in a threatening manner, spear in upraised hand. One of our men responds by firing at the man's legs. Undeterred, he keeps up the threatening gestures. Another man lets loose with a second round. Again, it has no apparent effect on the native other than forcing his hasty retreat. But lo and behold—he returns with a large shield. This he holds to cover most of his body while peeping through two small eye holes.

The men ignore him and stroll into the village. One of them attempts to give a few small gifts to the mother and child, while others expropriate two spears and a shield. They linger for a while, still trying to communicate with the natives. Oddly enough, the natives ignore them and go about cooking, canoeing, and walking on the beach—all the while keeping a wary eye on the newcomers. A few of the younger males approach unarmed, consumed with curiosity. They look at Joseph intently but then scamper off. Eventually, our men withdraw with their booty. They show it now for us to admire. How it fascinates, to hold one of those spears in my hand. How compelling to imagine stepping so far back in time. The shield, too, I examine closely. I think of it as a shell that a vulnerable naked man might hide behind. Naturally, talk of the encounter goes on for some time. It has stirred the men's blood and more than a few imaginations.

Late at night, as I sleeplessly mull the encounter, several other things occur to me. First, it appears we head in the same direction as our last native encounter—initial reception a hostile one. And yet, I cannot help but feel the attack, if that is what it truly was, had been of so weak a nature as to be pathetic. A naked man shouting and hiding behind a primitive shield did not conjure a truly threatening image. I begin to wonder at the necessity of having to open fire. Had the native actually thrown a weapon, it may have been an appropriate response. As matters stood, perhaps we had let emotion rather than reason dictate our response. I wonder, too, why the inhabitants here feel no need for even the most rudimentary of clothing. No other native peoples we know of go about thus. Try as I might, no satisfying explanation occurs to me.

I think again of what one of the men had said about the woman he had approached. She had looked at him in an unfriendly fashion while making the universally understood "go away" hand swish. Ha—so on the bright side, here was mutually comprehensible communication. Then too, on a hopeful note, the woman had assumed that our man would understand what she communicated. On the not-so-hopeful side—and firstly from her perspective— she had been totally ignored. Then too, the making of this gesture likely came about from more cogitation on her part than the others suspect. From her perspective, she understood at once that our intrusion was unwelcome and threatening in nature. Was she right about this? Do we pose a threat to her and her people?

Lastly, I think the natives might interpret our expropriation of the spears and shield as a simple case of theft. From their perspective, it would be the most natural assumption to make. After all, we ourselves bristle with arms, and yet, by implication, insist they be defenseless. This could be interpreted in some rather frightening ways. On the other hand, from our perspective, safety comes first—with us so many thousands of miles from home and any hope of aid. We simply must protect each precious life in our expedition with all due care. So there one has it: an unfortunate prescription for further misunderstandings.

The next day, while still passionate about carrying out my research, thoughts of the native encounter begin to nudge out my attention to detail. For some reason, I think of the shield with two eye holes and the man behind it. Curiously, this gives me a sense of what it means to be one of these unusual humans. By noon, I decide I simply must sneak off for a look at that village myself. Knowing it's a foolish thing to do, I override manifold objections by convincing myself that one lone man, concealed and observing the natives from a distance, might hope to witness their daily life as it truly is.

So off I go. Approaching the village, I quietly position myself on a small rise and lie down flat. If any of the natives have observed me, they do not let on. So I take out my spyglass for a closer look. Ah, it does indeed appear that I have not been seen. A woman continues to cook shellfish with evident delight. A man rubs some kind of substance into his beached canoe. Two men wade into shallow water, upraised spears in hand. One of them lets out an exclamation as he strikes. He and his companion laugh with delight as he next holds up the speared fish. Ah, what's this? Back in the village, I see a woman making what appear to be garments of fur. So, perhaps they do wear clothes after all—at least when the weather becomes cooler.

Most rewarding of all, I note a man with a large wooden tube sitting down next to the woman cooking. He begins to blow into it. Is it a musical instrument of some sort? I lower my glass and strain to hear what I may. Hmm, yes, I do hear low and mysterious tones produced in measured fashion. I listen as best I can for about five minutes, trying to absorb enough of the sound to imprint a memory. Looking through my glass again, I see that several natives have gathered around to listen—evidently, this type of music is quite meaningful to them. With my mission concluded, I prepare to sneak off. Ah, but then I have a thought. I fish around in my pocket for a coin. Still shiny from lack of use, I place it on the spot I had rested on. "A parting gift," I say with a smile.

That night I lie awake, eyes closed, as traces of the day's scenes flit about before fading away. Then my attention turns to the fantastical array of Southern Hemisphere stars. Alone with them, I feel oddly tilted, as if facing some other universe. How, then, can this new world fit into the one I have known? Only time would answer this question.

Chapter 5

The sun rises. My doubtful mood fades in its light. The task of collecting new plants calls forth my efforts. The weather turns cloudy, and the temperature drops somewhat, yet I find this refreshing. Soon, I am lost in fascinating observations. On my own again, I wander into a lush forest, its pungent scents a delight. With cries of alarm, various colorful birds give way before me. It begins to rain, but lightly. Undeterred, I continue my search. Finding a gorgeous new specimen, I stoop closer for a good look. Then I feel it. Someone is watching me. With a start, I turn around—and there stands a native.

A young man, he has white, chalky marks daubed over his upper torso. He carries no weapons, but rather a small wooden container in his right hand. His eyes shine with intense emotion—one of them, wonder. I, in my turn, feel wonder.

Stepping forward, he extends his right hand and nods. Hand now open, the small container lies on his palm. He wants me to take it. Without hesitation, I reach out and accept the gift. He nods again and makes an upward motion with his hand. Following this cue, I open the container and look in. There is a clay-like substance inside. It looks similar to the substance on his body. I take a pinch of it and rub it between my fingers. He smiles. How I wish I knew his language. Clearly, this substance has a special meaning to him—one that evades me. He laughs at my perplexed look and beckons me to pass him the plant I have just plucked. Then he holds it next to his body, spreads the roots so as to resemble two legs, and points to the sky. He next takes a pinch of the clay he gave me and points to himself. Still baffled, I feel the need to reciprocate. So I take off my hat and present it to him. He gives me a solemn no head-shake. I'm offended, and it shows. He laughs again and opens his other hand.

Ah, there it is: the coin I had left behind the other day. Even under clouds it shines a bit. Apparently, I had been observed after all—at least by one. And of course, this trifle to me is for him a rare piece of life. His mission complete, he nods once again and vanishes back into the forest, this whole exchange a thank-you.

That night, I lie awake contemplating our encounter. How odd to think, on the one hand, that a face-to-face meeting with a tribesman had taken place. Who could say what they truly believe—these men whose lives entwine with the wild? But then, my suppressed fear bubbles up. Yes, he might just as well have put a knife in my ribs as handed me a gift. Oh, but no—instantly, I am repelled by this thought. Something much more understandable had happened. In its essence, one of the simplest and most gratifying acts of a human being: the exchange of gifts.

I open his present again and take a whiff, foolishly thinking a scent might cue me as to its meaning. But no—it merely smells of earth. No clue here. Earth, earth… what does this mean? Ah, he had related it to a plant. Was he telling me this earth is good for growing plants in? If I planted a seed in it, would it sprout into some fantastical thing? Just like in the story of *Jack Spriggins and the Enchanted Bean*? After all, the plants here grow with a robustness not known in our England. I could perform an experiment and see… and yet, we would not remain here much longer. As well, the season here was tilting towards winter. While undoubtedly mild in this region, it might not be the best time for planting. At any rate, this fanciful explanation leaves me wanting.

I next do a most curious thing. Quietly rising, I fetch the native shield from a nearby storage enclave. Returning to my room, I lie down and place it over my body, peering out the two eye holes. Inhaling the scent of the wood, I close my eyes and imagine myself as a tribesman. Yes—there I stand by the sea, spear in hand, waiting to impale a fish for supper, my vocation an elemental one. How must that feel? Rising with the sun, we men head out to hunt and fish while our women remain behind to cook and weave. Hmm… perhaps the women also gather herbs to flavor our catch, causing oohs and ahs of delight as we feast around our campfire.

The next day, several marauders approach our village. How we rouse our collective manhood in defense of our own! Spears in hand, we approach the strangers with shouts of warning and gestures of martial prowess. They hurl back defiance and raise spears of their own. But we have one clear advantage: we defend hearth and home. This sends fire into our hearts. We roar and gesture with a surge of new energy. The intruders sense our resistance is too stiff, and—while still spouting bravado—slowly back off. We have won the day for our own. So we relax, and with pride, resume our daily activities. I spear a marvelous fish and know it to be a true prize—so much larger and more colorful than any my fellows spear. How this makes me smile. What a delight to the eye, my catch. How it reflects the sea from which I've just plucked it…

After our evening feast, the village musician begins to play his… whatcha-macallit. We listen on intently, swept away into living dreams of the land's beauty and power… Horizon, yes, that's it — that's what that sound now suggests to me: horizon stretching out more vastly than anyone in England could ever imagine… a horizon defining my people…

"Hullo, Ben," a voice next shatters this image. "Are you all right, lad? You haven't gone daft on me, have you now?"

There stands my Joseph. He has come for the specimen I'd promised to have ready for him. I quickly place the shield on the floor and stand up.

"No, no, I'm quite all right, I can assure you. I was just, um, examining this shield up close for a— a clue as to what these natives are about. That's it. That's all. No need for alarm, rest assured."

"If you say so, Ben," he replies, with a still-cocked eye. "But no more shenanigans. I need you up bright and early tomorrow."

"Of course. Bright and early."

With a slight scowl, he picks up the shield. I hand him the specimen with my notes and sheepishly return to bed. Restless, my imagination reenters the forest. Eye alone could spend considerable time analyzing its depths. Indeed, our artist Sidney does just that.

One day, while showing me his drawings, he made an interesting observation. He noted that while my work is quite valuable, his was too. He went on to relate what my own Joseph had said — about analysis beginning with the eye. What the eye first perceives, the mind later grasps.

With such thoughts coursing through my mind, sleep at last overtakes me.

Oddly enough, for the next few days, I find my research somewhat less alluring. This disturbs me greatly. I have let the novelty of our new surroundings get the better of me. So, I redouble my efforts and focus even more intensely on my work.

Even so, by noon, with my concentration once again scattered, I slip away to the beach for a time. Sitting on the sand, I study the bay and note a native canoe not far off. Its occupant appears to be fishing. A companion on the shore waves to him — evidently, he wants the other to come fetch him so he can fish as well. His companion, in a playful way, ignores him.

In exasperation, his fellow simply lunges into the water and begins swimming to the canoe.

"Oh my God," I exclaim with a start while squinting.

"Can it be?" Yes, a fin above the water closes in fast on the unsuspecting swimmer. Instinctively, I rise and shout a warning. The youth becomes aware of the danger and begins to panic. His friend paddles madly towards him, still some ways off.

Then it happens. Several dolphins appear, jumping with spirit into the air and landing with splashes. They fearlessly bear down on the shark, and after a few moments of struggle, manage to drive it off. By then, the swimmer's companion has fetched him onto the boat. The dolphins linger on, heads out of the water as they make laughing sounds. With great emotion, the youths wave their arms about and speak to the dolphins.

This spectacle takes me back to my own observation of dolphins on the high seas and how they appear to have an affinity for humans. At any rate, relieved that the youth has been rescued, I sit in wonder for two whole hours, even after the players in this drama have departed.

Some time after this episode, our crew gathers on that same beach for a sort of, well, farewell supper—although an open-air one. Soon we must sail northward up this coast for further exploration. Now, while autumn in this land slowly gives way to winter, the weather is still mild and pleasant, especially when compared to the same season in England.

So, under a crystal-blue sky with the sound of slight waves lapping, we seat ourselves on improvised chairs. Some few even remove their boots to allow their feet the freedom of sand. Our cooks set up a fire pit to prepare various dishes. For, in addition to fish, we will sample the meat of one of the large hopping creatures yet unnamed. Grog cups clink, and a surprisingly buoyant mood takes over. Something about the combination of sun, sand, and surf strikes all as uniquely appealing.

"So, young Ben," Charles smiles as he approaches, "have you quite gotten over your fit of native distemper?"

Sheepishly, I smile, yet feel discomfort. All know only too well of my shield episode. Once, upon falling asleep at a meeting, I had awakened to discover my face daubed with white paint. How they had all roared with laughter and made jungle sounds.

"Yes, quite. And as I have told you all many times, it was no fit of whimsy but rather an experiment of sorts."

"Right, an experiment," Joseph adds while joining us. "And just what, young man, did you deduce from your experiment?"

"I rightly deduced my fellows would never understand my motivation."

"An evidently successful experiment," Charles notes.

Uncomfortable now, I try to change the subject.

"Yes, well, we have had some stunning successes here, have we not? It's hard to say what our most important discovery is."

"Stingrays," Richard jokes. "You, Joseph, named this place after them—Stingray Bay."

"Stingray Bay," he sniffs with disdain, "Yes, Stingray Bay… That name is dated, Richard. In the time we have been here, a new array of plant life has been discovered. I will now change the name to Botany Bay."

"How humble of you," Charles responds. "And yet I suppose that with no further astronomical discoveries to be made, it sounds appropriate enough… although young Ben here might have other ideas…"

"No, no, I most certainly agree. All our most original discoveries pertain to the order of plants."

"And yet I sense hesitation in your voice…"

"Perhaps he thinks something more globally evocative of this land would sound better," Sidney, who just joined us, puts in.

"And just how might that be possible," Charles responds, "when no such well-rounded impression exists? Indeed, what in this God-forsaken land could an Englishman of right reason and good taste find to love? It is, you cannot deny, a forgotten land at the ends of the Earth, by all appearances in a state of advanced decrepitude. Even the animal species here strike me, for one, as bastard offshoots of animals in more accessible lands. There is something odd about them. All clearly see this."

"What about the birds?" I object.

He pauses here and pictures them in his mind.

"Yes, well, perhaps some of the birds here have a certain charm. As for the mammals, I suspect that isolation has led to an unsavory tendency to inbreed. And as far as the men in these parts are concerned, well, one would be hard put to name a more debased offshoot of humanity."

"In what way debased?"

"Debased in their total ignorance of the proper order of nature, for one. They live as do some of the dimwitted animals here. Just look at their homes, Ben! Back in England, one would find pack-rats in such haphazard heaps of sticks."

"Granted, they are hardly beautiful to look at…"

"Oh, I don't know," Sidney objects. "Something in their very compactness suggests an austerity that in other cultures you might find admirable, Charles. Think what one of your beloved Stoic philosophers once said: 'All that I have I carry with me.'"

"But what do they carry besides spears? The Stoics carried pen and scroll. Can these specimens write at all, I wonder?"

"Perhaps they act more as blank slates than pens. Perhaps nature herself inscribes her script upon them to the point of overflowing," I put in.overflowing," I put in.

"And just what do you mean to suggest with that bit of frippery?"

"I merely suggest that more ways than one exist for men to convey meaning."

"I should be delighted, young Ben, if you could but master just one such way."

Here, I fancy telling Charles that the sharpness of his mind vastly surpasses that of his wit, but then quickly sober. He is my senior, after all—brilliant as well.

"Oh, but Charles, just think—nature speaks to us in a language science seeks to decipher. As a man of science, you understand this. There may be types of languages at work here that we simply don't understand."

"But no written language, Ben! Yes, nature conveys meaning, but if a given race has no medium to express this meaning, then it is simply lost to them."

"So it would appear. But now, concerning the land itself, I would fight you on your observations. Surely you must admit, as we sit here eating and drinking under blue skies while the sounds of the sea charm us—surely you must admit it all a pleasure and a good."

At first he frowns, but then lifts his cup.

"Aptly put, young Ben, aptly put. Indeed, I cannot find fault with your latest observation. Cheers."

Our festivities continue thus for some good while. Absorbed in it all, I still cannot help but picture the scene in my mind's eye. For here we assemble, a band of explorers, having the chummiest of get-togethers on the shore of a land the extent of which we may only imagine—blithely discussing its fate while consuming its fruit. Truly, too, the food has appeal. In fact, we end up overeating, a forgivable sin considering all we have endured.

That night, scenes of the day flicker on in my mind. Our newly christened Botany Bay has witnessed much drama in the last stretch of time—starting with our stingray catch, continuing on to our raising the flag, and culminating in our astonishing finds. Ours is a colony of sorts, and a most animated one. Driven by dreams far exceeding the actual size and power of our expedition, we had—in our own minds at least—marked out this land for future exploration and eventual settlement by the British Crown.

So this is how such matters play out… Yes, take a measure of recklessness, combine it with ambition and a thirst for knowledge, and the concept of a new land is born.

Almost it seems too much has happened in too short a time for me to successfully integrate it all into my warp and woof. That will take time and reflection. Yet an impatient host of impressions bangs away at my fortress gate with a battering ram, with force wanting in. Manfully, I resist opening the gate to let this foreign host take up residence in my plot of interior England. I may only, at this point—and as Sidney would put it—consider it all in its visual and undigested form.

So here it is to date: A band of hearty Englishmen exists side by side with natives whom I suspect desperately hope we will forever go away. We know precious little of who they are, where they came from, and what their sensibilities are. Some few of us suspect they have none. Yet based on my own, for-now-private, observations, I cannot come to this conclusion.

There is much at work here in nature and in nature's children, the truth of which evades us at the moment. Yes, round a bend in the sky we have whipped, and now stand face to face with past and future.

Chapter 6

After several more days of exploration, our departure date nears. And yet, having just scratched the surface of this new world, I have somehow formed a bond with it and its people. And so, while walking alone by the bay, I lovingly stroke this or that newly cataloged plant. The chatter of tropical birds above makes me smile, their calls now familiar. Even this forest's rank scents now smell more enticing.

With this new frame of mind, I take a last tour. Back at the place where I had witnessed the dolphin rescue, the scene appears calm. Oh, but what might this be? Bending down, I pick up an unusual piece of wood. About six inches long, it is covered with some curious characters, or perhaps a script of sorts. Could it possibly be connected with the incident I witnessed? Might it have been deliberately placed here for me to find? No… But if yes, why? Why would I be the recipient of another gift from these people? Did they somehow connect my crying out to the timely appearance of dolphins? Or do I merely let imagination run wild? Yes, quite possibly so, as this land has a way of stretching all my known categories to the limit. Having exhausted these, the fanciful tends to seep in. Yet undeniably, I now possess another native article. And, in keeping with the mood that has overcome me, I will keep this gift too a secret while probing my mind for its meaning.

All of this private speculation comes to an abrupt end when we weigh anchor and put Botany Bay behind us. Normally, with my Joseph, we man the prow at such departures. Yet today I stand alone at the stern, looking south while the horizon swallows up our one-time home. It is true, on the one hand, that out of sight equals out of mind. For as all dissolves into the ever-shifting boundary of the sea, Botany Bay becomes almost a fiction of sorts—something that now exists only in our specimens and notes. It transmutes into the letter B, to be looked up again in the library within, as occasion demands. And yet, on the other hand, that night I have vivid dreams of the colors, scents, and sounds of our now-vanished encampment. And so, as the *HMS Endeavour* finds its way northward, my sleeping mind rests on that one fixed point.

In days to come, however, consciously at least, thoughts shift forward, as with my Joseph we stand at the prow and scan the hitherto unseen world before us. The coast on our port side—we watch as it languidly moves to the south. How striking to think that by going north we now approach true tropics and the Equator itself. How the land must be changing. How lush tropical beauties must be thriving year-round, unfettered by even a hint of seasonal change, except perhaps in the peaks beyond. The sea as well begins to change, though far more subtly. Then again, perhaps my imagination alone suggests this. For as the sun grows more intense, the sea sparkles with a vibrancy unknown in our more overcast north. It almost mesmerizes with its blueness, light, and expanse.

Oh, but then a dramatic and real change occurs as we approach a region of many coral reefs—or perhaps one vast reef. At times, as the water becomes shallow, it appears more a glass shell than murky depths. Yes, in this crystal blue, we see tantalizing hints of the lushest undersea landscapes. Of course, this beauty is lost to Captain Cook and our navigator. For they must now, with the greatest of care, ease our way through this navigational hazard. As our danger becomes more apparent, I too cease from aesthetic speculations and act as another pair of warning eyes. Many now perform this duty with nary a thought of a stingray supper.

We proceed in this tense fashion for some days, hoping with all our might to at last approach an end to this potential ship grave. Day after day, our hope is dashed, as the reef begins to appear endless. It only becomes more complex and convoluted, dazzling now green with a plethora of tiny islands. In spite of our danger, we cannot help but gaze in wonder as our ship eases past these miniature tropical worlds. With the most pristine of beaches, dense jungle looms in the background. Often we spot large tropical birds flying from tree to tree. If natives inhabit these isles, they remain out of sight.

One day, as we ease past one more such island, the most feared of scenarios happens. With a terrifying grinding sound and a deadly lurch, at once all know we have struck the reef. Even so, we do not panic. Each man quickly reacts, as we have in fact drilled for just such a possibility. With skill and good luck, we stem the flow of water as best we may and continue to sail. Our captain plots an emergency course straight for the mainland. As we approach the beach head-on, he deliberately steers us aground onto soft sand. Good fortune is with us in one respect, at least, as with high tide we more or less safely beach away from the action of waves. With immense relief, we evacuate to the safety of land. Only now do we begin to shake and experience the fearful emotions we had managed to stave off. These quickly pass as relief and a type of euphoria overtake us. Yes, we have survived a crushing disaster.

In the days to come, aided by pulleys and ropes, we actually haul our ship to drier ground to effect repairs. A perilous and, under the circumstances, monumental project, it absorbs every ounce of our will and sinew. Yet nature has blessed us with an abundance of trees from which to procure lumber for the needed repairs. Unfortunately for me, our effort begins with an accident. While helping to secure a load of lumber on board, I fall and land hard. My leg, though not broken, has been pulled out of joint. Our good Doctor Solander manages to reset it. Even so, now having to move about with a crutch, I have been rendered useless for our improvised project. Thus begins my adventure within an adventure, so to speak.

At first, I tell my Joseph that this need not be slack time for me. I insist it remains possible for me to explore using a crutch. With new species likely on this stretch of coast, here is an opportunity for more discoveries. Reluctantly, he agrees and returns to his duties. Off I hobble into yet another new world portal. As I survey westward from the beach, a horizon of low hills stretches north to south. A vast inlet winds inland. How the sea sparkles under that intense tropical sun. With effort, walking inland a ways, lush forest greets me. Not unlike the one at our Botany Bay, it nevertheless appears more verdant owing to its location in the tropics proper. Ha, yes, funny—I almost feel at home again. The same sense of intertwining levels of life does me in. I simply cannot resist its allure.

Back on the beach, I note a plume of smoke in the distance and know at once natives live not far off. A strange thought seizes me. Why not stride alone and unarmed into their village? Surely by so doing they would interpret no hostile motive. Seeing me walk with a crutch would emphasize my vulnerability and openness to their presence. This gives me pause, as indeed I would be quite helpless in the face of attack. But then another thought occurs to me. I will show them the engraved branch I often carry with me, imagining it a good luck charm of sorts. So, even while chiding myself for lingering superstition, I resolve to walk into their village. Only years later would I learn that the stick represented a type of inter-tribal passport.

Considering my condition, I make good time and soon approach the village. It lies in a river valley that abuts the inlet. I stand on a rise some ways off and survey the vista. Their village resembles the one at Botany Bay. Low huts of branches surround a central fire. People come and go in the midst of daily activities. Yet before I begin my descent into the valley, out of nowhere a tribesman pops up to confront me. He reminds me at once of the youth in my first encounter: strong upper torso, lightly bearded, short curly hair, and animated, deeply set eyes. For one breathless moment, the nature of our encounter hangs in the balance. My unexpected companion cannot quite decide how to react, since my appearance defies all known categories.

The finest moment arrives. Taking the carved branch token out of my pocket, I hold it out to him. His expression shifts into one of wonder. He eyes the token first, then me—and closely at that. Unblinkingly, he looks me in the eye for one full minute. Then, he slowly extends his hand, takes my token, and inspects it. Satisfied by what he sees, with an almost pleasant look, he beckons for me to follow him. This I do as best I may in my condition. Noting this, he obligingly slackens his pace.

We enter his village. As I am accompanied by one of their own, they react differently here than at Botany Bay. They do not challenge or ignore me. Instead, all eyes fix on my face for a careful reading of my expression. Apparently lacking enough for them to form a judgment, another breathless moment hangs in the air. When, however, my companion holds up my token, the moment unfreezes. Inexplicably, they appear prepared to accept my presence.

Breathlessly, I enter into the midst of them. A truly unique and jarring moment ensues. Before me stand villagers without a stitch on them. Yet oddly enough, what I notice most are individual faces. Each of these tribesmen appears, first of all, an individual—despite all having the same complexion and overall characteristics. They look at me with such intensity that I almost feel the impacts, the overall mood one of nebulous expectation. Yes, I think that about sums it up. At this point, they only know my presence means something of an unclear sort has happened. So, as is common to our human nature, they put the best possible face on an unknown situation. Perhaps I am the harbinger of some great good. At any rate, they choose not to raise the specter of the opposite possibility—at least for now.

To sum it up, I am treated as a guest. And, as it appears to be mealtime, I am led to a gathering of villagers by the fire. They bid me be seated on the ground. I smile, nod, and point to my leg. Hand to forehead, I pantomime pain. Instantly, they understand and fetch me a small log to sit on. I smile gratefully and sit down. Next, they serve cooked shellfish. I accept one, pry it open, and eat. As they watch, I rub my stomach and make *mmm* sounds. Instantly, they understand, smile, and proceed to eat themselves. As I finish my meal, one of the villagers brings me a bowl of some kind of thick reddish liquid. In response to my puzzled look, he dips a twig into it and licks off the thick stuff clinging to it. Next, he pats his stomach and says "mmm." I laugh while accepting a twig and do likewise. The taste is pungent, yet sweet. I like it.

Meal finished, my new companion acts as guide. With a *come on* hand swish, he bids me follow him. We arrive at a spot where the river meets the inlet. He points to this, claps his hands, and then clasps them. I quickly grasp the gesture: river meets sea in a type of union. I gather this is important to him and his people. I nod a yes, and he smiles. Next, I point to the water and, with my hand, mimic the side-to-side movement of a fish. Laughing, he points to a canoe. We get in and paddle out a ways. Not far from shore, he throws a small fiber fishnet into the water.

Excited by the thought of this rudimentary communication, I try some more. Pointing to the water, I use my hand and arm to mime a dolphin jumping out. I then shake my head up and down and make a laughing sound. At once, he grasps the meaning. He first points to his heart, then the water, and lastly clasps both hands together. Clearly, he feels a strong emotional attachment to these creatures. And so, another link is established between us.

Later, we catch a few fish and return to the shore. It is time to head back to his village. There, our catch will be part of the evening meal. I watch in wonder as two men hold a rope at opposite ends and start to swing it. A third begins to skip and makes elaborate movements in the process. How astonishing to think of the game of jump rope here at the ends of the Earth.

After our meal, some men begin to dance as all present sing. One man in particular holds my attention. His dance is more than mere dance—I sense a tale here as he imitates the movements of various animals. The singing too must be part of the account. I next take note of the circles, dots, and lines painted on his body. These marks are symbols of sorts; their meaning somehow relates to the dance and song, or so I begin to imagine. I turn to my companion, shrug, and upraise my hands. Understanding that I question the meaning of the dance, he takes me aside and begins to draw the shapes from the man's body in the sand. Next, he points to the sky, the river, and himself. With me still puzzled, he holds out two hands and moves them slightly forward. Does he mean *wait*? I think so.

This turns out to be the case. As the sun begins to set, he rises and beckons for me to follow. Into the river valley we wind as a full moon rises. I note the sound of flowing water and watch pale white light flit across its surface. The warm air carries scents of bough and blossom. Birds chatter joyfully while preparing for sleep. Oh—and what's this? A flock of bats now silently passes overhead, hundreds and hundreds of them. Vastly larger than any in England, I marvel again at the face of nature in these parts. How fittingly my host blends in with it all. He evokes land and creatures in an unstudied fashion, and yet I cannot quite discern the connections here—or their actual import.

At last, we stop and sit in an open expanse by the river. He closes his eyes for a moment, as if striving for the means to relate his account. Ah, he appears to have found his muse. Eyes open as he looks my way, folded hands go to his right cheek as, closing his eyes, he again tilts his head. He sleeps.

With eyes still closed, he puts his hands on his head and next goes through a pantomime of bird and animal movements. Ah, he dreams. Alert again, he looks for some sign of understanding. I nod a yes. He proceeds to draw in the sand—first a small man, then a huge one with a crown of rays. He points first to the small one and then to himself, next to the large one and the sky. Likely, he refers to some kind of deity.

I put both my hands together and hold them before me in a gesture of reverence. He appears to understand, nods, and continues—pointing one hand at the stars and slowly moving it over them in a winding fashion. With his other hand, he points to the large figure in the drawing. Vaguely, I grasp the meaning and nod for him to continue.

He gestures to the river and makes the same winding motion. Again, something registers and I nod. Once more, he mimes sleep. Hands rise from his head and again suggest bird and mammal movements. He looks up at me. I nod a yes.

At this point, he breaks into song as both hands continue to indicate animal movements. A vast drama unfolds which my imagination only dimly grasps. Pleased, he points to himself, spreads his arms, opens his hands, and brings all into his chest—shining eyes reflecting reverent emotion. I nod him on.

So, lastly, he puts both hands over his heart, slowly extends them skyward, and spreads his fingers wide to indicate release. Inexplicably moved, I nod and smile. Having concluded his silent account, he rises. It is time to return to his village.

When we arrive—quite overwhelmed by my experience—I clasp his hand, shake it, and point to my own encampment. Yes, we both agree—it is time for me to leave.

I arrive back at camp amidst a celebration. Our crew has successfully completed an important task to further repairs. All well pleased, mug clinks mug as some sing snatches of song. They move about in a rapid, haphazard fashion—in contrast to the native's more choreographed movements.

Various emotions bubble here: joy, sadness, anger—but mostly just an energetic enjoyment of the evening. And yet, it all lacks the focal point which had given a certain grace to the tribesmen's comportment.

My Joseph greets me with a concerned look. I return late and with empty hands.

"What of the specimens I had promised him?" he asks.

I hem and haw, and at length tell him that my leg had bothered me so much that I ended up taking my ease by the water. His scowl reads *lazy lad* but then softens. He genuinely worries about the impact this land's novelty appears to be having on me.

Placing his hand on my shoulder, he bides me have something to eat. I decline, saying rest is more called for. He only shrugs as I bid him good night.

No, I think while walking away, there is simply no way to relate my encounter coherently, so best to keep it secret until I understand what took place.

And so I lie awake, trying to distill meaning from this latest episode. On the one hand, it does make sense in an intuitive way. On the other hand, I cannot quite put it all into words. Images—an array of images—flow yet through my imagination.

I think first of my Joseph and his notion of a visual knowledge of one's object of study or contemplation. On that level, raw images had stirred my imagination. But imagination may often be a free-floating affair that reason must wrest to itself in order to extract meaning.

I think too of Sidney's notion of the land shaping its inhabitants. This makes some kind of practical sense to me now, as I had just witnessed a symbolic interaction of man with his environment—and cosmos as well.

And so in the end, our last and our greatest adventure drew to a close. We then set our course for dear England, our cargo impressions in wax that with luck would endure. Still, for all of our hopes and our hurts and our gains—and the royal displays to uphold them—only the wind-driven rain late at night would herald our passage.

"Thoughts, the slaves of life..." This line from one of Shakespeare's plays pops into my mind. What might be the truth hinted at here? And just what might a slave insurrection on this level lead to?

Perhaps in my case, it would lead to a more linear approach to life. My years of study and training had conditioned me to approach the world in an oblique and intellectual fashion. All my words, observations, and internal quibbles dance around the true nature of this event.

It was, simply put, the encounter of one human being with another.

Chapter 7

For the next few weeks, I am in turmoil. On the one hand, I long to sneak off and visit my new friend and his village again. With so much to learn, it seems almost a shirking of my duty as a human being not to do so. On the other hand, I simply cannot process the first encounter. Turning it over in my mind, it makes sense and yet doesn't—quite. It seems to me that in order to learn more about these people, I must first grasp the meaning of our initial meeting. That would serve as the foundation upon which to build further knowledge.

In addition to this, my Joseph keeps a wary eye on me now, sensing something afoot that badly affects the performance of my duties. This, in the end, is what dissuades me from further contact. My true duty lies with Joseph—my true object of study: botany. I simply cannot let him or the crew down.

In any event, with our repairs soon complete, we continue our northward voyage of discovery. By now, we have more or less acclimatized to this part of the world, and its panorama no longer overwhelms. Yet for me at least, an unusual process continues unabated, as I faintly sense my mind developing another pole of experience from which to interpret our world. Of course, we in England understand this effect and so consider travel to the Continent part of a well-rounded education. Raw exploration, on the other hand, alters perceptions just as much as it increases conventional knowledge. I would find this both a gift and a burden in the future—but I get ahead of myself here. For indeed, the most crucial part of our voyage looms on the horizon.

On the morning of the 22nd of August, 1770, the *HMS Endeavour* approaches its rendezvous with destiny: a rocky island at the northern extremity of the coast just explored. We drop anchor as an expectant mood descends. Rumor has it Captain Cook has something special planned to commemorate our successful exploration of this immense and hitherto uncharted land. All on board pause in the midst of labors to consider the Herculean task we have just accomplished—at the cost of no little blood and toil. As the heartiest of Englishmen, we cannot help but burst with pride.

Then too, many are the great and hazardous endeavors that go, if not unmarked, then certainly less celebrated in the annals of our national records. This would be no such occasion. All now are keenly aware that we have engraved ourselves onto the tablets of history. Most fittingly then, our captain will commemorate the occasion with dash and pageantry.

Still—and as always, on the other hand—I cannot help but feel a sense of trepidation as well. Though none on board fully knows what the captain has in mind, we understand it involves the subjugation of new lands to the British Crown. This has the effect of tearing me in two, so to speak. Yes, I understand full well that this act crowns our mission with imperishable success. We not only cover our nation with glory, but ourselves as well. Then too, this audacious act will open new regions to future exploration and eventual colonization. Might this not, too, give me the opportunity to return to a land that—dare I say it—I have grown to love?

However that may be, this new reality is forked and no straight branch. For us, it means our future as a nation has been marvelously extended. For the natives, it means control of their national destiny will soon be taken from them. Yet the pageant must go on. England must claim what is hers by right of discovery. So Captain Cook and his coterie array themselves in His Majesty's finest attire. Not only do they look their best, they appear as very England itself. They wait until near sunset before setting out for shore.

On the ship, I watch the unfolding drama through my spyglass. They land and assemble with order—no haphazard poking about here. Then, with military precision, they fire three volleys of shots while an honor guard plants our flag in alien soil. Ranks on board precisely match those three terrestrial volleys. Captain Cook takes out a document and begins to read it. One may well imagine his words from here on the ship. No lengthy harangue—rather, he sums up sparingly what all know to be self-evident: King George III augments his power and authority in this uttermost end of the Earth. We know, too, that as ship's captain, what he has just proclaimed on land he will ratify on the *HMS Endeavour*.

Historic deed done, they return to the ship. The crew bandies about the island's new name: Possession Island. How succinctly this sums up what has transpired. Now all know full well that this deed, duly accomplished, will set certain forces at liberty—forces of a national and moral nature. This accomplished fact can in no wise be undone. Even so, the moral aspect of this proclamation seizes my imagination and will not let go. The nature of this new moral imperative must be explored before our captain submits it for adjudication.

And so, I formulate a plan of action. Joseph and I will meet with the captain that evening to discuss research. Our recent discoveries consume him with curiosity, for in addition to being a commander without peer, he passionately delves into every aspect of our exploration. Yes, this will be my angle of approach...

Soon we sit in the captain's august presence. With keen delight, he examines a specimen while asking Joseph of its nature. Appearing satisfied, he hands it back and pauses in thought. Here is my chance.

"Captain Cook, I in my turn am curious about one thing. Today's proclamation… Now, just how would you sum it up in a sentence or two?"

He gives me a quizzical look. Off-topic, his focus scatters somewhat. But then he considers the question with something like relish.

"*Terra Nullius,*" he pronounces with a hand swish.

"*Terra Nullius,*" I echo. "*Terra Nullius…* So what you mean to say is that this land has in some sense been declared null and void?"

"Not the land, Ben. Its inhabitants."

"The inhabitants… I see. And yet, might I be so bold as to ask you to expand upon this somewhat?"

Here Joseph kicks my ankle under the table. As little escapes our captain's attention, he notes this and smiles.

"Oh, it's quite all right, Joseph. In fact, it is good that the lad asks so many questions. It denotes an inquisitive mind. Wouldn't you agree?"

"Oh yes, inquisitive, quite… But unfortunately given to fits of laziness. My Ben is prone to walking off on his own and shirking duties from time to time—but yes, I do forgive him. He can be the most diligent of assistants when he wants to be."

Captain Cook smiles at this indication of affection and proceeds.

"By that expression, Ben, I mean to say that judging from the individuals we have encountered here, this particular race of men is in a most unfortunate condition. In fact, they appear to have no conception of just who and where they are."

"Might you give me an example of this?"

"There are many, Ben. Let us consider just a few here. First, they have no concept of private property or of their right relationship to the land they inhabit. And of course the most glaringly obvious— they don't cover their bodies at all. The natives we previously encountered had enough modesty to at least partially dress. And yet this race roams about freely without the slightest awareness of the abject state their nakedness implies. Would you agree, Joseph?"

"Yes, I do agree in principle, except for one omitted detail—if I might be so bold as to point it out to you."

"Please do."

"Ah, yes then. As I employ my eyes extensively in all manner of observation, I could not help but pay close attention to the designs painted on their bodies. Now granting these designs elementary, I yet suspect they have importance to this people. Quite possibly, they indicate relationships to each other—much as your uniform indicates my relationship to you. And so, you see, we cannot simply conceive of them as stark naked."

The captain thoughtfully digests this observation.

"Would you agree with that assessment, Ben?"

"Um… well, based on our limited information of these people, that is a hard question to answer. And yet, it would appear that some sort of hierarchy exists in their society. If so, such designs could well come into play. Then too, they may denote an even broader relationship of these people to the world they inhabit— and the cosmos, even…"

"Oh come now, Ben. I am willing to grant that Joseph might have a point, but now you stretch it beyond the realm of credibility by adding cosmological connotations."

His last remark gives me the opening I look for.

"Well, why not get an expert opinion on that matter? In fact, Captain Cook, if I might be so bold as to suggest—why not have an inquiry into the nature of this people before you finalize your *Terra Nullius* pronouncement? In any event, it could prove a most interesting debate for us to engage in."

Captain Cook eases back in his chair with a faraway look. This notion captures his fancy.

"Continue, Ben. Press your case."

"Yes, well, along with our esteemed astronomer Charles Green, might I further suggest including our talented artist Sidney Parkinson and our ship's clerk Richard Orton to form a tribunal of sorts, to more perfectly inquire into this matter?"

"A compelling notion, Ben. Go, fetch them at once."

This I do. At first bemused by it all, I explain as they assemble around the Captain's table. They begin to grasp the goal of the proposed proceedings and so perk up. After all, what true Englishman can resist the notion of jurisprudence? We agree that the object is to arrive at an accurate estimation of these people from which to base a judgment. Captain Cook begins the proceedings by asking each member the nature of his personal evaluation of the natives.

"Tell us, young Sidney, what impressions have you formed of this land's inhabitants?"

"A most difficult question, Captain Cook. Ah, but in my humble opinion, even though the impressions in question may not be deep, they are, how might I put this—illumined."

"Illumined? Illumined, you say? A baffling answer, young man, as you cannot have it both ways. You cannot state your impressions humble while at the same time suggest them a type of illumination not shared by others here present."

"Begging your pardon, sir, I meant to suggest nothing of the sort. By 'illumined' I merely state the obvious. I observed these natives under the bright sun of their land in an unencumbered way. This is how I study all subjects of interest to me. It could, in fact, be a surface and superficial way of arriving at an evaluation."

"I see. Well, let us hear your conclusions to date."

"I have concluded, Captain Cook, that I really have no right to conclude anything beyond this: These people, through their outward appearance, bearing, and behavior, somehow blend human traits most naturally with this rare and original landscape."

All pause for a moment in thought. Charles speaks first.

"Oh, come now, my good fellow. That is precisely the kind of frippery we must avoid if these proceedings are to have any real merit. I mean really, what does that say about this people other than that they are primitive beyond compare?"

"Are you saying that the landscape here is primitive?" Richard jumps in.

"Yes, indeed I am. This land, beyond measure, is more rustic than any other on the face of the globe. The trees shed bark rather than leaves, the animals appear odd and dull-witted compared to the usual, and so it follows that the natives would fit right in."

"Then you agree with Sidney."

"I give no such assent!"

"But you just said that the natives blend right in with the land and its creatures, although you stated it as a negative rather than Sidney's positive."

"Oh, for heaven's sake, are we to split hairs at this inquiry?"

Captain Cook smiles and decides to move on.

"Go on now, Richard, offer us your own assessment. Doubtless you have something worthwhile to add to this debate."

"Perhaps I do, Captain Cook, and yet I would prefer not to give my opinion on the matter until later, if you don't mind."

"Very well. As you wish, Richard, as you wish. But come now, Joseph, please do expand on your earlier comments."

"Oh, well, I would very much like to expand upon them, Captain, and yet must frankly confess to not having a clue as to the truth of what I said. All I can really say is that the designs painted on their bodies suggest some kind of meaning to me."

"And yet not Ben's cosmological meaning…"

"Cosmological meaning?" Charles interrupts with impatience. "Cosmological meaning? How might any man in his right mind suggest that these human oddments have even the most elementary grasp of the cosmos? Just think for a moment on the absurdity of such an assertion. Just consider the fact that we men of Europe only slowly and painfully, over a period of centuries, at last comprehended the true movements of the planets, for example."

"Oh, but Charles," I object, "I did not mean to suggest that they grasp creation in a scientific way as we strive to. I merely suggested an intuitive understanding that they have about their place in the natural order."

"Intuitive, my eye. Men use that concept when all other rational functions break down. What is man without the light of his reason? How could any propose an understanding of creation bereft of this crucial ingredient?"

"And yet, I cannot help but feel that reason as we understand it has been erected on a foundation of precursors that make it possible."

"Precursors? Fiddlesticks! No man can arrive at an understanding of the nature of our universe without the focal point of thought that reason is. Consider what Plato, an apostle of reason, said on this matter: 'Man is a tree with his roots growing heavenward.' This, my good Ben, is what makes us wholly human: our quest to grasp the Heavens. This can only be accomplished through much toil and applied reason. These natives can scarcely navigate through the bizarre wilderness they inhabit, let alone even tenuously grasp matters cosmological."

"I have one question for you, Charles," Richard says.

"Oh? And what might that be?"

"Some time ago, you claimed the Book of Genesis as the blueprint of creation."

"Yes, I did."

"And yet, Charles, that blueprint was not arrived at by reason, now was it?"

Charles appears uncertain how to answer, but before he can, all my impressions and ruminations on the natives at last find their focal point.

"Everyone, listen, I have something to confess. I… I have been holding back. The truth of the matter is that I have had two personal encounters with these natives. Not only that, we actually managed to communicate in a rudimentary fashion."

"What? You have been holding back from me, your mentor?" Joseph says. "Do you mean to sit there and tell me that all those times I thought you lazing about, you were making contact with the natives?"

"That's what I just said, isn't it? Oh, and of course I do apologize for the secrecy involved, but I needed time to put it all together."

"And have you put it all together, Ben?" Captain Cook gravely inquires.

"Yes. Yes, I believe I have, as best one may under the circumstances. And it all came into focus, Charles, when you quoted Plato."

"Oh really? Would you care to make it all clear to us?"

"Yes. You see, in my first encounter, a young man gave me a gift. It was a small container filled with some kind of earth. When I looked puzzled about the meaning, he performed a pantomime of sorts. He picked up one of my specimens, spread the roots to resemble two human legs, and then pointed to the sky. Next, he took a pinch of earth and pointed to himself."

"And just what do you now suppose those aimless gestures meant?" Charles inquires.

"They meant, renowned astronomer, firstly that clay or earth has a divine meaning for these people. The clay equals the man— man created out of the dust, if you will. Secondly, mankind in turn is rooted in the heavens through our relationship with the Divine, as your esteemed Plato once maintained."

"And our young botanist appears to be rooted in a pot—a rum pot! I have never heard such rubbish in all my days! No true man of science could ever make a conjecture of that nature based on so little evidence."

The gathering listens on. Charles, of course, has a point and is highly respected. Even so, the image I had planted in their minds does not wholly fade. They yet envision one of our natives holding the plant roots up and pointing skyward as he explains the import of his gift. This proves the clincher—the giving of gifts, a universally understood transaction. Our captain had tried in vain to give them gifts which they had refused to accept. He then concluded that sharing and hospitality were unknown to these people. They now know otherwise. This renders them at least partly amenable to the rest of my account. I take hold of this and press on.

"Wait, it gets better. In my second encounter, I asked about the meaning of the designs on their painted bodies. The native began to draw in the sand, but when this didn't work, he took me out to a river valley at night. He began his account with a gesture that equaled sleep and dreams…"

"Oh, come now, young man. Enough of this nonsense! Could you please render in rational terms how one might convey such a concept without speaking?"

"Yes. Watch."

I put folded hands to cheek, close eyes, and tilt head. Then, eyes still closed, hands touch head and move out as palms slowly open. With fingers I mimic various bird and animal movements. I then look up to see their response. They had watched on, rapt, and appear to equate the gist of the movements to my account—all but Charles, that is.

"Pure nonsense! You use some kind of native magic to beguile us—you, with your hand tapestry. I still maintain gestures of that nature are meaningless."

"Finish your account, Ben," Captain Cook interrupts.

"Yes, well, he next swept his hands across the night sky and pointed to a large figure of a man next to a small one that he had drawn in the sand. I surmised the large one represented deity and clasped my hands in a gesture of reverence. He nodded a yes to this and continued, pointing now to the river valley. He repeated the dream gesture and animal movements and actually began to sing. I interpret this now as the creative process of his deity as he descends from the Heavens to the Earth. Next, he holds out both arms as if to embrace all thus illustrated, and then slowly brings his hands to heart. Lastly, he moves his hands out in a release motion to the night sky. I interpret these last gestures to mean he embraces the all in his heart and returns it—and himself—to his Creator. Of course, it goes without saying, my interpretation but approximates the actual meaning."

Whether convinced or not, the assembly has thoroughly enjoyed my little production—again, all but Charles.

"All right, young Ben, clearly you have convinced yourself of the truth of this eye-and-body drama, so I will treat you gently. I will merely point out the flaw in all you say that undoes your premise and leave it at that."

"Oh, well, by all means enlighten me."

"Let us suppose that what you say is true—that the native relayed to you a thumbnail sketch of his beliefs. And yet, by your own admission, they in fact appear premised on dreams. Is that not so?"

I consider this for a moment. In truth, it does appear to have been the case in both native encounters. Both had started with the sleep and dream gestures.

"All right, Charles, perhaps what you say is true. Perhaps the natives base their beliefs on dreams—or maybe the concept of dreams. What does this lead you to conclude?"

"It leads me to conclude, young Ben, that any society which bases its beliefs on dreams is, in fact, as a child lost in the woods."

"What about Joseph in the Bible?" Richard casually notes.

"What about him?" Charles snaps back.

"He was a dreamer of dreams that came true. Similarly so in the case of Daniel, who interpreted dreams which came true."

"You know, I liked you better as the silent, thoughtful type—with emphasis on silent. But surely you are not suggesting that Ben's accounts portray reality as truly connected to dreams. That is simply poetic fiction. Furthermore, biblical events took place long ago and so reflect a different mentality altogether."

"A more... primitive mentality? Or to state it positively, a more primary mentality?"

"You artfully dodge the central question here, Richard."

"And just what is the central issue here, Charles?" Captain Cook interrupts.

"The central issue here is—do we, as rational Englishmen, treat as equals a people who just might in fact believe their dreams real? Would you, good Captain Cook, make a serious and binding agreement with a representative of such a benighted people? Are we in England not beyond base superstition of this nature?"

Swayed by this argument, the Captain strokes his chin. Ah, but inspiration strikes me. I beg the Captain's pardon and, quickly fetching a book from my cabin, return.

"I would like to read from this, if I may."

Puzzled, he gestures: go on.

"Here it is:

'Our revels are now ended. These our actors,

As I foretold you, were all spirits and

Are melted into air, into thin air;

And like the baseless fabric of this vision,

The cloud-capp'd tow'rs, the gorgeous palaces,

The solemn temples, the great globe itself,

Yea, all which it inherits, shall dissolve;

And, like this insubstantial pageant faded,

Leave not a rack behind. We are such stuff

As dreams are made on, and our little life

Is rounded with a sleep.'"

My audience now misty-eyed, many a wistful thought turns to home. Yes, they dream of home even while consciously watching on. Slowly returning to the present moment, they perceive how their minds had been split during the recitation of these familiar words. Then too, while our Shakespeare begins this summation by referring to his play alone, by its conclusion the meaning has become global. Even Charles had been carried off in his mind, although he now impatiently fidgets.

"Well, young Ben, you seemingly put me in a bind with your eloquent summation. None here now will dare deny the power of words to conjure dreamlike images. But this raises a rather serious question. Do you see it?"

"Perhaps I do, Captain Cook. For if in truth we interpret these words literally—and life is spun from dreams—then what we do or do not do in life has no lasting meaning."

"Yes. Can the good barrister rebut this?"

"I will try. You rest your case, noble Captain, on the premise that dreams are not real. The natives—and perhaps inspired figures important to our own history—on the other hand, assumed them, at least at times, somehow connected to what is."

"Ha! A clever enough rebuttal. But as I am certain you must realize, young Ben, as a representative of the British Crown, I am honor-bound to uphold its interests, however much your production might have beguiled me. You do understand the nature of my dilemma, do you not?"

"I—ah—I believe that I do, Captain Cook, much as it pains me."

"Very well then, young Ben. What must be, must be."

"As we decide to see fit," I dare add, prompting a silence that crackled.

And so in the end, our last and our greatest adventure drew to a close. We then set our course for dear England, our cargo: impressions in wax that, with luck, would endure. Still, for all of our hopes and our hurts and our gains—and the royal displays to uphold them—only the wind-driven rain late at night would herald our passage.

China Creek

Chapter 1

The 1858 gold strike in British Columbia had an electrifying effect far and wide. The main strikes in the Fraser and Thompson Rivers, gold seekers had to traverse a mountainous region to get there. This forced them to fight wild nature—and sometimes, each other.

Now, a few of these seekers were men of renown, who studied rare events to filter out insight. Others longed to break free of their pasts and start over. Yet many were just adventurous regional men, who merely had to hike a ways from home to try their luck.

Vancouver Island was a rugged land too, although with its long coastline, it was more open to probing. Peaks formed a spine through its central part, exposed to winter gales and blowing snow. The island's sheltered east coast—facing the mainland along the Strait of Georgia—had mild and wet winter weather. But on the island's unsheltered west coast, Pacific storms struck hard, making seaborne approaches a hazardous venture.

After the news of the mainland strikes, rumors began to spread of a small island find. Up Alberni Inlet way, a creek was said to have yielded some gold. At first, the gold seekers there were mocked—coming all the way from distant China to search the wrong spot. Yet even with the mild allure of a rumored strike, the savvier island men had set their sights on the Fraser and Thompson. A few, on the other hand, chose the island site as their best bet—Frank McKenna among them.

Frank didn't know much about that inlet. Even so, armed soon enough with an accurate map, he decided to set out alone. But while buying provisions, Ted Knight and Sid Weston offered to join him—both men Frank had thought were mainland-bound for the big strikes. Puzzled, he asked why the change of heart.

Ted said he just couldn't bear the thought of his buddy alone against orcas. They laughed and shook hands.

Now, Ted was a tough but kind-hearted guy whose presence would help Frank immensely. But Sid's decision truly surprised him. Sid was a man who thought big—or talked up a legend, at least, that he longed to live up to. In fact, he was high-strung, like a cat who'd lapped up tea.

At first, loud and proud, he'd proclaimed the strikes up Fraser way were of epic proportions. Why had he now chosen to think small? Had he bought Frank's line about drawing a bead on one target, not pointing a shotgun at twelve?

Whatever the case, Frank shook Sid's hand too, making them a team of three—or maybe just two and a half. Time would tell.

Next, they decided to set out in a native canoe. It seemed odd at first—the craft being cedar and bulky—but with three men at the oars, it was safer than a small boat. Satisfied on that point, they studied the Alberni Inlet on Frank's new map. Not too far from their Fort Victoria home, it opened on the stormy west coast. At its far eastern end lay their goal—China Creek.

Finally, with all their gear assembled and ready, they loaded up their canoe to challenge the waves.

With surprising ease, their voyage began—clear blue skies all that day. Soon Fort Victoria faded from view as nature took over. A different world awaited them—or maybe more of a fore-world, nothing formed for sure but sea and sky.

By noon they'd established their rhythm, chatting as the shoreline rolled by, the rumble of breakers close.

Late that afternoon, they beached and pitched camp. Ted snagged a fish with his improvised rig. Sid tried, but caught nothing. He mumbled and cursed as Ted gutted his catch—a fair-sized sockeye salmon.

With the salmon roasting over a fire, they swapped a few yarns while they ate. Being in the wilds had that effect—got thoughts to churning. Pausing at times, they peered into the timber up the beach. Cool even in the fading light, its moisture and life flowed onto the sand.

They reacted with coolness too—not sure what its dark depths held for them. With luck, only gold.

The next day out, they made fair way. A few great ships passed by—canvas clouds catching the wind and driving them onward. The crews' task then was this: milk pure nature's force, avoid the kick.

Our seekers did likewise, in a sea-level way, paddling their stout cedar boat.

By the third day out, excitement grew as they approached the inlet. What would it be like in there, that narrow passage twisting inland? Soon they'd find out.

In the meantime, a mass of nasty grey churned in from the south. Waves picked up—and with them, their apprehension. Yet being close to shore, they could land the boat and sit out the storm.

Even so, by then they were of a mind to challenge the sea. Oars tearing into water, the wind at their backs, the first drops splattered about. Waves began to swell, turning their stomachs.

This only firmed their resolve—at least Frank and Ted's. Is this how some men die at sea? Gamblers refusing to retreat from a high-stakes game?

Rounding a sharp slice of land, they felt great relief. At last in the inlet, to their north lay an islet chain stretching northeast.

Inward they plunged, on a captive sea stilled, leaving a streak on its surface. Soon, flowing clouds dumped rain—but they were safe.

Wet and bedraggled, they beached their canoe and pitched their tent in the rain.

By dusk it was only drizzling. They ate a cold supper.

Sleep proved neither deep nor long, but still the sun came up—grey clouds broken.

It was early March now, and the northward-arcing sun pushed away at the grey skies.

Still damp and stiff, they got up to survey a wet world. Not quite to their liking, they ate hastily and moved on.

The inlet narrowed. It now resembled a wide saltwater river, winding through peaks of thick forest. Eagles glided by from time to time.

Here too, they spotted the orcas of Ted's warning—dorsal fins slicing the surface, spraying out wet breath.

A riveting sight, Frank scarcely felt the danger of their presence.

Slick and shining bodies churned past as they neared their goal.

According to their map, the creek to their right must be China—a funny name, Frank thought. In this land of orcas and original tribes, brave Chinamen had pushed into its course.

Who knew their story? Who knew what had brought them so far from home, seeking gold?

They didn't plan to ask questions.

So up the creek they went, still at their paddles. The world around them dim and cool in the shade of huge trees, Frank sniffed the air—crocus, cedar, and mulch, like a wind-stirred broth of scents.

At length they reached their goal—or overreached it.

As paddles dipped into the water, wary eyes from the north bank followed their moves.

Ceasing their strokes, their boat slowed down till the current held it static.

Pig-tailed Chinamen, like statues with sharp eyes, watched on.

Frank waved. They glared, as Sid glared back.

The current began to swish them downstream—just as well, they figured.

Down from the Chinamen's camp, they set up their own.

Mere seconds after completion, Sid started to pan.

Smiling, Ted and Frank watched on.

"That Sid—he's like a big kid," Ted noted, chuckling. "He just can't wait to pocket some gold."

"Yeah, me too, now that you mention it."

"No, wait a minute, Frank. I want to see what happens here."

They watched as Sid, near frantic, swished gravel in his pan. Minutes later he yelled—

"Hey, yo, guys, yo! There's something shiny in my pan!"

Rushing to the creek, they took a look. Sid fished through the grit and grabbed something shiny, lofting it into the light.

"Yee-haw, Sid! You struck it rich! A whiskey bottle shard," Ted exclaimed.

Ted and Frank laughed loud. Sid threw the treasure and cursed.

"Damn Chinamen! Drinkin' our whiskey 'n stealin' our gold."

"Cool off, Sid, cool off," Frank spoke calmly. "We've only just arrived—and it's a big creek. Just like I said, most have headed inland up the Fraser."

"Yeah, where the real gold is," Sid snarled. "Should never have listened to you, Frank. I should be standing right now where real fortunes lie—not in some piddly little creek full of Chinamen's piss."

"Boy, oh boy—five minutes into our venture and you're ready to throw in the towel? How you expect to make a name for yourself that way?

A man's got to have patience, Sid. It's just that simple. Got to stick with something he starts—stick with it all the way.

Come on, it's too late to start our search anyway. Let's cook ourselves up one fine supper. Bet this creek's full of fish."

"Ha. Then it's full of something, anyway," Sid grumbled on. "Shit. But I guess you're right. Let's start our dig tomorrow, bright 'n early."

They next prepared for supper. The creek was full of trout—in no time, they had several sizzling away. Ted scouted about for greens to garnish their main dish. He said a Salish friend had shown him the good ones to eat. So, even in winter verging on spring, he returned with a bagful. They feasted then, deep in the forest, as nighttime crept in. Soon, they sat by the fire.

"Damn Chinese," Sid flared up again. "For the life of me, I just don't know why we sit still for their kind stealin' our gold."

"Our gold?" Ted objected.

"Yeah, you know what I mean, Ted—our territory's gold."

"Doesn't belong to anyone till it's dug up," Ted countered.

"How can you defend the likes of them? First they steal our gold, then they mock us by smashing whiskey bottles in our creeks."

"I got some Indian friends who might disagree with that 'our' bit," Ted persisted. "And we got no way of knowing who threw that bottle. Could've been someone like you, Sid. Think back for a minute…"

"Hey, whose side you on, anyway? Know what I think? I think we should, ah—we should liberate any gold those skulkin' brown balls might've hid, that's what I think."

"Whoa," Frank said, sitting up. "We sure as hell don't need that kind of talk in this camp, Sid, even if you're just blowin' off steam. You got any idea of the hornet's nest we'd stir tryin' to pull a stunt like that?"

"Hornet's nest, my eye. One white's worth ten of them in a scrap. And hey, they're the ones who started this spat by bein' so damn unfriendly."

"Now look, Sid, just tamp down that crazy emotion, will you? Look—this is a gold-seeking situation. Anyone who claims a good spot has to be on guard against claim jumpers. If this situation was reversed, we'd be wary of newcomers too. As it is, we came here to look for gold fair and square. What's more, we wanna get outta here in one piece. Got it?"

"Yeah, yeah, I got it. Don't have much of a spine, do ya?"

"Sid, clam up—and clam up now," Ted put in. "We're partners here, and it's two against one that says we keep our noses clean. No more of that kinda talk. Ha, and look on the bright side—you're the youngest one here, never really done anything on your own. So here's your chance to do a little growin' up. Time for you to be a man, and rule number one is: work with your partners as agreed. You get that much, at least?"

Squirming, Sid looked away, then back at Ted.

"Yeah, okay. Sorry, guys. Just didn't expect to be competin' with Chinese, is all."

"But you knew damn well we were goin' to China Creek, right?" Frank objected. "How you think this place got its name?"

Sid threw his hands in the air.

"Alright, alright, enough already—I get your point. So tomorrow, bright 'n early, let's have at that gold."

"Amen, brother," Ted smiled.

"Right," Frank agreed.

And so they spent their first night deep in that wet island forest, spreading dry boughs on always-damp ground and nestling down for the night. The strand of sky the creek allowed quickly drew Frank's eye. Scattered clouds floated by, yet the stars appeared bright, hemlock and cedar treetops brushing them almost. Looking down into the dim woods, there was scarcely a thing to be seen. But when a three-quarter moon arose, lines of trunks and ferns appeared, with creatures rustling beneath them. Rising mists bore scents of leaf and spore. Last of all, the sound of the trickling creek soon lulled them to sleep.

Next day had clouds, but they broke—to our seekers' relief. Washing up and eating, they soon hit the creek. Oh, and what excitement. Not one of them had tried their hand at this—a true novelty. So even when they didn't find gold right off, with racing hearts, they zipped through their first day. Huddling around the fire that night, they mulled over their work. Frank, for one, had not expected this—sand becoming a world of its own. He could still see grains of it when closing his eyes. As for their haul, they had, in fact, found a few grains that shimmered enticingly. Then all three would cluster round and hold the find to the sun—groans to follow as it turned out a mere grain of crystal. This lasted but a second, as the creek called them back. Trembling and hot, into their pans they dumped sand and swished it with water.

So finally, on their third day of panning, it happened.

"Hey guys, looky here!" Sid called out.

Dropping their pans, Frank and Ted trotted over. Sid plucked a bit from his pan and lofted it skyward—a sight to behold: a gold nugget the size of a pinky nail.

"Whoa, that's one big hunk!" Ted exclaimed with a smile.

"Lemme see that," Frank said.

Pure amazement registered as Frank scrutinized their first find. Though tiny, it had discernible heft. In the sun, it shone purer than pure. What a marvel of nature, this metal that never rusts—and what a fine color.

"Ha! Amazing. You did it, Sid, you did it!" he gushed, slapping his back. "C'mon, back to work, men. There's more of those nuggets hiding out in this creek."

And so they panned away with ardent hearts, finding a few more bits. That night, around the fire, they spoke with excitement.

"So whatcha gonna do with your pile, Sid?" Ted asked.

"Ha, ya know, I haven't really decided on that, Ted, but ah— maybe I'll buy myself a boat. Yeah, maybe I will, at that…"

"A boat? What kind of boat?"

"Hmm, just not sure… Maybe a merchant ship…"

"Oh, so now it's a ship, is it?"

"Maybe it is. Maybe I'll skipper a merchant ship and sail the seven seas…"

"I like that thought, Sid," Frank said, misty-eyed. "Not quite sure of the nuts-and-bolts practicality of it, but it does sound nice… So, Ted, what you gonna do with your pile?"

"That's easy, Frank. I'm gonna buy myself a ranch. Don't ask me where—I'm not sure—but that's what I'm gonna do. How 'bout you, Frank?"

"Me? Well, think I'll start up a little business, right here on the island."

"What kind of business?"

"Ah, I'm not entirely sure, but ya know, somethin' to do with the newspaper trade sounds appealin' to me. Yeah, somethin' like that."

"Huh, yeah, you do like to ramble on, don't you? With a pile of gold, you can do it in print—much to our future consternation."

Here they laughed and prepared to bed down. Yet hardly did they sleep that night, so great was their excitement. But then, as day followed day and they found only gold dust, their glow slowly faded. No ships or ranches here—maybe enough for supplies. That hopeful emotion remained but surely felt stifled. Other feelings began to take root, like envy and spite, as they watched the Chinamen having more luck. Why did they find chunks while they found mere grains? Still, an unwritten rule was at work. They were there first and had the rights to their plot with a purchased license—or so they assumed. Warily, they guarded it too, not warming at all to their neighbors.

The next few days proved a mish-mash of emotions. They found a bit more gold, but not nearly enough to quench their growing thirst. Still, they had all their marbles. So even with the odd outburst from Sid, they reined in baser instincts—and yet it still happened. One fine day near noon, and in the midst of their panning, Sid, saying that he needed quiet time, wandered upstream. Next, Ted excused himself to take a dump in the woods. A short time later, Frank heard shouts as a shot rang out. Ted came out of the woods looking stricken. Both men stood stone still, listening intently.

What on earth had transpired? they thought. Then, hearts thumping away and hands shaking, they both hiked upstream. Peering through dense underbrush, they took in the scene.

Looking like an anthill stirred up, the Chinamen scurried about, several with guns. Peering under logs for some lost item, they chattered away in their tongue. Some pointed fingers of blame at certain others. Frank and Ted could only guess the words they hurled. They watched on, rapt, a minute—no sign of Sid. Then the Chinamen saw them. Dead silence followed, a dozen wary pairs of eyes nailing them cold. Frozen in a moment of time, they knew they had mere seconds to react. Frank had a pistol strapped to his hip; the Chinamen, three rifles. No option there.

It struck them both at once: time to make tracks. But first Frank pulled a ruse to confuse them, calling out to a clump of nearby ferns. All Chinese eyes impaling the spot, Frank and Ted ran off, hoping they'd check out that clump before attacking. Reaching camp, they grabbed a few things. Bolting for their canoe, they froze in their tracks—its marks there, but it missing.

"What the hell?" Ted exclaimed. "Where's our boat? Where's our bloody boat?"

Baffled and with mere seconds to spare, they tried to decipher the riddle.

"Wait," Frank said, "where's Sid? He wasn't up the creek or in the Chinamen's camp... Where'd he go?"

"Shit, oh shit, I think I have it, Frank. We know that guy's like a big kid, full of fibs 'n' bluster. But underneath it all, we know he's just plain afraid."

"So you think he's a coward, took off to save his own skin, left his buddies behind?"

"Looks that way. But we don't have time to debate. Damn, I hear shouts getting closer… Oh no, what's this? Didn't notice it at first."

They looked some yards off from where their boat had been, in back of some brush. Lo and behold, there lay another—like theirs, but not.

"What the hell goes on here, Frank?" Ted said. "It's not our boat but sure as hell's a godsend. Come on, get in. Let's get outta here while we still got breath in our bodies."

"We'd be stealing a boat, Ted."

"Hey, what's worth more in the grand scheme of things—a boat or two human lives?"

These words firming Frank's resolve, they both got in and stowed some gear before shoving off, paddling like mad, bullets striking nearby. One more shot rang out, followed by silence— them safely downstream. Yet as they paused to catch their breaths, they heard excited chatter 'round the last bend, getting louder. They looked into each other's eyes and then at their paddles—time for the race of their lives.

Chapter 2

On they paddled forcefully, not daring to look back. As they left the creek and entered the inlet, sounds of pursuit pushed them on. Back down their original route they frantically paddled, hugging the southeastern shoreline to avoid probing eyes. Nature turned into a backdrop, real life now in Frank's mind a bubble of light. In that sphere he pictured the sea, like in a crystal ball. Clearly, too, he knew that once free of the inlet, they must paddle north. For now though, they lunged across that winding snake of sea.

As dusk approached, Frank at last dared to look back. But then in the distance he saw it — a boat alive with spindly limbs, like an upside-down spider on water. Doubling their efforts, they hoped that night would shield their escape. Soon stars came out between dark shreds of cloud. On they strove in a rhythm of sorts. Time compressing and stretching at once, it seemed a short long while when they reached open sea. Raining now — this felt good on hot bodies. Frank nodded north to Ted, who understood. Northward their journey continued.

A dim grey dawn crept up. Passing one more inlet, they clearly saw a chunk of coast ahead. This new land too crept up, and with it, beaches. They wondered for a moment if they should stop there. Both said no and surged on as dawn showed them a clouding-up sky. Another inlet opened on their right, wide and deep. But then their eyes affixed to a block of land ahead just to their north, this drawing their eyes.

As they stroked on, winds picked up. Waves swelled up to scary size, impeding forward speed. Reaching the end of their strength, they made one last effort, taking them up to that coast. At last, they spotted a beach. But rain now fell in torrents and land disappeared. Their world had shrunk to one wet blot as a huge wave approached, striking Frank hard as it roared by. Splash — he fell in the water, felt a knock on his head. Confused but conscious yet, he swam for shore. Blackness and light stretched before him, and then just plain sand. Collapsing at last, his world swirled down a long drain.

Coming to, Frank lay sprawled on a desolate beach, about him huge rocks and much driftwood. Grey sky opened here and there, sunbeams striking the sea in shifting blots. Exhaling hard, he groaned while getting up. Gulls cried out in tones that mocked his efforts.

"Sorry to disappoint ya sea-goin' vultures," he seethed while shaking a fist.

Having no effect, the gulls mocked on.

Dazed and rubbing a sore head, Frank walked to drier sand and sat down. High waves crashed on distant rocks, giving off spray. The pounding surf — in the past so charming to hear — now sounded threatening.

"Huh," he thought out loud, "so the sea… she's kind of got two faces, like us humans. God, how she rages at me now — wonder what I've done wrong… But no, nature's nature after all, can be this way at times."

Looking about in a daze, he took stock — checking knife and gun, both in good shape. Ted had laughed at the sight, Frank dressed as a frontiersman. But they'd come in handy now. Likely bears in the woods about, and who knew what might drift in from the sea.

He sat a good while longer, sun parting clouds some more as spring returned. Then hunger drove him to the water's edge. Digging for clams, he found one, pried it open and ate, drinking the juice. Tasting of sea and of slime, it still hit the spot. He sat on a rock for a moment, scanning about — no masts in sight. So he turned and looked inland. A sheer rock cliff abutted the beach. Some ways south, it ended. Heading that way, his feet sank only slightly in the pebbly beach.

Reaching his goal, he paused by a forest as odors flowed out.

'Hmm, what brought me here?' he thought. 'Ah, freshwater, of course.'

So into dank dimness he plunged, going getting rough. Climbing a ridge, he rested on top. In a grove of cedars now, most appeared some ten feet wide. Then he spotted a tree that surpassed all the rest. Approaching in near reverence, he stroked its red bark and looked up — branches round its circumference, probing the sky.

'One can only guess at the age of this tree,' he mused in silence.

Next, a trickling sound brought him back in the moment. Clambering down the opposing slope to a brook, he splashed his face and drank. Next, cutting some ferns, he lied down and dreamed vivid. Soon awake, he came up with a plan. He'd gather wood to make a signal fire for ships to see.

Probing into the woods, he found enough. Back at camp, a new thought struck: no matches. Groaning, he sat in the sand and nervously rocked.

'Something's not right here,' he thought. 'That hit on the head must have rattled my brain, and what a bump now. Time to rest and focus.'

And so the day wore on, shadows under standing rocks lengthening northeastward. Rising, Frank found some clams and ate. Returning to his forest nook, he cut more ferns and bedded down in a blanket of green.

Next day dawned bright blue. Rising, he headed to the beach and scanned the sea — no ships in sight. Frank then thought of Ted.

'My God, yeah, Ted, my lifelong friend. How muddled my wits must be. All this time I've focused on me, but what happened to Ted? Let me see, we were heading north before the wave hit... Had it capsized our boat or had Ted pushed on? After a futile attempt to spot me at sea? If the first case, Ted wouldn't be far off, alive or dead. Yeah, but if the second case, he couldn't have gone much farther in that terrible storm. He'd have to beach the boat and head for shelter.'

Excited now yet fearful, Frank headed north, all along that broad wild beach seeing no sign of Ted. Soon he decided to climb a high rock, the better to survey for signs of life. Ascending its cool rugged surface, he reached the top. Gazing to the north, the beach stretched onward. A breeze swished over the rock, making Frank think.

'Wait a minute… Some time before that monster wave struck, the wind had shifted. Yeah, yeah, at first southeasterly — a sudden gale gushed in from the north. Only dimly aware of this shift, it had confused us… So then I fall overboard… One man paddling alone could never challenge that wind… So Ted must have turned south. I'm looking the wrong way!'

Jumping up with a surge of new strength, Frank descended the rock and headed south.

Towards late afternoon the land began to look different. Big rocks behind him now, the beach loomed smooth and dark. Forest thick on their slopes, distant peaks bore snow that dimly shimmered. Looking closer at the beach, he spotted a washed-ashore board of some sort, mostly buried in sand.

This made him wonder: might he be at Wreck Bay so recently named? Just one year ago the story had broken in town. The *Florencia*, bound for Peru with lumber, had gone adrift in bad weather. The *HMS Forward* tried to tow her but developed mechanical problems. So they cut her adrift. She hit a rock in the bay and broke apart. Everyone in Fort Victoria knew the tale.

Pausing to consider, this thought caused a chill. Yes, the nature here looks unspoiled, but disaster had struck. So, while no longer visible, that ship and its crew cast their pall. Death lingered here —

that of a vessel and men. Time, of course, had cleansed the sands of major carnage.

Then Frank spied a boat far up the beach. Forgetting the *Florencia*, to it he ran.

"Ted!" he called out; no one answered.

Slowly turning all way round he saw and heard but gulls and pounding surf. Next, the gulls guided his eyes to a bluff a ways off. Circling it in force, they made his spine tingle. He didn't want to look but knew he must. A hundred yards off from that hemlock-crowned bluff he saw the body, crumpled in the rocks below.

Forcing himself to the spot, the sight of the face made his throat click. Taking off his hat, Frank knelt down beside the corpse. Eyes closed with battered brow, there laid Ted. By the look of it, he'd died just a short time ago. Emotions built up. Heaving and writhing, Frank almost threw up, but calming instead, stroked Ted's brow.

Time faded into the background. When it returned, he wasn't sure how long he had been crying. But then the thought grew: Ted would want him to live. Even so, he had to bury him first.

With a stout tree branch, he dug in the sand for some time, dragged Ted to the pit. Next, he scooped the sand by hand over Ted's body, watching his friend disappear forever from sight. Last, he placed a rock at the head of the grave, said a prayer and sat down, head buried in knees.

Soon new thoughts churned up.

How did Ted die? Well, clearly he'd fallen from the summit above.

With a burst of resolve, Frank ascended that bluff, on the brink, beholding Ted's last sip of life.

Maybe he'd come up there hoping to spot a great ship… and then he had slipped?

Odd it seemed to him that a strong man like Ted had lost his footing…

Then again, that storm might've weakened him some…

Even so, suspicions grew that someone might've pushed him.

'But no, my reasoning's all wrong,' he thought. 'Must be that knock on my head… Yet might it be so?'

***

Returning to the beach, Frank sat on level ground, feeling safer there.

'Who on earth would kill Ted in the wilds?' he thought. 'It just could not be so…'

Still, pulling out his pistol, he looked at it closely.

Yeah, still packed with six rounds.

Calming down, he walked to the boat and checked its cargo.

Their dried beef, wrapped in waxed paper, had weathered the storm.

'Oh my God, what's this?' he thought, picking up two small but heavy sacks.

He opened one and saw inside gold nuggets.

In disbelief, he opened the other, eyeing it closely.

Shaking his head, he sank down in the sand, back to the boat.

How could this be? Two sacks of gold from thin air?

Questions now buzzed about him like wasps, with answers far off.

***

Pitching camp near Ted's grave, Frank found his presence calming.

Then, knowing his need for direction, he began singing songs.

They brought back faces of friends and feelings of home.

Smiling now, even the gulls sounded less shrill, and the surf more subdued.

'Ted, yeah, my old buddy Ted,' he thought, *'had stowed that gold in our boat? There's just no way to explain it unless… unless Ted had planned it all along… Could that possibly be? Him with his talk of fair play, all the while scheming on the Chinaman's gold?*

So he'd somehow snuck into their camp, found their hidden gold, and dashed off. But someone must've spotted him, let out with a yell… Ah yes, and that thump I felt on my head before my spill… Might it have been a paddle, not a knock on our hull?

So he'd have the gold for himself? Oh God, that whack on my head – how it's muddled my wits! What a crock of a thought, and it doesn't make sense. Our boat was gone when we got there, just stumbled on the other by sheer luck – or was it just luck? Had Ted engineered that feat to convince me Sid had run off? That Sid was the one to suspect of no good?

How perfect and clever, except that he's dead… But I loved him like a brother, and him me… Damn! Got to stifle this bullshit, mind addled yet. Time to eat and sleep, figure it all out tomorrow.'

***

Again he found some clams but ate jerky as well.

Oddly, the mixture tasted just fine.

Then he made a fern bed by the cliff, bid his friend goodnight, and soon fell asleep.

Rising next day with a throbbing head, it all rushed back in.

Ted was dead, and he was confused about what to do next.

This had a bracing effect—every minute now counted.

So again, he ate some jerky.

No way now to accuse his buddy Ted of doing him wrong.

That would strip him of his one last shred of comfort.

No, Ted was right from the start.

That Sid—he'd loudly threatened to rob those Chinamen…

And he the one a skitter bug, could never resolve himself one way or the other…

But it appeared he'd had enough smarts to come up with this scheme…

So he somehow found the Chinamen's stash, snatched it, and packed it into their boat.

Next, he snuck back to their camp to grab a few things before leaving, just as the ruckus exploded.

Then, in the excitement, he lost his wits, returning to board the wrong boat.

They were so close, after all, and he such a scatterbrained type—even lost track of left and right from time to time, and his friends knew it.

So off he must've gone in the wrong boat, thinking he'd pulled off his scheme…

But what about that second boat—how had it ended up there?

***

Mulling this scenario, Frank closed his eyes for a moment.

Whoosh! Thump.

A large rock landed beside him.

Up he jumped in panic, scanning the bluff.

"Something moved in the shadows!" he said in fright.

He spun and looked all directions, snapping off a few shots, then dashed for the beach.

"Someone on that damn bluff! Just tried to kill me."

Warily, he scanned again in a circle.

"Frank!"

Someone called out from behind.

He turned—no one was there.

Hands went to face as he cringed.

Sitting next in the sand—how his head ached.

"Oh my God, my shattered wits! Starting to hear things…"

***

Again he rocked back and forth.

This calmed him some.

Sound of surf now registered and evened him out a bit more.

Looking up again, he scanned the horizon—a beautiful sight.

This gave him fresh hope as it hit: he had a canoe after all.

All he had to do was get in and paddle home.

Still, he longed to know what had transpired here.

Returning to camp, Frank reexamined the supposed rock of attack.

Maybe it had been there all the time.

Almost relaxing, he began to think of the natives.

They lived their whole lives this way, plying land and sea for daily bread.

How must that play out over time? How would it build up a life?

Must be the elements themselves take on great importance—much more so for them than whites, or so he imagined.

Looking now out to sea, as a reddened sun neared the horizon, glints of the big picture gave him a dim sense of joy.

And so, eating several more clams, Frank bedded down for the night.

Chapter 3

At last the dawn crept up, and what relief. Frank's eyes drank up the light, making him smile. What a joy to be alive, to just see that light. At peace, he dozed for a moment. When he opened his eyes again, there stood a well-built man clad in a fibrous garment down to his knees, a conical hat on his head. Long black hair he wore in many braids. The sun on his face etched a light beard and dark, focused eyes. Rifle cradled in his arm, he took in the sight of a man on a desolate beach. Baffled, Frank shut his eyes. Open once again, the man remained. Could this be another dream, or had he gone mad?

"My name is Makanta," the apparition spoke, "and your name is Thief."

Dazed still, Frank strove to make sense of it all.

"Please, go way, whoever or whatever you are. Just leave me in peace, will you? For all I know, you're a bit of undigested clam, or a scrambled bit of brain."

The intruder's brow went up, but then he pressed on.

"Stand up. I cannot speak to a man whose eyes I cannot see."

Passing a hand over his brow, unsteadily Frank got up. Groaning at first, he next took in the dawn over snow-tipped peaks. Yet when he beheld the stranger again with his broad and stoical face, that dawn faded some. Still, he pressed on.

"Ah, good to meet you there, Makanta. My name's Frank, Frank McKenna."

Holding out his hand for a shake, the other, glowering, refused.

"I did not come here for friendly talk," he answered.

"Oh? So what did you come here for?"

"I came to punish the thief who stole my canoe."

Shaking his head while stroking a stubbly face, Frank pondered these words.

"Oh yeah, you mean back at China Creek, during that fracas…"

"Yes."

"A man of few words, I see. But look here, Makanta, we didn't in fact steal your canoe. It was, ah, just one of those things."

Here Frank recalled telling Ted that snatching the boat would be theft, and Ted's reply: *"What's worth more in the grand scheme of things, a canoe or two men's lives?"* Again he looked at the intruder.

"Alright, alright, I think you're real."

Again his reply disconcerted the native, who strove for its reason but then simply frowned.

"What do you have to say for yourself—thief?"

"Ah, that's one tough question there, Makanta. But you know, like my father always said, there are two ways of looking at things."

"There is only one way for an honest man to look at things—the true way. But as a thief, you would not know this. And so you lie about what your father told you."

"Hey now, just one minute here. This is between you and me. Don't you go bad-mouthing my father, or ah, implying that I now lie about what he said way back when—yeah, way back when, to my days as a sprout seeking sunshine…"

One brow dropped as Makanta sifted through this comment, liking, in fact, the slight poetry while still distrusting this man.

"And don't you go talking to me that way," he replied, shifting his cradled rifle. "I am already more angry than I like to be."

Realizing now this situation was all too real, Frank fully awoke.

"Alright. Let's keep this conversation on an even keel, shall we, Makanta? But now, my father is on record as saying that there are, in fact, two ways of looking at things—at least some things—with the situation in question one of them. That being so, can I explain to you what he meant?"

Makanta simmered on but then stroked his chin.

"Tell me what your father meant."

"Right. It's like this: On the one hand, we did take your boat. I cannot deny it."

"And what is on the other hand? The—left hand?"

Here Frank sighed at this ancient prejudice, even though right-handed.

"On the—other hand, two lives hung in the balance at the very moment we took your canoe. So, before you decide how you really feel about this, put yourself in our place. A throng of armed and angry men chase you, in no mood to chat. You want to escape, but you're boatless and trapped. Then you see a boat! On that boat, you can escape a grim fate. So, the question here is, what would you do, Makanta, mmm?"

Shifting from left foot to right, Makanta digested this thought. But then his look hardened.

"Why were those men angry at you? No, do not speak. I know the answer to that question. You stole their gold."

"Oh, but that's just a crude assumption on your part, Makanta, nothing more. Ah, and you tell me—what were you doing in the Chinaman's camp?"

"Curious, I was preparing to visit them. But then your rude interruption drove me off to chase a thief. And now you seek to distract me. The real question is why did you steal the Chinaman's gold?"

Frank thought for a moment. How could he convince this man he spoke the truth?

"Well, Makanta, it looks like we're on the horns of a dilemma."

"No. *You* are on the horns of a dilemma."

"What would it take to prove that I didn't steal the Chinaman's gold?"

"It would take the truth."

"Ah, a famous quote comes to mind… 'What is truth?'"

"Do not try cheap theatrics on me."

Impressed by Makanta's pliant mind, Frank pushed on.

"Look here, Makanta, you're partly right. One of my friends, whom I trusted, turned out to be a thief. He stole the Chinaman's gold and escaped. He left me and my friend over there to pay for his crime."

"I see no other man here."

"He's dead. He died here. I'm not sure how. His grave's over there," he said, pointing.

"Tell me the rest of your story."

"Yes, well, our partner Sid thought to make off with the gold alone. But somehow there was a mix-up between your boat and ours. They do look alike, and he's got scrambled eggs under his hat—a real scatterbrain. Here's how I think it happened: he stashes his stealthily stolen gold in your boat by mistake, runs back to our camp to grab a few things before bolting, right as the ruckus erupted. Excited and confused, he boards the goldless boat—yet again by mistake. Then he takes off."

Makanta pondered these words.

"There is an English word for your story."

"Is that so? And what is it?"

"Bullshit."

"Alright, I do see your point, but here's mine. This betrayer by now has discovered that he took the boat with no gold. I know how his mind works. At first, we thought him an innocent type. Truth is, though, he's double-minded and devious—but not very good at it. I'll just bet you good money that as we speak, he scours this coast for Ted and me. Winds were from the southeast when we left the inlet. So he'll figure this would be the natural direction for men in a hurry to go. So when he finds us—as I now think he will—he'll give us some cock and bull story to convince me he's still on the up and up, all the while hoping we haven't yet discovered the gold he hid in your boat."

"There was gold in my boat?"

"Yes, there was."

"But there was no gold in my boat."

"Oh yeah? Come and see."

Frank showed him how Sid had hid the two sacks, Makanta hefting the gold.

"So, you really did steal the Chinaman's gold. I was not sure at first."

"No! I wouldn't have shown it to you if I had, now would I? And it goes back to the Chinamen too, as soon as I'm free of this place."

Makanta stroked his light beard.

"So, you think your betrayer will come looking for this gold?"

"Wouldn't you, if you were a thief who'd risked his life for it? Even a chicken like Sid would be drawn back for it."

At last, Frank saw something in Makanta's eyes besides suspicion, but then he looked at Frank's gun. By now, having sized his man up, Makanta perceived him no killer and yet looked askance at his gun. Noting this, Frank took off his gun belt and handed it over.

"Here. It's only got three rounds in it anyway. Hold it in trust until you believe what I say. And you will—when the real thief pulls up."

Makanta handed it back.

"A man who would give me his weapon is innocent. I believe you now, even if I don't like you."

"You don't like me?"

"You still took my boat. You have caused me much, um… aggravation."

"Well… I do know how that feels."

They next established an uneasy truce. And after the initial shock, having company improved Frank's mood. Soon they set up an expanded camp and talked a bit more. Frank at last convinced Makanta to wait two days for the traitor—but then what? Sid's folly had cost Ted his life. Somehow, he must pay.

Makanta watched on as Frank simmered. At first, he calculated, then simply smiled. Frank asked him why. He said to wait and watch his actions. Puzzled, Frank turned to other tasks.

Later, he watched Makanta fish, his way with line and hook stirring admiration. At length, the skillful native snagged a salmon. Towards evening, they started a fire, the roasting smell making them smile. Frank's wits trickled back. Curious as they ate, he asked Makanta some questions.

"So ah, what tribe you belong to, Makanta?"

"I am Nootka, as your people say."

"Ah yes, the Nootka. Your English is excellent, by the way."

"So is yours."

Here they both chuckled.

"Ah, so Makanta, tell me the truth— you want to pan for gold too. That must be the answer to what brought you here."

"I have no desire to pan for gold. Your people's mad search for gold has only brought grief to the tribes off the island. And we on the island have already endured much at your people's hands. We wish that no gold be found here. If gold is found, we hope it is little."

"Well, some gold has been found."

"Yes, but not much."

"No, not a lot, but some."

"Yes, but with good luck, the gold will run out."

Their topics then changed to things of a more neutral nature. With much to think about, they then bedded down.

As they arose next morning—who but Sid should paddle ashore. Frank rubbed his head but felt fine. Sid, really there. Turning to Ted's grave, how his pulse quickened. Somehow, Sid must pay. Just then, he felt a hand alight on his shoulder.

"Watch my actions and follow what I do, Frank McKenna."

"What? What are you talking about?"

"I have a plan that will save us much grief. Watch what I do and follow."

Baffled again, Frank complied. After all, Makanta knew how to act in these wild lands. So up they walked to Sid as he beached his canoe. Looking up, he smiled at Frank but frowned at Makanta.

For a moment, Frank saw his old friend. Ha, yeah, Sid… Always did lack focus, but always tried hard. Too bad the wilds had revealed this hidden flaw…

"Ah," Makanta boomed in a big warm voice, "your friend has awaited you. He knew you would find him. He has been searching for you with diligence."

Frank's head spun a bit at this outburst. Was this Makanta's plan? Don't let on they knew what Sid was really all about? But why?

Puzzled, Frank put on a fake smile.

"Sid Weston, you son of a tree stump! Where you been, buddy? We've pried into every nook and cranny on this stretch of coast looking for you."

Up Frank strode and slapped Sid's back—maybe a little too hard. Sid righted himself and, gazing his way, looked relieved.

"So ah, where'd you disappear to at China Creek, mm?"

Sid's face went scarlet as he turned away. Then he looked Frank in the eyes.

"Frank, look, I am so sorry, but when I heard that shot and the ruckus I—I just lost my head, is all. I was so afraid, you see… It pains me hard to say this, Frank, but… I've always been afraid, and I've always tried to cover it up. So, I ran off. I ran off to save my own skin, paddled off in our boat. But you know, I've been looking high and low for you guys ever since. God, I feel so bad… Can you ever forgive me, Frank?"

Frank distanced himself from Sid and looked at him hard.

"Ran off, did ya? Couldn't take the heat of combat, eh? Ya know, in the army, if you do that… Ah well, never mind. We're friends, we are. No need to hold a grudge… But ah, I have some bad news for you, Sid."

"What? What bad news?"

"Ted's dead. He's buried over there."

"Where?"

"There, by that bluff."

Wordlessly, Sid ran to the grave and fell down before it. Both hands went to his face as he cried. Stirring Frank's grief again, he walked up and joined him.

Several minutes later, Sid looked up at him again, face wet and red.

"How'd it happen, Frank?"

"I'm not entirely sure, Sid. At first I thought he'd been murdered. But ah, you see, I took a nasty bang on the head, wasn't thinking all that clear. I dunno—now I'm inclined to think it was an accident. I believe he fell off that bluff while scanning about."

Sid groaned and turned away in grief. Too much for Frank, he walked off, heart twisting around. He only hoped this deception would not last too long.

So, even while bound up in the pains of contradiction, he made it through the day with this charade. At times he noted Sid look about, eyes darting here and there, and then at the borrowed canoe. Already a mass of emotion, this made Frank boil.

Makanta, looking his way, with his eyes conveyed purpose. This evened Frank out. And so, curiosity soon came to the fore. Just what would be the fruit of Makanta's ruse?

Chapter 4

Next dawn came with a fresh surprise. As Frank awoke to the sound of surf, his eyes turned seaward. A boat, some ways to their north, rode waves as it beached. Out jumped three Chinese—irate and armed—wanting to fight for their gold and quickly be off. Frank rousted Makanta and Sid, Sid taking fright. Makanta almost smiled, baffling Frank.

"Up, everyone up. It is time to bare our teeth," Makanta announced.

"What teeth?" Frank objected, while standing erect. "Three Chinamen with rifles beat us cold."

"We have two rifles and a pistol. It will be a stand-off."

"But Makanta," Frank objected again, "we have only your rifle and my pistol, with just three rounds left. They have us beat, but good."

"We have two rifles and a pistol," he repeated.

Frank and Sid looked puzzled, wondering what the native had up his sleeve. He then handed Sid a long stick of a branch with a flared end.

"Cradle this in your arms like so," he demonstrated. "From a distance, they will see a rifle. And you, Frank McKenna, take out your pistol and hold it up."

Blinking a bit, they obeyed. Next, they stood in a line facing the enemy squad, about two hundred yards off. They now stood in a line as well, weapons held across chests. Makanta was right. They saw three well-armed men, neutralizing their force. So, as is the Chinese way, they reacted with prudence. While sharply watching on, they calmed, awaiting their enemy's next move. Makanta too had his squad ease up, calling a huddle.

"What happens next, Makanta?" Frank asked.

"They will study us, look for our weak point. They will also wait for us to make a rash move. As defenders in an attack, they would have the advantage. They have a boat to hide behind and return fire from if we attack. If they attack us, they see the same thing. We could hide behind our boat and fire back. We are equally armed. No, we have more firepower than they do in a close fight. Your pistol can fire six shots without reloading."

"But I only have three rounds left!"

"They do not know that, do they?"

"No, no they don't."

"What's going on, Frank?" Sid finally asked.

"Ah, the Chinamen think we stole their gold…"

"See? I told ya! I told ya, didn't I, Frank? You can't trust their kind. We never should've gone to China Creek."

Cringing, Frank stifled a harsh reply.

"The time for shoulda thinking is over, Sid. Just clam up and follow orders, alright?"

Blinking in fright, Sid turned away. And so it began, the Chinamen playing it cagey, biding their time. The defenders likewise garnered their strength while eyeing their enemies closely. Toward sunset they ate a quick meal, the sky growing darker. That sky remained mostly clear as a full moon arose. Each camp could still see the other.

"We must post a guard so others can sleep," Makanta announced. "The Chinamen will do the same. Frank McKenna, you will guard first. I will guard second. Your friend will guard third."

"I, ah—right. Got it, Sid? You have third guard duty. Think you can handle it?"

"Sure, sure, Frank, I can handle it," he replied with a quivering voice.

Makanta and Frank exchanged a look. Frank understood. They prepared to bed down. Time crept by as clouds drifted in. The moon obscured, conditions now felt unsettled. On Frank's watch, the hours passed without mishap till he awakened Makanta. Frank then tossed and turned as slow hours wilted. After his watch, Makanta woke up Sid. Moving in jerks, looking fearful, he assumed duty. The wind began to pick up. Maybe the weather would turn stormy by dawn. As Frank thought on this, he heard muffled sounds—and then silence. He wanted to look, but Makanta's ruse called for noninterference. Something next happened up beach. Dimly Frank surmised what played out.

At dawn, Makanta woke Frank. Scanning nearby, they saw a boat missing—the one Ted had arrived in. They next looked up beach and noted the Chinamen gone. Makanta smiled.

"Do you understand what happened, Frank McKenna?"

"I believe I do, Makanta, and I must say it's a clever and, um, almost devious plan."

"Tell me what happened."

"It looks like my, ah, my good friend Sid Weston has skedaddled yet again. Not only that, he's taken the boat he believes the gold's still hid in… Oh no! Makanta! If Sid does manage to get away clean, he'll have gained from his crime."

Smiling again, Makanta walked to his bed and returned with a bag. Open, he poured out gold nuggets.

"I took these out and filled the sacks on the boat with pebbles."

"So even if Sid gets away, he gains nothing. But much more likely, when the Chinamen catch up to him, he's in for major trouble… with two bags of pebbles to barter for his worthless life."

"Yes. In truth, his situation will be harsh, but his crime merits it. He wanted to cheat you and your friend and the Chinamen. Worse than that, your friend is now dead because of his greed."

"Yeah, poor Ted. But with this revenge, maybe he'll rest easier."

"Maybe he will."

"And now we can leave without facing enraged Chinamen with more guns than us. We're safe. So later, when things cool down, we can somehow return the stolen gold."

"Yes."

"You are as crafty as a fox in the woods, Makanta."

"Yes."

But then, with their moods lifting, nature took a turn for the worse. Grey clouds united—it rained. So they propped Makanta's boat up on a long, low rock and sheltered beneath it. How pleasant it felt to watch rain flowing off of their hull, a curtain of wet. By nighttime, though, a great wind roared in, energized surf pounding sand in savage ways. Even so, they managed to sleep and dream of sunnier vistas.

The sun came up, and with it, calm, as grey clouds had lifted. Makanta, catching a salmon, cooked it for breakfast. He didn't like jerky, he said. Frank looked out to sea and cringed while picturing angry Chinese chasing down Sid. But no—justice merely played out, justice raw and ungarnished.

Next he strolled along the beach, drinking in nature's bright bits. For the sand was littered with shells that the storm surge washed up. An unusually bright, perfect pebble then drew his eye. Picking it up to inspect, in a flash he pegged it as gold. Scanning left to right, he spied other bits. Dizzy now at the thought, he sat down on the beach to analyze. The storm surge—could it have churned up deep sands, unearthing this stuff? But then he gave way to emotion.

"We'll figure this out later," he spoke aloud, "but for now it's time to hunt gold!"

Puzzled, Makanta watched on. Frank, ignoring his breakfast, grabbed his pan. Back at the beach in a fever, he swished away at sand, plucking out gold. All day long he continued his quest, powered by emotion. How his eyes widened on seeing those luscious gold bits, and how his hands trembled while panning. Makanta continued to watch on, shaking his head. And so, by day's end—yet trembling and exhausted—Frank returned to camp with two small bags of gold.

At last he ate some fish and washed it down with tea Makanta had made. Then, like a kid on Christmas, he opened his bags again and peered in with glee. Makanta's thoughtful look by now appeared grave. Something troubled him deeply. At first, Frank sloughed it off as cultural difference—gold not affecting the Nootka the way it did whites. Yet as emotions cooled, a grim new thought crept in. He looked at Ted's grave and thought again of Sid…

"Oh no!" he uttered while jumping up. "I just had a new thought, Makanta…"

"Tell me your thought."

"Ted… He landed here right after a storm. So, he saw what I saw, did what I did, and ended up with two small bags of gold…"

"What does this mean, Frank McKenna?"

"It means that—Sid was telling the truth! And what we've done is—oh my God! What we've done to him is too terrible to imagine!"

"Yes."

"Oh, but why would he sneak off like he did?"

"Because he is, as he confessed, a coward."

"But why in the boat with the rock bags?"

"I do not know. You told me he is an, um, scatterbrain. But now we must learn the whole story."

They next decided what to do, although it was risky — paddle through the night and overtake Sid. Makanta figured that one man paddling madly from dawn, who later encountered a storm, would have to beach. He estimated this spot would be the jutting land south of the inlet. So they ate a quick meal and packed up. Makanta regretted leaving his borrowed boat behind, but they needed to paddle in haste. Hauling it up the beach, they hid it with boughs and took off.

Fortune favored the foolish as conditions turned calm. The dip of paddles and sound of surf combined to form a rhythm their efforts clung to. Reaching their goal by dawn, they approached the point where swells turned into breakers. Carefully paddling southward, they spied boats on the beach — but no men about. They landed their craft some quarter mile south of that spot. Up they dragged her onto the beach, hiding her as best they could. Pausing from this effort, Frank looked around. The beach curved in a lovely U, with a hill and stands of timber beyond.

"Come now, Frank McKenna. It is time for us to make our great effort."

"Yes, the time has come. Let's go."

So first with care, they walked north to the unguarded boats — one of them Makanta's, the other the Chinamen's. A third boat hinted of reinforcements — they'd found the right place.

"Men nearby are very excited with emotion," Makanta noted. "Not one man thought wisely enough to guard these boats. Follow me. I know where the men have gone."

Up that timbered slope they climbed. At the summit, they saw hilly land stretching inland. Looking down the hill's far side, they saw a creek at the bottom. Clambering down to it, they followed the creek upward. The forest, dim and quiet, saw cedars edging out hemlock. In a grove of those towering trees, they paused for a moment. Makanta looked like a man alone in a great French cathedral, eyes ascending red trunks to sky-piercing crowns. Frank too felt the strength of this grove, but they had to press on. As they climbed higher, at last they heard it — voices rising in anger, but not in their tongues. They looked at each other and knew — Sid and the Chinamen loomed straight ahead.

With stealth they climbed on through that grove, and then at last saw it: gathered round the tallest tree, a clutch of angry men in silk and pigtails. Mesmerized, they watched on — till one of the men felt their presence and turned. Instant silence fell as all followed suit. But boiling rage cooled off a bit as they tried to cipher the puzzle of a white man with a Nootka. At length, one man stepped forward. Older than the rest, he had presence and bearing. Still, after a curious look, his brow descended. Then he hurled some angry words in his tongue. Makanta answered back in even Chinese tones. Never had Frank seen such a look of surprise. Calmer now, that Chinaman just had to learn of this wonder.

Makanta then strode forward and they conversed. Word followed word as emotions stirred up. Soon the Chinaman back-stepped a pace in sheer astonishment. Next, his expression changed into one of respect. Beckoned over, the angry host gathered round as their leader explained. They too eyed Makanta in a new light as he beckoned Frank over.

"Your friend," he said, finger up, "is in this tree."

"What?"

"Your friend is up in the boughs above. The Chinamen cannot see him. They cannot climb up after him. They are amazed that any man could climb this tree. But it has only made them angrier. You must now climb this tree and convince your friend it is safe to come down."

"What? Me climb this tree? Impossible! The Chinamen are right to wonder at this. I never knew such a thing even possible. The first limbs on this tree are like, what, maybe thirty feet up?"

"You are the only man for this, um, mission, Frank McKenna. I will help you. You can use two small sharp knives in your hands to bear your weight. I will work sharp spikes into your boots. Then you can climb like a giant squirrel."

"Ha, yeah, giant squirrel, alright. You'd have to be nuts to try something like that. How on earth Sid did it is beyond me."

"Fear can give a man wings, much as more desirable feelings can. But that is not the, um, point here. You must rescue your friend before he weakens and falls down. I now give you this coil of rope. Tie it to the lowest limb and lower your friend down."

Exhaling deeply, Frank put a hand to his brow as he pictured his plummet and impact. But then he pictured Sid up there alone.

"Alright," he said while shouldering the coil, "do your work on my boots and I'm off to climb this damn tree."

And so the most bizarre event in Frank's life began to unfold. Like some giant squirrel — and feeling like one too — he shinnied up that tree. A huge one, at that — about fifteen feet wide and a couple hundred feet high. Amazingly, Makanta's tools did the trick. Hands plunged in those knives as feet gained traction with spikes.

The sight he soon beheld almost made him laugh — Sid hugged a limb way up high like love at first sight. But then Frank simmered down, gearing up for his task.

"Sid!" he called out.

Sid hugged that limb with eyes closed — no response.

"Sid! Hey! Yo, buddy, it's me, Frank. Snap out of it, man. I'm here to save you."

Dazed and disbelieving, Sid opened his eyes and beheld him. For a moment he couldn't decide if Frank was real. Sadly, Frank knew the feeling.

"It's alright, old chum. It's really me. I've come up here to get you out of this mess."

"Frank? Is it really you, Frank?"

"Who else would be fool enough to climb this tree after you? I swear, Sid, you remind me of old Mrs. Carter's cat. Remember that? Damn thing was in that tree for two days before Roscoe shinnied up to save it."

He smiled a bit.

"Yeah, I remember that… Stupid cat. Should've left it up there. Dumb enough to climb too high, should've just left it there… You should've just left me up here, Frank. Yeah, you should've. I've been thinking long 'n hard in this ole tree, I have… So terrified at first I could hardly breathe, so dizzy I almost threw up… But I got used to it, you see, and used to the idea of dying. So you know, now I think it's not such a terrible thing, after all. I mean, look at the alternative… Even if I escaped from this mess, I'll be running and hiding from some other damn thing before you could say Jack

Robinson. So what kind of life is that? Huh? Can you tell me that, Frank? Well, I can tell you. It's not really a life at all. So then I get to thinking that by letting go of this limb, letting myself fall to earth, by doing that, I'd be doing the one and only brave thing I've ever done in my whole life."

"No Sid, no, don't you think that way. And look, I've really put myself out on a limb for you, buddy…"

Again Sid smiled a bit.

"Wasted effort, Frank, I'm sorry to say. I have nothing down there waiting for me but more humiliation. So please, do me a favor, just shinny down the way you came and let me die in peace."

"I'm not gonna let you do that, Sid, because, fact of the matter is — I put you up here."

Sid blinked a bit, looking puzzled.

"What? What do you mean?"

"I mean just what I said. I put you up here by what I did to you."

"By what did you did to me? What did you do to me, Frank?"

"You really want to know? You really want to know what I did to you?"

"Yeah, I really do."

"Then, Sid, you have to come down from this tree with me. Because the only way I'll tell you the story is over a hot cup of tea."

Puzzled, Sid thought for a moment.

"You really did something to me? Something bad?"

"Yeah, pretty bad."

"And you won't tell me about it here?"

"Nope."

Again Sid considered this notion.

"Aw shit. Then you'd better give me a hand 'n get me out of this tree."

And so, through patient effort, Frank led the way to the lowest limb. Tying his rope to it, they both rappelled down to safety. What joy they felt with feet on the ground. Sid, eyeing the tree, fingered its bark — wonder nudging out fear. Then he turned to Makanta and the Chinamen. He felt himself in some other world as former cruel foes now stood impassive. Makanta most of all drew his eye. That Nootka's look of contemplative calm almost fed his heart and gave him courage — almost. At last, with the sharp edge smoothed from the mood, the men set up camp, evening meal in the offing.

Chapter 5

In serene unease, Frank helped order camp. Thick clouds had broken. They stood on a sunlit patch of grass, a clear stream flowing through cedars. Makanta readied his line and began catching trout. Sid sat down on a rain-soaked rock, catlike, tense and alert. For he had entered a whole new world, his weakness out of the bag and new sprouts within seeking light. Frank, sensing his mood, wished Sid the best. Then he joined him by the stream to tell the story. Fearing anger and bluster at his summation, Sid took a good long breath and let out a sigh.

"I would've been tempted to do the same thing, Frank. Partner of mine pulling a fast one like that… and so it appeared. I mean, I did threaten to steal the Chinamen's gold, 'n all… Just crazy bluster, no more. But damn, ya know, I did run off and leave you and Ted in the lurch. That's almost as rotten. That's betrayal too."

"Well, Sid, it does look lowdown on the surface… But ya know, what I did was much worse. I gave in to the lust for vengeance. That came close to costing you your life."

"Ha. Not much of a life."

"But it can be, Sid, if you really want it to. And the thing of it is, if you worked up enough courage to let go of that limb, well, then you can use that in a constructive way. It's time for you to face life head-on. No more running away."

"Yeah, no more running away…"

Later, as the bright sun started to dim, Makanta joined them.

"So, Makanta, tell us what happened. How'd you change these Chinamen's minds?"

"By telling their leader the truth."

"Ah yeah, and… what was the truth? What brought you to the Chinaman's camp in the first place?"

"I was looking for the Chinamen."

"You were looking for the Chinamen?"

"Yes."

"Why were you looking for the Chinamen? And ah, what would you have done if you had had time to approach them before bolting off?"

"I would have asked them if they had any news of Lu Zong."

"Lu Zong, you say?"

"Yes, Lu Zong."

"Alright… So who is this Lu Zong, and why would you want to learn about him?"

"I knew this man as a youth. He stayed with my tribe a few years. There is a story behind this. Would you like to hear it?"

"Yes, I would."

"One day, many long years ago, Lu Zong came to Nootka Sound aboard a fur trading ship from China. When his boat departed, we were amazed when he walked right into our village. Standing still as he thought about what to do next, some of us realized that he longed to remain here. At first, we were shocked and didn't know what to think. But he said if we helped him, he would later help us when he returned to China. He told us he would trade valuable items with our tribe in return for furs—items we could sell to make money. So our chief allowed him to stay."

"What happened next?"

"Lu Zong told us about a time of trouble in his home, Manchuria. He told us how he had once been a dreaded warlord, one who had cowed many rivals. But then, one day, he saw another warlord attacking a peasant woman by a well. He said that some strange thing happened inside of him. He said the sight of the woman's distress made him feel as if his life could become a blocker of fate—or the lifter of a sad fate to a good fate. So he drove off her tormentor and set her free. The woman, happy and grateful, told her story to all people who would listen. Soon, many common people honored his name—so much so that Lu Zong began to act as the hero he was in their minds. This caused great anger with the other warlords, who united against him. He fought and defeated them once, but when they regrouped and later attacked him again, he was driven from his land. His rivals tracked him to a hideout, but he escaped again. He knew that he had to leave China if he wanted to live. So he boarded a fur trading ship and came to our land."

"How did you communicate?"

"Some of us spoke English. He also spoke a little English. I was fascinated by this man and became his friend. He taught me his language, and I taught him ours. He also taught me about his people's history. I, in my turn, taught him Nootka ways. He was very happy to learn of my people."

"What happened next?"

"When he thought it was safe, he returned to China. We waited for a message from him. No message came. Many Nootka wondered what became of him. Then, when I heard of Chinamen on our land, I decided to visit them and ask if they knew of Lu Zong."

"But then that ruckus exploded, and you bolted off to borrow a boat to track us down."

"Yes."

Bemused, Frank shook his head—this account the last thing he'd expected in the wilds.

"And then, Frank McKenna, when I approached the angry Chinamen by the tree, I asked my question. Shaken, they appeared, to hear a Nootka speaking Chinese."

"Yeah, I bet. So what did they say?"

"They told me Lu Zong fought against fierce Manchurian warlords for a few years. Finally, that brave man was killed. But many common people still speak his name in loving tones. He fought for his own rights, but he fought for their rights too."

"I see... So he truly is a hero to some."

"Yes, a hero to many."

"Then, when you told them the story of his stay with your tribe, they changed their hearts towards us, right?"

"You are half right, Frank McKenna."

"Oh. So what's the other half here?"

"I made a promise. I told them we will help them find the one who really took their gold. This helped to calm them down more."

"What? You negotiated a giveaway clause without my consent? I'm not sure you should have done that, Makanta. Time is valuable, you know. We have our own lives to look after."

"Do you want me to tell them the deal is off?"

"No, no, don't do that. It's a pretty high price to pay for peace, is all I'm saying."

"But it is important to find the real thief. That will seal the truth of my words to them. It will clear you and your friend of lingering suspicions."

"Ha. The real thief. What do you think our chances of finding the real thief are at this point? Pretty much zero, I'd say… Oh no, then again…"

"Then again, what?"

"Do you really want to know?"

"Yes."

"Then watch what I do, Makanta."

"What will you do? Tell me, and then I will watch."

"Sid and I are going back to that north beach. But this is urgent. We must leave now and travel through the night."

"What" Sid objected. "You want us to paddle through the night, back to that desolate stretch of beach? What for, Frank?"

"Courage, Sid. Courage—courage and faith. It's just a hunch, but we need to check it out, and right away. Tomorrow morning might be too late. So you think you can do that? Think you can trust me and work up the guts to paddle all night?"

"Yeah, Frank. I think I can muster up at least that much."

"Good. Let's get going. And Makanta, we'll need all the Chinamen too."

With a grunt, Makanta nodded, then beckoned the distinguished lead man to his side for a parley. He listened intently and nodded as well. So, puzzled but compliant, all soon took off. Out at sea again, the mood amazed Frank. Under the light of a bright full moon, a fleet of avengers paddled northward. Moderate swells proved no hindrance as they plowed through. Winds had calmed but hinted at stirring by sunrise. Even so, resolve put nature in context.

As dawn crept up, they spied their goal. *Ah,* Frank thought, *there's the bluff above Ted's grave. This is the place.* And so they beached their odd little fleet, stepped ashore, and scanned—no living in sight save for gulls. Time for a parley. With a come-on swish of Frank's hand, all gathered around. Carefully choosing his words, he began.

"Alright, guys, see that bluff overlooking the beach?"

All nodded yes.

"Good. Now, I could be wrong, but I think there's a man hiding out up there."

"What makes you think so?" Makanta replied.

"Well, um, on my first day here, I think someone might've thrown a big rock at me from the top of that bluff – maybe tried to kill me?"

"You do not sound sure of yourself."

"Well, truth is, I'd taken a nasty blow to the head and, you know, imagined a few things… ah, or not, as the case may be…"

"So we now chase phantoms of your mind?"

"He could be real."

"If someone wanted to kill you, Frank McKenna, they would have used a gun or a knife. What man would throw a stone hoping to kill?"

"Hey, it was a big rock! Ah, supposing, that is, it was in fact thrown at me…"

Makanta frowned with annoyance.

"Show me the rock."

Frank took him to the place as the Chinamen followed. Hefting the rock, Frank now knew it wasn't as big as it had first seemed. Again, Makanta frowned.

"I needed to return here for my boat, so this trip was not wasted. But the Chinamen will not be pleased to hear they paddled all night for this. Yet I will convince them to search the bluff for signs of a man."

Maybe Makanta was right. Maybe they were chasing a dream phantom. How could it make sense – a rock too small to kill a man, and no boat nearby? So how could anyone there be the gold thief? Supposing someone was there at all? Still, Makanta convinced the troop to search out the bluff.

Frank stayed on the beach guarding the boats. Sitting near Ted's grave, he mused on their adventure gone awry. Then he gazed out at the sea – still fairly calm, though the winds had picked up.

That steady pulse of waves just never ceases, he mused. How many things has it washed ashore over years uncounted?

A scream broke the thought. Tense and alert, Frank leapt up, eyeing the bluff. The troop soon returned. Ah – they'd taken a prisoner. Two men held her firmly by each arm – a Chinese woman. They made her sit in the sand and gathered around.

So she sat in a circle of men with harsh, sullen faces. She couldn't be much more than twenty or so. Long black hair caught the sun and shone radiant. Her face, first contracted in pain, next showed defiance.

And so a trial of sorts began on the spot. They made her tell her story. Then they mulled it over amongst themselves.

No longer able to bear it, Frank asked Makanta what gave. He communed with his Mandarin friend and got the story.

"Her name is May Li. She was the wife of one of the gold diggers – the man who found the gold-rich spot they now pan. Soon after that, he died of a fever. So, his share of the gold went to the other men, not to her. The Chinese have no custom of sharing wealth with a woman."

"Amazing. What else did you learn?"

"She has confessed to her crime. Not able to endure her husband's share going to others, she came up with a clever scheme. In her plan, she would make it look like you and your friends stole the gold. Then she would use you to make her escape. She knew she was too delicate to paddle away alone.

"At first, she was confused when one of your friends ran off in your boat. But she quickly seized the chance to hide herself and the gold in mine, knowing you would have no choice but to escape in that boat."

"Huh… She must have hid under the blanket… She's not big and wouldn't have made much of a bump curled around supplies… So, during that storm at sea… I wonder… Did she hit me from behind with something?"

"I cannot answer that question. She would never confess if she had. But look at her, Frank McKenna. Her limbs are slender and not strong."

"Yes, it doesn't seem likely… but one never knows. So, she made it ashore with Ted. When he wasn't looking, she escaped and hid on the bluff. Right?"

"Right."

"I wonder again… Did she throw the rock at me that night? A woman could throw a rock that size, after all."

"Again, she will not admit to this."

"And of course, she'd never admit to pushing Ted off the bluff…"

"No. She says he fell off. She says a huge gust of wind made him lose balance."

"She could be lying. But then again, the wind can do that at times in these parts… And Ted, weak from our ordeal… Just might be true… And I do see her point. Her husband makes the discovery, dies, and now they won't give her his share. Sad. But even in our own society, women must sometimes fight for what's theirs."

"So you think she is innocent?"

"I didn't say that. Even a beautiful woman may explode with the wrong kind of passion… And she did concoct a devious plot to get back her gold… Oh – and what about that gold? Did they find it?"

"No. She says she lost it."

"She lost it? Now that seems a little hard to believe."

"She says that one huge wave made her lose her grip on the bags."

"Hmm, possibly rings of truth – that was one hell of a wave… It's within the realm of possibility…"

"The Chinamen think she lies. They now discuss ways to punish her."

"That doesn't seem quite fair. I mean, way out here, having a trial and all. What might they do to her?"

"I do not know. But my translator, Wei Chan, argues for her. He says she was treated unfairly by them. They listen to his argument but still smolder with anger about the gold. They believe it was theirs by right of their company's agreement. And think, Frank McKenna—her scheme put you and your friends in grave danger. She did not value your lives."

"That's true, Makanta, but still…"

"Still?"

"Well yes, she's so lovely. And just look at her now—so helpless and vulnerable. I wonder… did she plan to share some of her gold with Ted and me if all had gone well? It would only be fair to compensate us for all our trouble. And really, as you mentioned, she'd need us to row her back to Fort Victoria—couldn't do it alone."

"The Chinamen have no interest in that part of the story. They have not asked her about it. But what you say might be true."

A sudden impulse seized Frank. Running up to their boat, he took out his two sacks of gold and returned to Makanta.

"Here, give this to the Chinamen. Tell them it replaces the missing gold they're after. Tell them we found it at China Creek. But tell them this too: the woman must get half. Yeah, tell them that or no deal."

Makanta looked shocked. He gazed long into Frank's eyes, then at the woman. Her head bent to her chest, she quietly sobbed. Then he grasped Frank's motive.

"I will do as you ask."

A dumbfounded clutch of Chinamen soon turned Makanta's way. They rose to their feet, Wei Chan seizing the moment. He argued with great passion for the woman's release. Some loudly objected while others considered the gold. That's really all they'd wanted to begin with—their missing booty. Yet the thought of taking but half made some faces redden. They wrangled on. Wei Chan, though, proved good with words and forceful as well. At last, and with reluctant nods, they all agreed. And, as Makanta had said that Frank found the gold at China Creek, they longed to return and find more.

The deal finalized, with a bow, Wei Chan bid Makanta farewell. Makanta bowed back. Then Wei Chan bowed to Sid— an apology for the pain caused. Sid just stood there at first but then did likewise. Finally, bowing to Frank, he wryly smiled at the thought of him as a small version of Lu Zong. As they left, the stunned woman looked up, scarcely believing her tormentors gone. Then she looked at Frank—and looked away.

"So why'd you give away all that gold, Frank?" Sid then broke in. "And where'd you find it, anyway?"

"Let me show you something, Sid."

He took him to their boat and fetched the other two sacks.

"What? More gold? Where'd you get all that?"

"Right here, Sid. Right here. Just wait for the next storm and I'll show you."

"Unbelievable! Who ever heard of finding gold on a beach?"

"Well, we have now."

Makanta walked up.

"I must return to my village, Frank McKenna."

"You mean right now?"

"Yes. I have learned what I came to learn—the fate of Lu Zong. I am not happy with what I learned. No—I am a little happy. He died fighting for what he believed in. That is better than growing rich and idle."

"Come on, Makanta. It's not all that bad to look for gold, is it?"

"Your people's search for gold has hurt the tribes along the Fraser and beyond. Their way of life is shattered forever. My own people have also endured much grief in the past. We fear what will happen if much gold is found on our land."

"Well, China Creek is quite a ways off from your village. And it's not really a big strike like some on the mainland."

"This beach is nearer to my village."

"Yes, it is at that—although I suspect it's no big strike either. The force of the waves can only churn up so much for so long."

"Even so, it causes me great uneasiness."

Exhaling new emotion, Frank looked at the sand, then back at Makanta.

"Alright, Makanta. Here's what we'll do. We'll stay here for one more storm, collect what we can, then head for home. We'll tell everyone we found it at China Creek. They already know about that strike, and it's pretty far from your village on Nootka Sound."

Makanta managed a smile—though not a great one.

"It will be as you say, Frank McKenna. And now, I must say goodbye."

They shook hands. Makanta nodded to Sid and looked once more at May Li. One more look Frank's way put a smile on his face. Then he strode through the surf and paddled off.

Frank saw new dots in his life that only time and reflection would connect—and he saw May Li.

Red On a Rose

Chapter 1

Sarnia, Ontario – Tucked in a southwest nook on Lake Huron, it's where the three upper Great Lakes empty into the St. Clair River. A small city of about 70,000, industrial plants churn out car parts. The air is fresh with a breeze from the north, hazy when summer digs in. The lake—well, the lake is something else, stretching out forever, or so it seems to kids there. It could be the sea, they think, except for the frozen desert look in winter. Come spring, though, when the sun frees pent-up waves, lake freighters and salties from the Atlantic ply their trade, carrying grain, ore, and oil to various ports.

Vic Thompson has fond memories of that lake, from an assortment of family picnics to moments alone with its nature. On the family side, autoworker dad Greg Thompson and wife Faye liked to spread a blanket on the beach and take in the view. Radio turned up loud—Dad tuned in sports and news while Mom favored pop songs. Later, Vic and Dad would toss around a football. Lastly, they'd all dig in to fried chicken, conversation light as the afternoon waned.

On the solitary side, as Vic entered his teens, he'd taken to hiking up the shore alone. There he'd sit to view it all and practice his new guitar. Quite self-conscious then, the thought of others watching made him nervous. Oh, he'd get over it, especially when his skill picked up. At that time, he found his guitar a thought-absorbing magnet—just as well. For his buddies, then messing with drugs, were looking for trouble. Yet due to his all-consuming love of music and nature, Vic mostly steered clear of fiascoes.

But then his dad was laid off and took it hard. It seemed the job defined the man, and without it he lost his bearings. Morose he became, and abusive, this persisting in time. One day, though, when Mom had had enough, she just took off, leaving Vic a note. In it, she said that she loved him and that in time he'd join her.

Vic thought on this long and hard as at last he found the truth of blues. Oh, he and Mom wrote for a while, but the legal wrangle and pending nature of it all finally got to him. Come the spring of 2000, then, after an all-night beer bash with his chums, he bid them farewell. Onto a morning train he next stepped, bound for Alberta. Why Alberta? Well, for one thing, hero Gordon Lightfoot sang of its sweep and its beauty. Filled with inspiration then, he figured it was the right place to start a new life. Soon he roared by deep blue lakes and sweeps of pristine forest. Then, as the train turned straight west, a horizon of windswept grass tickled his eyes. "This is more like it," he sighed.

Strathmore, Alberta – Oil rigs sprouted like industrial trees, yet just beyond their reach there's sky all over. This became Vic's new home. During the week he'd toil on a rig, grinds and thumps and scrapes defining the soundscape. While truly hard work, he rose to the task and swayed to the roar of it all.

On weekends he'd party and play his guitar at the High Prairie Inn. Here he changed his loyalties, musically speaking. In Sarnia, he'd mostly played rock and pop, with a smidgen of folk. Now, though, the names of country crooners nudged out past favorites, Stompin' Tom amongst them. How could it be otherwise? How could he live in that land of tall grass, rippling like waves in the wind, and not feel its pulse?

By now, as well, his voice and playing had ripened. While not of country-star caliber, he had a way with songs that went with beer.

But then one day Vic's world swerved right off the road. He stumbled under a pile of worked-loose piping, badly crushing his right leg. After months in hospital and several surgeries, doctors said he'd never regain its full use. Scornfully, he swore a vow that he'd walk like before in one year.

With pluck and determination, Vic recovered enough in a year to get around with effort. He took a bartending job at the inn and of course continued his singing. His income took a nosedive, but with his long-range goal a return to the rigs, he took it in stride.

Renting a little place nearby, he had more free time now to take in nature. On Saturday mornings he'd sit on his porch to glean as much as he could. But people, too, figured much more into his inner equation. For now he took a closer look at their comings and goings, picking up on the daily life things he hadn't before. And so he grew to appreciate the power of kind words and hope for the future.

Montreal, Quebec – A city straddling an island on the Saint Lawrence, it bustled under the summer sun and grey winter cloud-cap alike with unquenchable life. An old city, here's where much of North American history began as French fur trappers moved in to stake a claim. Three million souls called it home—this city with Mount Royal at its core. That sightly hill rose flanked by green, and many lapped its nature on the weekend.

Lisa Moulin grew up here with her single mom. Struggling always to find a good job, Mom finally enrolled at a noted beauty college. Graduating at the head of her class, she found a job near Mount Royal, matrons of note on her slate. So Lisa spent time in the hair shop, listening to customers seated, dryers for crowns. She'd picture their lives in her mind, the perks and pitfalls. Yet in spite of the glamour involved, she found their lives wanting.

But then one day she discovered the city's glass-domed Botanical Garden. Entering that urban oasis—vines winding up trees, rare beauties abloom at their feet—greeted her eyes. Colorful birds flapped about, voicing distant places in their songs. The heated, misty air within somehow felt soothing. Even a trickling stream wound through, pleasing the eyes like a real one. Blending all together then, Lisa could picture a tropical isle, far beyond the confines of her everyday life.

And so as a child, Lisa progressed, making all the right moves. But then struck adolescence. Feeling hemmed in once again, the black and white of city life dimmed the topaz sky of her rainbow-crowned isle. For a time, she turned anorexic. When challenged on this matter, she'd holler that she had to watch her weight. The doctors, though, told Mom another story. They said she clung to childhood in her mind and wouldn't let go.

Distraught for a while, Mom fished for a cure, finally deciding to buy her a Burmese kitten, a ploy twofold. First, it would satisfy the kid in her with its promise of chocolate-brown cuddles. Second, it would engage her with tender emotion instead of her fears. So she handed Lisa a burger and held out the cat, telling her to eat before a cuddle. It worked like a charm, as Lisa took a bite and held out her hand for the furball. Next, she offered her kitty sweet dill from the bun, which it nibbled—and so, the name Pickles.

So Lisa bounced back, did well in high school, and made some new friends. Sadly, though, in her senior year, she met a guy who got her to sample cocaine. Lisa's world contracted again, even as she imagined a new universe. Later she moved in with her beau, a small-time drug dealer. Poor Lisa, not wholly aware of this tragic choice, just savored the rush and the color that next flooded in. And yet, at times, she'd imagine her tropical island—but with dark clouds now that muddied up the horizon.

This went on for a while, straining relations with Mom to the point of rupture. But then one night, in a fit of rage, her drunk and drugged lover flung Pickles across the room. Lisa flipped, and he slapped her around. Stunned, she fell into a frozen sulk, rocking and cradling her cat, beau drinking on till he passed out. Imagine his surprise next day when Lisa had vanished, along with a pile of his loot and a not-so-new car.

It's the ragged edge of April, 2005, cold and rainy in Montreal. Crossing the Saint Lawrence, Lisa had but a vague notion of reaching the west coast. There, the cry of gulls and a breeze from the sea would hint of the isle of her dreams—or so she imagined. Ontario blurred by green and wet as she now headed north and west on Highway 1.

Next day dawned bright but cold. Waking up with a start, fear hemmed her in. But she closed her eyes, breathed deep, and somehow felt strengthened. Steadier now, she got up, continued onward. Still dazed and dreamy, at last she reached the prairies. More on the rebound now, she took in the flattest of vistas—patches of snow under bare aspen trees, brown grass daubed with spring green, all capped with sharp blue. Not quite to her liking, she still found the sweep of it all at least picturesque.

Next day, after a comfortable snooze at a Saskatchewan Holiday Inn, with Pickles fed and purring, she reached Alberta—prairie higher and drier and more starkly grand. Then she saw it: the High Prairie Inn. Calling it a day, she checked in self and cat. Standing by a bathroom mirror, she brushed her long blonde hair and put on red lipstick. With growing ease, she passed her hands over her breasts and decided she looked fine.

"Time for dinner," she smiled.

Into the diner she walked, sitting at a table next to the stage. She ordered a steak sandwich and salad as out walked Vic with a guitar. The few Tuesday night patrons gave him a hand as he nodded back, smiling. How he loved those moments. They took his mind off the future and placed him right there. Then he spotted Lisa, who, curious, turned his way. She prepared for dinner only— that was the sunrise she looked for, not some cowboy balladeer. But life's full of surprises. So, as eye met eye, emotion flowed—just a little, like trickling water.

Vic, in fact, was not a bad-looking guy—tall with dark hair and brown eyes. Lisa's red lips caught his eye, but then her eyes alone touched the hull of his love boat.

"Green-eyed lady, ocean lady," he mumbled aloud with a smile.

Attraction here had to be expressed, yet he wasn't sure how. But then, with a light in his eyes, he thought of Alan Jackson's song *Red on a Rose*. Vic's style, while never causing swoons, that night sounded fine. In fact, faces turned his way from plates as eaters put dinnerware down. For just one precious moment, that haunting country ballad touched their hearts.

Now Lisa liked music—who doesn't? And while seldom considering herself a country-western fan, she blushed as Vic sang her way. She still felt pained inside, emotions all scattered. Maybe that explained the tune's soothing power. It splashed over hidden parts, like Vic was watering some wonderful plant. She lapped it all right up as dinner arrived.

This she picked at now with Vic's song over. Soon Vic moved to the bar to assume his duties. Glances, however, persisted, until—with steak gone but bun intact—Lisa oh-so-slowly walked his way. With a fetching smile, Vic made her a pina colada and they started to talk. Topics light at first soon filled with meaning.

Lisa said how she longed for the sea and the feel of wind in her hair, free of the confines that bound her. Vic in turn spoke of his passion for the land, and how at times it stirred his pilgrim soul. Shift over, place winding down, he sat by her side at her table, bought one more round, and took the time to say at least a little of what flowed from his core.

Still feeling pained and unsure of herself, Lisa listened on to a little past midnight. And so, when two hands clasped and boundaries blurred, they saw each other.

Next morning Lisa awoke with a start, Vic snoring by her side in his less-than-grand homestead. Panicking at first, she began to calm down. Then, when Vic awakened with a smile, she felt more at ease. Moving closer, they kissed. Lisa next backed off as thoughts intruded.

"Pickles," she mumbled while shaking her head, "my poor little Pickles. She spent the whole night alone!"

"Wahh… Pickles, you say?"

"Yeah, Pickles, my cat Pickles. She's my sweetie, and a spoiled little brat, too."

Vic smiled inside and out, this tender attachment completing a one-night thumbnail sketch of the woman he was falling for. Later and with gravity, she showed Vic to her cat, which he lightly stroked. Pickles ate it up and purred for more. Lisa watched on with approval, lingering doubts now erased.

"She likes you! Pickles really likes you. That's good, real good."

And so their two lives joined. Lisa took a job at the inn, and Vic proceeded to give her a tour of the region. Grasslands waved with fresh spring green as the Rocky Mountains wore bright caps of snow. Weather at times changed fast as northern blasts swept through. Squall lines appeared, casting shadows of night at noon, wind and hail beating down. Yet in the end, of course, the sun won out.

Later in the season, thunderheads crowned the land with billowing white. At one such time, Vic regaled Lisa with one of his favorite songs—*When the Rain Tumbles Down in July*, by Aussie country crooner Slim Dusty. Vic said that emotion shrank distances, and music combined with raw nature, no matter the land.

As autumn approached, cold winds blew and people more and more remained indoors. Vic sometimes went for walks alone while Lisa nuzzled close to hearth and cat. She read, then thought, then read some more, all the while digesting summer love.

Yeah, she mused, I'm changing, growing up, and about time, too. My poor mom—we'll have to get back in touch, reconnect. Yeah, we'll have to do that…

Vic mulled that season over too in early morning walks. Lisa, he imagined, walked by his side or thoughtfully faded out as he absorbed lonely nature.

As the season deepened, Lisa sheltered in books, turning over thoughts with novel pages. Ah, a story of life in Sumatra… She set the book down, looked about, and sighed—her world now so contracted that four walls defined it. Outside, cold winds howled and night ate chunks of day.

Now, Lisa had never liked this season in Montreal, but exposed to winds on the plains, she felt it like never before. More and more she hid in books and took in life less often. Vic, on the other hand, saw the beauty of it all—that austere charm of winter. He tried to transmit this to Lisa, with little success.

And so, as cabin fever took its toll, Lisa dreamed of the sun on sea and wind that didn't hurt when it brushed her face. Vic decided she needed that world of books, needed that space to grow in—at least for a season.

But then it happened. One dark morning, she awakened as the wind outside built drifts of snow that Vic had to shovel. This was just too much. Panic-stricken, she nudged him out of his sleep.

"Vic, oh Vic," she began, "I know you love these high plains, changing seasons and moods—I know that, and I respect you for it. It takes a rugged type to take all this in stride, but um, you know, when I left Montreal… You know, like I said before, my goal was the coast, the BC coast, where right now it's about 25 degrees warmer.

Please, don't interrupt, let me finish. I know, I know, maybe it's raining there, maybe it's no tropical paradise. But still, wind blowing in from the ocean—even in a cool season—has an, um, sweetness to it. Do you understand what I'm saying?"

Vic absorbed this bolt from the blue—that in fact, he had seen coming. Withdrawing into his thoughts for a bit, he mulled all the cherished events that had led to this moment. Then, as a fresh thought seized his mind, he sat up straight, eyes reflecting resolve.

"Lisa, darlin', you know I only want you to be happy. That's my main mission in life. So tell ya what, let's cut ourselves a deal here: you marry me, become my wife, make me one happy man, and then come spring we'll move to the coast. And look, I still have some oil rig savings. We can buy ourselves a little place—maybe no castle in Spain—but it'll be our place, our little nest by the sea of your dreams."

In silence, Lisa pondered these words and pictured the scenes that they conjured. Her smile returned.

"Oh, Vic, yes, I will marry you. You know I love you too, with all my heart. And your offer of moving—it's real noble of you to put me first that way. Yes, I'll be your wife, and you'll be my husband."

Closing his eyes, Vic savored this thought. And then they embraced.

Chapter 2

And so, with spring just several weeks off, their wedding day came. Now, a winter stay on the high plains could not compare to a honeymoon in Tahiti. Even so, the couple's radiant warmth made up for the geographic misplacement—that, and the tropical plant Vic had bought Lisa. As another nice touch, the festive mood of friends, blended with drinks and back pats, had all present basking in some kind of sun. Later, when Vic promised to take Lisa to Tahiti once he'd saved enough, they almost made it there that very night.

Soon April rolled around with welcome sun. Tall grass sprouted again—and with it, time for goodbyes. So after all present had packed up the newlyweds' snuff, they embraced and back-patted. Off they next zipped in a new old car, trailer in tow. Vic then glanced at the rearview mirror with a tear in his eye. For hanging in his friend John's barn were his silver spurs—a parting gift. Heartache and hope for the future just about summed his mood.

Into the Rockies they soon plunged, as if into a wall of frozen waves of rock. For here they crossed that stark divide—plains on one side, range after range on the other. Vic, tamping down his doubts, soon felt like a trekker, occasionally stopping to take it all in. At such times, he could almost feel the grind of glacial ice on rock that had carved out these valleys. This gave him a sense of the scope of it all—like a breath of fresh air. But some ways down the road, clouds forming over high peaks dumped their rain. Windshield wipers clacked, smoothing splats on glass—but just for an instant. The wind, too, played a tune he didn't much care for—it hinting of struggles to come.

Lisa, on the other hand, looked about as bubbly as the cola she sipped. So as she stirred her ice with a straw, she lightly in her mind passed through the storm. Then, standing on a sunlit beach, she smilingly got her bearings. Her joyous thoughts next stood on a yacht, bound for who knew where. Finally, sitting down all comfy, in her mind she played a song she loved—*Beyond the Blue Horizon.*

But then, as at last they neared their destination, Lisa's flights of fancy hit a cold front. She began to note the sights that spoke of sharper edges than Sumatra. On an expressway now, laden rigs roared by as rain fell harder. Warehouses dotted the scene, as well as stacks of lumber. Radio songs only partly masked this gritty new mood. For while love, in fact, makes the world go round, shipments bound for market foot the bill.

Driving into an industrial nook of Surrey by the churning Fraser, more and more her dreams condensed into rain.

Turning onto Scott Road, they passed by SkyTrain Station. At a red light, they watched as people rushed in, gratefully folding umbrellas to board the next train. Then they would swoosh over

SkyTrain Bridge, Vancouver-bound. The light turned green and they turned down Old Yale Road. Passing under a train trestle, Vic ground their car to a halt. Ah, there it was—their goal: the Fraser Trailer Haven and Pub.

Vic turned off the engine to take in the sight. A row of white rose bushes marked the outer boundary of the park, behind it a pub of tough cedar, to the left a laundromat. Rows of RVs and trailers lined narrow dirt lanes. Finally, scattered trees and the odd Canadian flag defined the skyline.

Breathless, Vic started the car again, turned left, and entered. They proceeded down a narrow dirt road, now muddy and puddled. He stopped and looked left at a trailer—about it, a small yard with one picnic table. Not far off was a high plank wall, sawmill behind it, smell of cedar shavings filling the air. Still, with a flourish, he noted the trailer and called it their home.

Now, in all fairness, Vic had said all along that their new home would be no palace. He'd added, though, that the sea wasn't far off and a nice river beach was steps away. He'd taken pains to explain it as the first step of their new life. With love's labor, he'd concluded, that patch of home would yield its fruit—all in due time.

Vic, basically an optimist, knew there were two ways of looking at things. On the one hand, through rain he saw trailer by a sawmill, not-so-grand abodes housing new neighbors. Then too, their river beach would never have the look of Waikiki. And a flock of hungry crows cawed away—not one flamingo in sight. Yeah, it looked like humble pie all right, fresh from the oven. But then again, rain here cleansed the air, green grass sprouted, and budding trees glistened—all in response to the rain.

The compact homes of new neighbors inwardly bubbled with life. Couples nuzzled close in front of TVs, yakking about this and that as the Fraser rolled by. Inside their new home, Vic imagined like scenes. And so, while some doubts lingered yet, he thankfully embraced it.

Lisa, on the other hand, hovered on the other side of the last mountain pass, somewhat removed from it all. She struggled with the clash of her dream with what lay before her. Sure, she had the same man by her side—that hadn't changed. The same deft hand that strummed a guitar now sweetly stroked her shoulder. Feeling too a few chords plucked, she took another look at their new place. The two discrepant pictures had, in part at least, merged into one. So, while carefully eyeing her husband, she managed a smile.

Pleased, Vic jumped out into the rain, removed his coat, and held it over his sweetie as she stepped out. With Lisa clutching Pickles, they crossed their new home's threshold. Vic clicked on the lights. What they saw, while truly not impressive, didn't upset Lisa overmuch. Sure, it's no castle in Spain, but other than a shrunken look, everything looked pretty normal—living room, kitchenette, bed, and bathroom. What's more, the place was furnished with presentable stuff.

So, easing up on her grip, Lisa set her cat on the floor. Bluish eyes then widened with fear, whiskers curling out, all tense and alert. But then she spotted the purple toy mouse Vic had secretly placed there. Playfully, she jumped the toy, spun about three times, and then turned to Lisa.

"Pickles, she likes our new place!" Lisa chirped. "And if Pickles likes this trailer, then it must be okay."

And so they began to unpack their precious belongings. Soon enough, the place had a homey look. Lisa whipped up plates of juicy burritos while Vic scrubbed out a grouty bathroom sink. At last, they sat down at their table. And, while not exactly *Strangers in the Night*, they nevertheless exchanged romantic glances. Finishing off their Twinkie dessert, hand met hand. And so, nestling next on their small but plush sofa, Vic loaded the VCR with their favorite movie. Far-off scenes lit up the room, for a time dissolving boundaries. This then set the stage for their new home-defining first romantic encounter.

They woke up the next morning to a whole new mood. Clouds had parted in the night to reveal fresh spring blossoms. Still cool, the air warmed fast in the sun. So after a breakfast of scrambled eggs, toast, and coffee, they decided to check out Fraser Beach.

Walking down the puddled-up road, they passed the pub and entered a park. Through parting trees, they found the river beach. Being a Wednesday, they had it all to themselves. So, sitting down on a big old log, they took in the scene. Imported sand covered riverbank mud—a nice effect. The river, a beautiful sight, rolled placidly by. On the other side lay New Westminster, but Vic and Lisa saw it as greater Vancouver.

Several hundred feet overhead, SkyTrain Bridge—its great concrete pylons buried deep in river mud—arose, drawing their eyes. Then they heard the click and whir of two commuter trains crossing it at the same time. Lastly, some ways off, they saw a berthed ship, making Lisa smile.

"Wow, a freighter! What do you think it's loaded with, Vic?"

"Oh, lumber, I expect."

"Where do you think it's headed?"

"I dunno—States, maybe."

"Or maybe India."

"Yeah, maybe."

Silence for a moment. They soaked up their new world. How different from the plains it appeared—this coast of wet and green—and how the ocean fed the land with its life. Mountains caught incoming clouds and milked them for rain, thick forests covering their slopes. And in the city itself, sweeps of trees connected grids to nearby primal nature, at least in a piecemeal way.

Then, having eyed the scenes enough, Vic turned to Lisa.

"Look here, Lisa, I know this isn't quite what you had in mind—beach on the sea and fancy house—but remember, like this river, things always move on. Nothing stands still in this world, really, and you know that. So, honey, be patient. Anyway, ya know, right now it feels comfortable to nestle in this little nook we've found."

Lisa considered his words as she again eyed the ship.

"I know, Vic, I know, and you worked hard to make it all happen. And you know, I feel like I've been carried way beyond my small world in Montreal."

"Glad to hear it, honey. Real glad."

Here she looked straight into his eyes, then back to the river.

"The river is beautiful, but it's not just a river, is it?"

"What do you mean?"

"Well, it's a boundary too. It divides Surrey from Vancouver beyond."

"True enough, honey, but look at the bright side — at least we don't need a passport to cross to the other side."

"The other side… Makes me think, Vic. Makes me think life's a little like a coin in the air — you know, a flipped coin."

"Huh. A flipped coin, spinnin' away in the air… Yeah, but ah…"

"The two sides — different, of course — but as the coin spins they blend into one thing."

"Aha! Maybe like yin 'n yang, like in some of those books you read all winter?"

"Maybe something like that…"

"And our lives in the air — air meaning spirit?"

"Mm, one way of putting it…"

"Course, we want to land heads up… or does the coin of a life actually land? Could be it dissolves in the air, like sugar in water…"

"Or salt, in your case," she teased.

They both laughed a bit. Lisa smiled. Nuzzling close, they took one last look at the scene and headed back home.

That evening, they went to the local pub. Its dim-lit main room had sturdy walnut tables, as well as more intimate booths a few steps removed. Soon, they made the acquaintance of Keith O'Connor, the owner. A congenial guy hard not to like, he gave them helpful hints on life in the park — which he said had its perks.

Vic and Lisa paused to consider the sheltered nook feel of the place, removed as it was from the main parts of town. With Surrey large and busy, here lay a place to catch a welcome breather. Vic right off picked up on a friendliness more country than urban. In other words, for him, it fit like a comfy old glove.

Maybe this had to do in part with his disability. True, it had slowed him down, but it also gave him space to observe life's daily graces. Now, he truly struggled to regain full use of his leg and longed to take a good stout whack at life.

Still, when he mentioned he sang country in a place back in Alberta, Keith asked him to sing in the pub on Saturday night. This made Vic smile. Right off, it lessened the pressure of new expectations. As always too, losing himself in the moment blunted the future's sharp edge.

Lisa shared this feeling to a point. Sure, she saw the park as one big yard to relax in. She pictured herself outside when Vic was at work, chatting with a neighbor or tending a garden. On the other hand, the new strengths she had talked about gave her new perspective. And so she noted that while laid-back, the park had boundaries. So in the end, the place fit her too — but with a slight pinch.

At any rate, they nestled in, feeling comfortable. Soon, they made the acquaintance of next-door neighbors Bill and Alice Evans. Bill worked at a lumber yard just up the road. Alice stayed at home with their toddler, Bobby, whom she proudly displayed.

A chubby little guy he appeared, rosy-cheeked and cute. But when he upchucked his snack, blushing, Mom wiped his mouth.

"A real chip off the old block," Bill crowed, in spite of the sideshow. "And soon to be hockey all-star."

Vic and Lisa eyed the tyke, each relating what they saw to their own aspirations. Keith next named the local men for Vic, claiming them all stalwart types — "more or less," he added, while eyeing a skinny guy playing pool.

"That's Darren McMasters — basically a good guy too... Just a few funny ways, is all."

Vic's curious look prompted him on.

"Yeah, well, ya see, unlike most here, he lives by himself, and ah, when I stroll by his place I sometimes hear Korean pop songs playing."

"Korean pop songs, you say."

"I do say. But other than that, he's a good enough guy."

"Well, it takes all kinds to make a world."

"Yeah, takes all kinds."

And so, tone of the season set, a gorgeous spring unfolded. In contrast to the plains, this place busted out with flowers. In fact, its multitude of blossoms made Vic sneeze. Lisa, on the other hand, just ate them up. Taken by it all, she planted a garden — a mix of favorite flowers plus summer squash. This she swore tasted better than steak when smothered in butter.

Then too, with new friend Bill's reference, Vic got a job. Now, some might grumble at lumberyard work, but not Vic. He liked the feel of tools and their various actions, and liked as well the thought of visible fruit for his efforts.

So summer unfolded in near pastoral ways: barbecues with Bill and Alice, beer quaffed and tales swapped with kindhearted slaps on the back. Then too, the purring couple found the river beach a little love nest. On Sunday afternoons, Vic liked to sing to his Lisa. Lisa listened, eyes closed. She now saw the many hues this style added to life, felt its tenderness — though more than once Vic came home to Led Zeppelin.

Autumn arrived. Lisa picked and cooked her squash as summer heat faded. Now, it is a fact that moods change with the season. For Vic, autumn affected him in poetic ways that he sometimes liked to write of.

In fact, one afternoon by the river as a shower fell, he wrote a poem entitled Wet on Red. That night in bed, he read it to his Lisa. Chin in hand, she listened as words painted a picture. It tickled her that a few scribbled lines could do that. She smiled and gave Vic a kiss.

Next morning, with Vic off to work, Lisa thought of his poem. She understood what the season did for him — but still didn't like it. Longer nights and colder, winter to follow. That season here, while mild, would be wet and grey.

How she loved the summertime and hated to see it fade out. Winter was winter, after all, and autumn's the guy at the gate who lets it in.

Yeah, time moves on. Once she thought she'd be a kid forever. And now here she was, married and so far from home.

The season dug in. One day, Lisa walked alone in falling rain, umbrella in hand. She slipped into their summer beach, now so different in mood. Looking across the river — Vancouver beyond — she felt empty and aching.

But then, standing as the shower stopped, she imagined summer memories forming a prism of sorts.

'Yeah,' she thought in wonder, 'all those bits and pieces of thoughts and emotions forming one thing… But what is it?'

With a shrug, she went home, fixed dinner for Vic. In he stomped, smile begetting smile as lasagna was served. Lisa's mood changed as she savored Vic's solid presence. He shared the best of his day as she listened and nodded.

For an instant in her mind, she touched Vic's wellspring, drawing refreshment. Lastly though, when she noted how satisfied her husband appeared with his new life, smiling, she sighed.

Chapter 3

Now, all is not rain and reflection in autumn on the west coast. Sunny days still abounded, or at least lingered on. On one such Saturday morning, Vic and his buddies went fishing. For the Fraser teemed with salmon now—or so they had been told. Even so, at first they plied her for hours, catching nary a fish. At noon, with salmon still dodging their hooks, the boys had pizza with beer. Soon they laughed with glee and began catching fish. By day's end, happy and exhausted, they headed for home.

Vic pulled up with delight. Walking up to the door, he hoisted his scaly prize for Lisa to see. "Funny," he thought, "guess she didn't hear me pull up." So he opened the door and sniffed for hints of dinner. "Hmm, no taste in the air… KFC tonight?" Then it registered: TV off, curtains drawn, no pesky little furball running about. In a growing mood of unease, Vic flipped on the lights. Then he spotted a letter on the kitchen table, his name on it. Grabbing it, he sat down on their sofa. In suspense, he eyed the envelope and then broke the seal. Paper crinkled as he unfolded the note. Good thing he'd sat down, as what he read aloud about knocked him flat.

"Unbelievable," he mumbled while shaking his head. "Unreal," he added, sinking into the sofa. Stunned eyes froze straight forward as the letter dropped from his hand and landed with a swish. "Lisa, my darlin' Lisa—she left me, just like that."

Shadows lengthened into night as Vic sat unmoved, the weight of pain on his chest holding him still. In time, he pondered the contents line by line. "Need to test my wings," he mumbled. "You gave me the gift of freedom," he added flatly. "And we'll see each other again, in time." One line though burrowed into mind and heart to ever remain: "I left because I love you." He just shook his head again and again, trying to un-contradict it.

"Ha. If I live to a hundred, I'll never figure that one out."

Then he scanned about his empty home and almost saw Lisa's trace, just for an instant. TV off, he wondered what tonight's Check movie was. This thought summed his emotions—something played but the set's turned off. At length, he looked at the salmon by the sink, awaiting his knife.

"Looks like you died for nothin', bud," he said, smiling wryly.

Too stunned for anything else, Vic hit the sack. Later, lying wide awake, he saw and felt nothing. Sunday dawned; he left the curtains drawn. Dreams seemed to flit on the ceiling his eyes had affixed to. Outside, a breeze kicked up as the sun climbed high, but in his dark cocoon he couldn't connect. Up at 2, as breakfast burned, he tuned in his country station, JR FM. Steve Canyon sang of his true love—Vic switched it off.

At 7:15, he answered his banging back door. There stood buddy Keith, smile quickly wilting.

"Vic, you okay? You don't look so great."

"Oh, hey, Keith, good to see ya. No, I'm okay, no problem."

"Then why aren't you at the bar for your 7 p.m. strumming? Remember, it's the long weekend. You agreed to come on Sunday night. And you know, you got a bit of a following here."

"Oh yeah… Sorry about that. Just slipped my mind. But look, Keith, um, actually, I'm not feeling all that charged—maybe a touch of the flu."

"Yeah, that's going around, isn't it? You just rest then. The gang will understand. Say, where's the little lady and that furry little scamp of hers?"

"Ah, yeah, well… I'll tell you about that later."

Sensing pain and looking concerned, Keith didn't pry, but rather eased out of the scene. Vic went to the kitchen cabinet and pulled out the 20-year-old Jim Beam he'd been saving for a special occasion.

"Time to break this seal and drink to love… Yeah, to love. Good thing tomorrow's a holiday."

So he poured a shot and popped their favorite movie into the VCR, plunked down on the sofa, and grabbed the remote.

"Oh yeah, my magic wand, for sure," he laughed while clicking scenes into being. Dreams of love soon lit up the screen, tears at last flowing. Drained by the end, Vic threw his bottle at the fridge, leaving a dent. Last, he crawled into bed, and contracting, soon slept.

Next morning, Keith stopped by to see how Vic felt. Vic invited him in, and over a cup of coffee, told him what's up. Stunned for a moment, Keith fished for a thought. And while he wanted to help, he sure had no cure to proffer. He could only say that shit happens and that in time it would all work out.

Vic smiled, nodded, and accepted Keith's offer of a good fried egg breakfast. So he went to the pub and hung out for a while but didn't feel much like talking. Back home, he lay on his bed and dozed off. Waking in the afternoon, he listlessly stared out the window. The high beams of Skytrain Bridge then grabbed his attention as steel cables shined in the sun. Then, windows glinted on a train that sped to Vancouver, destination bound. Lisa had said in her letter she'd take such a train—precise destination unstated.

'Huh, just where does that arc end for her?' Vic wondered. 'And with what force of gravity did that destination pull her from my side? That damn Skytrain represents the first flaps of wings Lisa said she had to test… Wants to be free… Our home a prison, then? Or maybe a nest a baby bird flees when it can fend for itself? Lisa, yeah, Lisa, she was kinna like a baby bird when we first met, hungry, sad-eyed, just fallen out of her nest—so vulnerable then… And that cat of hers, she's like a little kid with her cat… But she's stronger now, moved past all that, said so herself… But what about me? Am I stronger now? I felt strong in Alberta, yeah, all that hard work, but then things just crapped out… But I got my second wind, worked on my leg, made a comeback… And now, our comfortable home… Okay, so it's dinky, no one said it's our final destination… I mean, the people here are great 'n all, job's okay, maybe not making a bundle, but ah…'

And so it went, as thoughts tugged and pushed at the boulder on his chest. Still, Vic made it to work. Not only did he make it, but two reasons nudged him on to greater effort. First, he could lose himself here as muscles pumped and heart beat away, all to the rhythm of rock. More important though, he felt the need to make a greater effort at life in general. Maybe, unknowing, he'd been a slack hand and let the love of his life just slip away—so he had to fight back.

Days passed into weeks as Vic struggled on. Then one day he pushed too hard, strained his bad leg, and had to slow down. At quitting time, he limped past the office while leaving. Nat Adams, the owner, knew Vic pushed too hard. So he took him aside and suggested dropping back to 40 hours a week, just for a while. Testy at first at this notion, Vic recovered his wits and took Nat's advice. He couldn't risk aggravating that leg. Well, his buddies felt real bad about this, tried to cheer him up, motivate him for another comeback, but they couldn't do much beyond that.

Vic slumped even more, what with pumping up income crucial to his comeback goal. In this state, casual acquaintance Darren McMasters called him one Saturday morning, suggesting a meeting at McD's. Puzzled, Vic accepted. Mumbling to himself, rubbing an unshaven face, he headed for those vaunted golden arches. Pulling up with a slight twinge of pain, Vic spotted Darren at an outside table. Smiling, Darren jumped up to shake Vic's hand. They both went in to order and returned to the table. A wan October sun lit the scene as laden rigs whizzed by. Darren inhaled his first Filet-O-Fish and worked on a mountain of fries. He ate a lot, even as his wiry build and lean face hardly showed it. Vic, finishing off his Big Mac, sipped coffee in silence. Sensing it time to break the ice, Darren spoke up.

"Damn, you know, I don't care what they say about fast food—these fish fillets really kick ass," he beamed while wiping his mouth.

"Yeah, they're okay."

Looking at his tray as he unwrapped his second fillet, Darren started to read its cover.

"Hey Vic, fact or fiction: The apple is a member of the rose family."

"Fact," he mumbled, napkin to mouth.

"Right on. No foolin' you, is there? How about this one: In 1995, the potato was the first vegetable grown in space. The goal was to feed astronauts on long-term voyages and eventually feed future space colonies. Bet you didn't know that, huh?"

Chin in hand, Vic eyed a guy munching his fries with abandon, wondering if Korean pop songs were just the tip of the iceberg.

"Where you from, Darren?"

"Fredericton, New Brunswick. Moved out here five years ago, and ya know, I really love this place—even learned a smidgen of local history. See, the Salish Indians lived here first. Just picture the place back then, Vic: tall timber everywhere, the Fraser just boiling with salmon, bears in the woods, 'n all…"

"Ha. Well where else would they be?"

"Right. But just bear with me, Vic," he answered, grinning.

"Yeah, right, bear with ya…"

"So anyway, white settlers move in, clear a patch or two in the wilderness. Mm, yeah, sad how the Salish got edged out, but maybe they'll make a comeback... But you know, Surrey here was an important settlement till they built the bridge. Here's where people would board ferryboats bound for the New West side. Surrey gets its name from one of those great boats—the *Surrey*. Bet ya didn't know that."

"No, no I didn't. It's a little interesting. So, ah, where you work?"

"At the spring-making plant just down the road. I make springs—you know, the big ones for heavy-duty equipment. I really like it there. See, I worked in a lumberyard first, but the sawdust really bugged me. So I switch to the spring works and feel lots better. Then I figure it out: I have a more natural affinity for metal than wood—ha, a little funny, considering how much I love the deep dark woods here... But there you go, just one of the wonders of nature."

Vic paused here. There's something he just had to know.

"So, ah, Darren, you like music, right? I mean, you seem to be at the pub pretty often when I play..."

"Oh hey man, I love music—all kinds, you name it; rock, country, blues..."

"Blues and..."

Here Darren looked bashful and turned away.

"And..." Vic egged him on.

"Okay, okay, I like old Barbra Streisand songs. There, you made me say it."

A little exasperated, Vic went direct.

"You like Korean pop songs, Darren?"

Darren, at first shocked, then smiled, looking wistful.

"I don't know how you found that out, Vic, but yeah, I do. See, I had a Korean girlfriend a while back. She just loved that stuff, and ah, I loved her. But then her family moved to Ontario and she with them. You know how it is for Koreans family-wise—they're real tight."

Vic digested this tidbit and smiled, easing back down in his seat.

"I get it now. You're okay, Darren. I mean, it's not exactly country, but your grounds of approval are just as sentimental."

"Yeah, sentimental. And you know, those Koreans, they have a presence in our parts these days. They work hard, built lots, put in their fair share."

"Yeah, true enough. So tell me, Darren, what's this all about? You said on the phone you had some info that could benefit us both. Want to tell me about it?"

Darren pulled a folded page from his shirt pocket. Plunking it down on the table, he then beamed in triumph.

"Take a look at that, Vic. You play the guitar. You'll really appreciate this."

Vic unfolded an article from the *Vancouver Sun* and began to skim through it. Soon he looked back at Darren, in the know.

"Amazing, isn't it? Just think, Vic—right up the Fraser there they are, Pacific Coast Maples, just taking root and doing their thing like ordinary trees. But see, their wood is super special—has a nice color, density, and grain. It is, beyond the shadow of a doubt, the best damn wood in the world for making fine musical instruments."

"Huh. Never knew that, to tell you the truth."

"Yes sir, it is," Darren continued his pitch. "I mean, they're beautiful to look at—tall and stately, finely shaped leaves, the whole bit. But ya know, just like people, it's what's inside that counts. And like I said, their wood is just so damn fine it about wants to sing out loud. Says there musicians just love it—it's like they're made for each other. No wonder the best players own such fine instruments. Ah, but getting down to the nitty-gritty, like all true love, it calls for self-sacrifice—in this particular case meaning that these guys shell out top dollar to get their hands on one of those polished beauties. Hard to imagine, isn't it, that mere kilometers off stand trees worth fifty K a pop."

"Huh. So what you suggesting here? That we, ah, that we cut down a fancy maple?"

"Ha! Cuttin' to the chase, I see. No fooling around for you, right, Vic? But now, before you give me your answer, just think— fifty thousand a pop…"

"Well yeah, Darren, according to the article that's true, but it also says some are only worth a few hundred and that it all depends on grain quality."

"That's right, Vic. It takes top-notch, finer-than-fine curly-twirly grain to fetch top dollar. But see, I'm working on this theory— there must be ways of judging from outward appearance which trees have that golden grain."

"Aw come on, Darren, all those trees look the same, and that's a fact. Finding that one perfect tree is like a gamble, pure and simple. Why, you could cut a hundred before hitting the jackpot, which brings me to objection number two—that without a proper permit, cutting such trees is illegal."

"Okay, Vic, ya got me," he said with a grimace, smacking hands to his heart. "That's true, that's true. Without a government stamp of approval, we cross that thin line. But look on the bright side— this way, there's no messy paperwork and expense. Furthermore, we have the element of surprise working for us, and that, my friend, can mean the difference between winning and losing a battle. Ya know, life's like that too—it's a battle. Now, I don't want to touch any sore spots, but I know you're hurting for cash and that it's part of the ammo you need to make a comeback. I mean, think about it—25 K… You could make a down payment on a bigger place, maybe invest it, but no matter how you slice it, cash can only help your situation. See Vic, I can sense these things. You're not resigned to this split business. You mean to win your sweetie back, don't ya?"

Vic winced a bit and bit his lip, not so swift to answer.

"Alright, okay," Vic finally replied. "Here's how I see it: The love of your life—it's a one-time-only deal. Once she's gone, once you let her slip away, well sir, you live on the wisps of a vaporized dream—not for this boy. She hasn't slipped out all the way yet."

"That's the spirit! Like my ironworker dad used to say, *It ain't over till it's wrought.*"

Vic once again looked at his new friend askance, not used to this kind of remark. But then he chuckled, in spite of himself.

"Well put, Darren. It ain't over till it's wrought."

Amazingly then, and against his better judgment, on the spot Vic signed on board. After all, he was hard-pressed, wits still muddied up by conflicting emotions. Darren, for his part, was a gambler to begin with. So he proudly displayed the king cobra skin wallet he'd recently won in a card game. Beaming like the sun, he went on to say that he later scooped fifty on top.

So as Vic walked home alone, second thoughts suppressed for now, he viewed the scheme at least as a welcome distraction.

Lying in bed, again he studied Skytrain Bridge—sinewy cables, concrete, and rails with trains swishing over. Somehow, some way, he must cross it too. But no, he shook his head. That bridge had become a symbol for him—not just a link to Vancouver. No, it's not a matter of riding a train from point A to point B. It had more to do with personal vision.

Just what was his vision, his dream, Vic wondered. Alberta had once been his dream—still was in a way. Did he want to go back to define it? Ah, but no. Now, the bits of prairie that still shined in Lisa's eyes from time to time defined his old dream. He knew as well that, like lifeblood, his dream flowed ever onward and now hooked up to the Fraser. So, still at loose ends with himself, he concluded that Darren had made a good point about money.

"Yeah," he mumbled, "at rock bottom it takes cold hard cash in the tank to drive a life. Dreams in the backseat, passengers safely belted in front, forward. And, well, shit, everyone knows that if you're not moving forward, you're moving backwards. Huh, yeah, and furthermore, since the past is gone, you really end up nowhere."

Chapter 4

Work week followed weekend. At the saw again, Vic pondered what transpired and almost laughed. "So this is what it's come to," he thought, "hacking down trees to see the forest, or some damn thing like that. Oh boy, whatever I've been roped into, at least it provides a little comic relief. Just hope it's worth risking a hefty fine…"

But as the fateful weekend approached, distant clouds rolled in. Now, stage two of the rainy season here meant green sidewalks and glum demeanors for the sun-seeking set, which equals about everyone. Resisting this liquid fatalism, Vic noted that abundant rain meant a plush green feast for the eyes, plus the semi-musical sound of falling rain. Even so, that night he dreamed an Alberta sky so blue that weighty chunks fell down to earth. "Funny," he mumbled while picking one up, "that high plain sky in my mind actually surpasses the real thing in beauty. Some kind of mystical process at work here, I expect…" Waking up to grey skies, he plopped down for another five.

Still, after a shower and shave, he was raring to go. Entering the grill, shaking off his umbrella, he looked around. Ah, there sat Darren, flatware in hand. He looked at his breakfast and chafed at the bit, but waited politely for Vic, who sat down and ordered. Then he dug in. Plate now clean, Darren, wiping his mouth, wore a serious look. "Uh oh," Vic thought, "he's gonna add a layer of verbal padding to this venture. I just know it."

And so he did, thinking a little knowledge of the Fraser in order. So he told Vic it starts way upstream and then gushes through Fraser Canyon. During the last ice age, that famous gorge had lain beneath one vast ice sheet that melting left a fiord behind. But then the land rose up and presto, a new notch in mother earth. "So at last," he concluded with relish, "you got your Pacific Coast Maples and a host of flora and fauna surrounding this crown jewel of Fraser nature. These beauties tend to congregate near stands of tall Douglas fir, so that's what we have to look for first."

Briefing over, they moved out. Boldly they'd attack in day with rain rather than at night, the usual time for such dubious ventures. Their buy contact would then meet them at 5 pm in a tucked away nook. Darren had dug up his number through an underground grapevine. Vic asked no questions. They'd rented a U-Haul truck for the job, buzz saw in back. Sitting high and feeling so too, Vic fired her up as grim met grin as into the din of Scott Road traffic they plunged. Soon they rolled into Langley, bustling town at the Fraser Valley's mouth. Grey sky and glassy road formed buns that a patty of rain sizzled through. They stopped at a red light. Vic saw one crumpled driver listlessly watching on as the swish of windshield wipers replaced summer's hum.

At the junction of legendary Highway 1, the valley now appeared a notch in mountain slopes as the Fraser snaked east. Through misty gloom, tall trees clothed slopes — hemlock, spruce, cedar, and Douglas fir. Darren told Vic of a fair-sized stand of Douglas fir near Chilliwack. Later approaching their target, Darren pointed Vic to a side road. They slowly lumbered up an asphalt way till a dirt track forked off left. Onward and upward they wound. Then, with a wild wave of his arms, Darren yelled, "Stop!"

"What is it? What is it?" Vic asked in alarm.

"It's lunchtime, man."

Vic shot him the look and checked his watch.

"Darren, it's 10:45."

Ignoring this observation, Darren reached into a bag and pulled out a grease-splotched wrapper wrapped treat.

"Oh man, these bacon double cheeseburgers really kick ass," he mumbled with mouth full. "Good thing I had that two-for-one coupon."

Vic resigned himself to the intermission. Too wound up to eat, he sipped coffee and peered through the woods. 'Ah,' he thought, 'could those be maples dead ahead?'

"Hey Darren, take a look over there."

His partner looked, shading eyes even with the sun obscured.

"Yeah, fiery red leaves and shapely, bright still in falling rain… Yeah, maples, I think. Let me finish eating and we'll have a little look-see."

So they put on slickers and headed out. 'Aha,' Vic thought, 'what luck,' as several of the beauties rose up large. He scanned the bunch and picking the biggest grinned wide.

"That's our tree," he decreed. "Let's break out the saw and do it to it. The sooner we clear outta here, the better."

Hand to chin in contemplation, Darren slammed on the brakes.

"Not so fast Vic, not so fast. Take a good look at this bark."

Vic glared at his partner.

"Darren, what gives with you, anyway? A tree is a tree and this is the biggest one. Let's cut it down and make tracks."

"Look Vic, I know you're all hot to buzz 'er down and skedaddle, but remember, some of these trees are worth a few skins, some a pile. They gotta have that curly-twirly grain to fetch top dollar, and well, the outer configurations of this particular specimen just don't jibe with the insides we seek."

"Are you nuts? You can't tell the grain by the outside. Let's get going."

As Darren begged to differ, an argument broke out. Vic began to shout before catching himself, thinking it not good to make noise. Finally, seeing that Darren had latched on to this cockeyed notion, he backed down. So with Vic red-faced they checked other trees, none meeting Darren's standards. Vic stomped back to the truck, Darren following shortly. Then up the dim-lit track they inched as tires squished mud. Some ways up, again they spotted a stand of maples. Again they inspected; again Darren snubbed. At this point Vic wanted to call it all off, delays like this making it more likely they'd get caught. But then he decided to give it one more try.

Up again that narrow road they inched, necks craning left and right. Ah, they spotted another stand. Vic pulled up, yanked the emergency brake, looking first at the trees and then at his squinting partner. Darren got out of the truck, circled round one tall and stately maple. Vic watched from behind the wheel as his partner circled again, each line and wrinkle scrutinized. Lastly he leaned over and took a good whiff.

"Vic! Come on out and take a look at this tree."

But just as Vic's boots hit spongy turf, the dreaded scenario happened: an RCMP patrol car inching up stopped as a folded law enforcer extended his full and awesome height. Looking first at the nervous pair then their ride, he stiffly walked up. Stationary now and well clear of personal space, he fired off the feared declamation.

"Wet day to be in the woods, eh boys?"

Eyes now roved them up and down, burning off a layer of deceit.

"Yeah, well," Darren began, slight askance wink at Vic saying I'll handle this, "you know how it is, gotta keep the little lady purrin'."

The officer shot him a quizzical look.

"Would you care to explain that?"

"Yeah, sure. It's like this: See, my wife, she's Korean. Now, on a rainy day countrified Koreans like her have a custom – they make mugwort tea. They say it wards off feelings of damp 'n dank, which are a bit like yin 'n yang, but in this case they don't complement each other. Anyway, she says 'Darren, you fetch me fresh mugwort or you're cut off.'"

"Cut off?" he asked with a face scrunch.

"Well, yeah," Darren added leaning forward a bit, lowering his voice, "you know, no nuzzlin' tonight sort a thing."

The officer smiled a bit but remained rigid.

"So I say, okay sugar pot, you got it. I'll go out this very morning, find the freshest mugwort on the coast for you. But you gotta promise me a big sloppy kiss when I get back. Well, she smiles coy and I'm out the door. You know how it is, man."

Easing his statue-like pose for a bit, the officer stiffened again, scanning the truck once more as his eyes flashed a "Gotcha!"

"Ah huh... Pretty big rig for hauling a handful of mugwort – don't you think?"

"Oh, that. Yeah, okay, here's the thing: My sweetie, she goes on to say that ordinary mugwort won't cut the muster. She said it must be picked near the biggest fish in a stream. See, that's another countrified custom: mugwort near the biggest fish is the most potent, if you know what I mean," he ended with a brow twitch, the officer still looking baffled.

"Well hell, just look at that U-Haul, man. Got a salmon painted on the side near as long as you are tall. Not gonna find a bigger fish than that! So I kill two birds with one stone. I have a roomy truck for stocking up on the stuff so's I don't have to do this all winter. Then I'll just tell her that I stood right near the biggest damn salmon in BC! She'll never be the wiser."

Finally, the grand enforcer couldn't help but smile in earnest. Vic couldn't tell if it was because he believed Darren or if the yarn had tickled his ribs. In any case, he backed off.

"Yeah, okay, you boys have fun in the rain."

Ambling back to his car, he turned and drove back down the road. Much relieved, the rain-slicked pair turned to each other and laughed.

"That was some impromptu line of BS, Darren. My hat's off to you."

"I do have my gifts, Vic."

"Whatever you say, Darren, whatever you say."

In the clear for the moment, they walked up to the tree for a look. A real beaut, it appeared, about 30 meters high and a meter and a quarter wide. Darren, stepping forward, tenderly stroked the bark and then gave it a whiff.

"Damn shame, really, that we got to cut 'er down."

"Hey, let's just do it and get the hell outta here before that cop's coffee wears off."

And so they did the deed, Vic wincing at the racket. At last, with a crash, the tree fell. Eyeing the stump for ring configuration, Darren gasped in wonder.

"Man oh man, just take a good look at this curly-twirly grain, so rich and intricate it practically sends musical notes into the air."

Looking closer, he too saw the fabulous pattern.

"We hit pay dirt, Darren. Don't know how you did it. Must be some kind of fluke… Anyway, let's chop 'er up and make tracks, double time, before it gets dark."

So with that dreaded buzz saw whine, they cut it into several long chunks and loaded them into the truck. Without further ado, they headed back down the mountain, Darren driving. When he pulled into a roadside A&W, Vic only grinned. Next it was off down the highway, out valley ramparts onto a stretch of land near a now lit-up Langley. Here they pulled onto a frontage road and into a nook behind cedars. Early for their rendezvous, Vic tuned in JR FM while Darren stoked what he said was one fine Havana. As the smell of a cut-rate cigar wafted by, Vic glared his partner's way and cranked down his window.

As darkness deepened on that rain-soaked day, their contact pulled up. They popped out again, slickers on, holding flashlights. A shifty-looking guy named Len asked to take a look. So they opened the back of the truck. In triumph, Vic pointed out the fancy grain. Wonder showed on the buyer's face, which he quickly masked. But the boys had caught this risky shift and so concluded: no way to dicker us down, we gotcha but good.

"Now don't you deny it," Darren began, "we saw it in your eyes. You know damn well this tree is top of the line, so let's skip the Wall Mart routine and go straight to Berks. We want top dollar for this baby. Holler away all you want, we're gonna get it."

Assaying his marks for a moment, he sighed, ready to cut to the chase.

"Okay gents, it's a fair enough tree. Let's not waste any time here. I'll pay you 25 K; double my usual price for a tree of this type."

"Whoa now, hey there, ho there, hi there, you're as welcome as can be — but not without the price of admission."

Both buyer and partner here shoot Darren the look.

"Hey there, yourself, ya goof. I'm offering you top dollar. What were you smokin' in that cab, anyway?"

"Top dollar?" Darren shot back. "Look ah, Len, I can see that you really dig the slick little hustler routine, and, well, you wouldn't be too bad at it if you were dealing with a couple of drunken dumkoffs. But seein' as that appears to be your action plan here, I hope ya haven't ruled out other career options. I hear that health care aids don't do too bad these days. How're you at dumpin' bed pans?"

"Yeah right, ya frickin' smart-ass, and I hear that telephone call rooms pay cue balls like you minimum wage to annoy people at home," he fired right back.

"Okay, alright, looky here, Mr. Bean, to make a long story short, we know for a fact that a tree of this magnitude fetches 50 K. So don't even think about rippin' us off."

"Hello, earth to choppers, do you read me? Yeah, okay, the instrument people will pay that much, but as everyone knows the middleman takes a risk and thus takes his cut. So no more smart ass lines, okay? It's 25 K, take it or leave it. I got places to be, other deals to make. Don't waste any more of my valuable time."

Vic and Darren gave each other a look. Of course, they knew the middleman got a cut, but they hadn't thought it through. And so it sank in: The guy had a point and now that he mentioned it, 50%, while an ungodly steep commission, sounded about standard. So, with disgruntled shrugs they sealed the deal.

The last scene of their venture soon unfolded: two guys less than ecstatic whizzed into Langley neon as the night throbbed away, steady swish of wipers counterpoint to Paul Brant's fleshed out version of *Alberta Bound*. Vic almost laughed as Darren pulled into a Wendy's drive-through. Back on Fraser Highway, they too were homeward bound, though victory's song lacked oomph. Vic noted too the nonsense at the core of this transaction: haggling over a fallen tree with a would-be wheeler-dealer. 'Hard to believe a few logs have spawned a woodpecker mafia,' he thought with a sigh. And so, at half the hoped-for price, the door Vic longed to open jarred but slightly.

Chapter 5

Next morning, Vic awakened to the usual view with a twist. Through breaking storm clouds, Skytrain Bridge shone against a dark sky backdrop.

"Huh, looks like some kinna painting," he mumbled in wonder. Closing his eyes, he next replayed their adventure. Dumb, real dumb, he concluded. Yet in spite of it all, he smiled at the humor daubed scenes. Then too, while no major break from his past, this episode had in fact created expectations. Yeah, he'd inched up the stairs to that platform of departing trains, destination bound, wheels that had spun in the mud at last gaining traction. And while the results disappointed, they had cut a deal. The shadiness still bothered Vic, but he knew deep down that no such dubious scheme would be repeated. Still, that harvested tree had left him with its bounty, a prized gift of nature. More important, the light of ambition now shone on his nebulous dreams. Yeah, just once, Vic had crossed that plain of passing scenes to catch at least a glimpse of the land of ahs. Now he had to follow through before returning reason told him to play it safe, man, play it safe.

"Ha, yeah, money... Money's just pretty paper, colored tokens in a game. You roll your dice, scoot up the board, scoop it up here 'n there, the whole point being that you left Go and for better or worse must make the rounds to the game's objective, or player's destination. Aw crap, that word again," he frowned, deciding it was time for breakfast.

Vic worked hard all week, absorbed in tasks while he pondered recent events. Impressions ripened. With Friday night's performance done, this thought hit home: Somehow he had to make up the difference between last week's expected payoff and the actual score.

"Yeah," he spoke aloud, as insight hardened to goal, "got to up the ante here, go for that brass ring missed. Got to play the angles," he sighed, aware again of the silence that awaited him at home.

In that motionless space, he tuned in JR before bed. Then, he heard it: Vegas Days at Tulalip Casino in nearby Washington State – come one, come all, have a blast and win a pile, to boot. His arm pulled, tumblers rolled. Up came cherry cherry cherry then whoosh, clink clink clink, as out spilled the missing difference with a bonus, the cherry on top. Now Vic was no gambler, just playing the odd card game for friendly stakes. Still, he needed to find an outlet for his new longings. It wasn't the thought of winning cash but the symbolism that hooked him. Now he pictured in his mind risking his all in the hope of just once breaking more than even.

"That's it," he concluded, sitting up in bed with a start, "that's the nub of my dilemma. I've always been happy to break even, avoid loss, shore up the walls of my little fortress and not stride too boldly. Maybe carried through over time in a dedicated fashion, such an approach might yield life's fruit... but then again it lacks pizzazz and daring do, qualities that attract." Rising now inspired, he called Darren and shared his idea. Naturally, he caved in right away. The mere thought of flowing casino gold, to say nothing of Jose Cuervo, set his tongue into motion.

The scene: near dusk and only partly cloudy, two guys whizzed pell-mell down Highway 15 for the U.S. border. Passing through customs, they proceeded on I-5. Arriving at night, into another world they strode, a world of loud music, fast girls, words of advice, but precious few pearls of wisdom. But the latter's not the point here. You leave your brain at the door, switch to hormone drive, and cut loose till the sun comes up.

And so it began, gin fizz begetting another. The glitter, the noise and the laughs soon loosened Vic up. Each had brought 7 K. Vic reached for a mound of chips as Darren eyed a shapely serving girl. With a wink he grabbed a shot, loaded his gun and strode to the Blackjack table. Vic joined him as the game began, sharpie dealer losing some as agitated throngs now lusted for more. Ye ha! Vic won hand after hand before with a thud his new wad hit the floor.

And so it went for the next few hours, rock songs blasting away. The boys, now in the swing of things, began to bet more. It's cash flow high tide for a while. With trembling hands they paused for drinks while counting mounds of chips. But later, hubris led to a drubbing at the poker table. Fighting spirit ebbed. Casino lights became just like the burning Sahara sun. They wiped wet brows and looked for signs of water. As their camels pictured green they pictured lovely maidens serving wine – yet the sun just grew fiercer. At last at 1 they spotted palm trees and water, winning a few more hands at the Blackjack table. Tempted by this whetting to place larger bets, each lost a layer of hide, and how it stung. Three now, the crowd remained thick but not so our boys' wallets. Still, each had about three thousand in chips. Vic wanted to call it a night. Darren, at last overwhelmed by it all, dozed for a moment in a chair. But then, with a sudden whir of limbs, he woke up.

"Vic! I had a dream, I had this dream…"

Eyeing his friend, Vic thought he'd had enough to drink, and himself as well.

"Look bud, it's been fun 'n all, but the time has come for us to head out while we still have gas money."

"Hey, no, wait, Vic, hear me out. This is important. See, I had a dream, a dream with my departed uncle in it."

"Really time to go, Darren."

"Yeah, I had this dream," he continued undeterred, "and in this fantastical dream, my dear ole Uncle Jimmy, clear as a bell he says '14, 7, and then just plain red.' Ya know what that means, don't ya?"

"It means that last whiskey sour has soured your brain. Time's up."

"Oh man, Vic, don't you get it? It's just like what I read in the news one time. See, this woman in the States, she had a transcendent-like dream – her departed father told her the winning numbers for some state lotto or other. So she buys a ticket the next day and presto chango, whop de do, she wins man, she wins! It's a mystery of life, I tell ya."

"You're a mystery of life, Darren. Your cock 'n bull story sounds like something right out of a supermarket tabloid."

"Hey, the search for truth can take you there, man… but that's not where I read it."

"No matter what your damn source was, Darren, a dream's a dream and this is reality."

"Vic, now don't get mad at what I'm about to say, but your spine has done turned into Jell-O, right at the very moment destiny knocks at your door."

Having just heard his latest buzzword spoken, Vic paused, but then shook his head. "Not gonna fall for this," he muttered, feeling duty-bound to save Darren from himself. Still, once a notion lodged in the guy's brain, no amount of poking seemed to free it. Thus, undeterred, Darren headed for the roulette wheel. A small crowd fought for cash and laughs, groans, and rolling eyes where matters stood. Beautiful dreamer dug deep, plunked down his all on number 14. The crowd gasped, like he'd just grabbed an adder. The dealer eyed him hard, then cracked a grin. 'Oh yeah,' he thought with glee, 'another drunken sheep to fleece, can't wait to hear 'em bleat.'

"Darren, look," Vic persisted, "you've flipped, okay? Just grab those chips like lightning before this guy spins and takes you through the car wash."

"I'm stickin' to my guns, Vic."

Quite the scene unfolded. The dealer eyed his mark and Darren likewise. Our hero heard a tickled laugh from the drink-bearing lass by his side, cleavage abundant. Boy oh boy, no stopping him now. So he turned to the lady and twitched his brows while saying he's hotter than hot. The dealer smirked as he pictured this Romeo nerd trip on his laces. 'Hard to feel pity for a jerk like him,' he thought while twirling the wheel. All eyes watched as colors spun, ball bouncing around. When the pinging stopped, that tiny orb of destiny nestled under 14. "Whoa!" the crowd gasped as one. The lady by Darren's side lightly stroked his shoulder.

"Easy, honey," he said, "or I'll lose my cool." Watching on, Vic's eyes rounded in wonder as grabbing a shot from a tray he downed it fast.

"Darren!" Vic said, "just what the hell's going on here? How'd you do that?"

"Hey, get on the stick and get with it, Vic. It's just like I said. You think I'm all bluff 'n bluster, don't ya? Well, let this be a lesson to ya, man. Sometimes ya just gotta shut off the ole brain and go with your gut."

Darren grabbed another drink as the crowd nestled closer. Lady Luck breathed warmly on his neck, "Take me, I'm yours," her soft whisper. Ha, all think, this is more like it, the house getting drubbed for a change. Through their new champion, losers and small-time winners alike sought righteous vengeance. Stand-off now tense as a packed Skytrain, the dealer wiped his brow, trepidation flowing out with his sweat. 'No way that grinning goof wows Jennifer, not on my shift,' he thought with a snarl. Darren scowled right back, eyes ablaze. 'Little does he know I know kung-fu,' he thought in silence.

"Let 'er ride. Number 7," he spat out hot while scooting over his chips. The crowd ate it up, way better than reality TV. Admiring eyes roved him over. The guy has balls of brass, all concluded. Lady Luck now tenderly traced her name on Darren's back.

"How many kids do ya want?" he responded, voice cracking a bit.

Vic had one of those moments when time stood still. Okay, so he's drunk and upset from his recent loss and maybe this muddled his wits. Still, in a bubble of inner silence, he weighed the moment on a scale poised just so.

'Is this the essence of life,' he wondered, 'moments of monumental decision with the rest mere icing on the cake you win? Or do such risky shifts amount to no more than a cakewalk mirage that you lose your shirt in?'

Unsure, he hesitated. But then, imagination plunked him down in Skytrain Station, awaiting a train. Does destiny expect him to remain bench-bound, twiddling his thumbs?

"No way, no how!" he shouted out loud. So, steeling nerves with one more shot, he plunked down all his chips on number 7, oohs and ahs filling the air. Delighted witnesses now getting a double dose of daring-do drama.

The dealer, taken aback at first, grabbed a pair of dice from a nearby table. Rotating them to snake eyes, he pointed them at his target and flicked out his tongue. In truth, Vic gulped while Darren mocked by putting two spread fingers in front of his mouth as if to say, "White man speaks with forked tongue." The dealer's head recoiled an inch before righting.

'Hope nobody saw that,' he thought, as he grinned a fake grin. 'But no,' he added, 'no need to sweat bullets now, this guy's dead meat. Odds work in the grand scheme of things to level down fools, and no amount of bluster sways her, ever.'

He spun the wheel. Imagine his pain when the ball stopped under number 7. The crowd went wild, aware now that a dream played out before their eyes. Darren, unfazed, scooted his mound of chips onto just plain red, the easiest shot of them all, Vic doing the same.

The dealer's brow beaded up: this was no dumb luck he's up against but some slippery contravention of laws writ large in every rock, tree, bird, and man – laws that state what can be in this visible world. The crowd too sensed otherworldly intervention. Darren read their signal clear and now rode a wave of emotion. There he stood, ten toes hanging off the edge of his surfboard, as poised on a mound of curling sea with upraised arms he yelled out, "Frickin' amazing!"

Not one person present batted an eye: all knew this his moment. A hush descended as all held their breaths while the dealer hoped for a riptide. How he'd love to thump this knobby-kneed surfer of fate who dared to ride its brink just a moment too long. He spun the wheel. The bouncing ball pinged here and there, at last falling square onto black. Like a wind squelched, all present gasped out "Aww…" and a lifeguard attended the wiped-out surfer. As a mystical ambulance carried him off, Lady Luck left for another club, longing to please, to a point.

The crowd began to drift off, but with the knowledge they'd witnessed one rare event. A few patted the boys on the back. Others said tough break, but you guys have spirit, all right. Darren stood there yet, wet and disbelieving in his wipeout. Vic's teeth ground away as he absorbed this cruel blow. Only the dealer now smiled, sweat on brow replaced with shining oil, the anointing of champions. Downing one more shot, Vic mused sadly that snake eyes in the end had stared him down.

Chapter 6

Vic woke up the next morning in a motel room, eyes red and head thumping. Showering, he skipped the shave. They tossed a few things into the car and drove to a nearby Denny's. Sitting by a window, Vic scanned the scene. Ah, one stroke of luck: only scattered clouds after night rain. Cars stopped at a red light. Face upturned, one guy drummed the wheel with glee as the autumn sun equaled cherry cherry cherry. Slurping coffee, the sun also rose for beleaguered Vic. Not so for Darren, who, after one bite, tossed burned toast onto his plate. But then his scowl melted away as he cracked a grin.

"What you smiling about?"

"Oh, nothing really, just remembered something."

"Yeah? And just what might that be?"

"My Uncle Jimmy – he had a twisty-turny sense of humor. And see, he liked to joke about always ending up in the red…"

Hearing this, Vic plunked down his knife and fork and eyed his friend square on. After a pause, it hit him too as they both laughed out loud.

"Hey, you gotta admit, Vic, that was one night to remember. How often in life do you risk your all on one wild hunch? See, now that I'm sober it occurs to me the whole dream thing could've been a tequila-induced sleight of hand trick and nothing more."

Vic gave this some thought. Darren could well be right, but then again, even two major hits out of three defied the odds.

"Normally I'd agree with you, Darren, but ah, this little episode has thrown normality out the window. So now I say, who knows? Whatever the case, I expect we'll carry the marks of this whipping for life, for better or worse, although strangely enough I now incline towards the former."

Silence fell for a moment. Vic again stirred.

"Ya know, I was really drunk last night and not so familiar with the game. How much did we lose, anyway?"

Darren winced hard. Hand going to his brow, he looked down.

"Let's just say more than loose change," he replied, looking up again.

"Oh yeah, way more."

"It was a price hike, alright, but what a view," Darren grinned with one trickling tear.

"So who's gonna leave the tip? It's that bad for me."

"I got this one, Vic."

Scooting over the border mostly quiet, implications only now seeped in. Home, Vic lied down and eyed the last of his maple jackpot. "Well, it wasn't a total loss. Still have a whittled-down wad left," he half-smiled. This tiny glow faded out as he thought of the lesson involved. Yeah, there had to be a lesson at that price. Might it be that his ill-gotten maple tree gains had demanded a fiery comeuppance? If so, had it burned him clean through or did it reveal a nugget of truth? Then, eyes inevitably turned again to Skytrain Bridge. "Yeah," he groaned, "I'd pictured that bridge last night, thought my ride had arrived, yet here I lie, stranded in a world that somehow looks a touch shabbier than before. Might there be two lessons here? It's best to stick to honesty being the first? Maple tree rustling, of all things... But then again, that casino scene... Yeah, once the ball is rolling, maybe it's best to throw your all into the venture, let what's pent up inside gush up to the surface. Then, win or lose, at least you can say you died trying – end with a bang, not a whimper. Ha, that bridge, yeah, that bridge..." Vic now realized he too had a bridge to cross. He didn't know quite where it pointed, but he knew he must cross it.

All week at work he thought of this as everyday scenes appeared different, like he hovered in the rafters looking down. Man and machine did a two-step dance as the river flowed on. Yet by and by the music dimmed and though ceasing not to please, lacked fulsome body. Then, late Friday night with a rip to his chest Vic woke up hard. "Some damn dream," he mumbled, hands shaking, blood still flowing from a psychic wound. He lit up a smoke, its tiny ember quenching the night ever so slightly. Pfff... A cloud stalled in midair. Vic got up to ventilate his place. Window cracked, smoke flowed into the clear night sky as Vic watched. "Well whatta ya know," he said aloud, "stars out for a change, real bright, pretty. Ha, yeah, gems in a vault… Ah, and over there, one so bright and twinkling... How worthwhile is it to consider a star way up high? Maybe quite a bit. Funny, wouldn't have seen it either, but for a few nasty blows…"

That weekend Vic did his thing at the pub. And, although he sang his favorites, no tune seemed a grabber then. After some applause, he sat in a corner sipping a beer, not his usual style. A little concerned, Keith joined him.

"So… That windfall fiasco's got you down, eh?"

Vic managed a smile.

"Aw no, Keith, I got over that pretty fast. And ya know, Darren and me, we can actually see the humor in it all – some wild ride, for sure."

"Yeah, couple of drunk drivers," Keith chuckled. "So ah, you okay money-wise?"

"Oh hey," he answered embarrassed, "don't even think about it, Keith. I'm doing okay and my leg's not hurting so bad these days."

"Huh. Guess in your case the rain might help."

Smiling, Vic took another gulp of his beer, plunked it down straight-faced.

"Yeah, I know, I know," Keith continued, "you must miss Lisa like your own breath. Wish I could help you out there, but ah, with a pending divorce and the little lady after a strip of my hide, I'm really not the guy to give you advice in the romance department."

Vic paused. Sure, he's hurting, but pain it seemed made the rounds, didn't pick on one guy. So consoling his friend in his own grief, that upward ascent began.

"You know, Keith, you've done okay for yourself. You've made it, bud. I mean, you own this plot of land, park and pub, to boot. And our city grows like a weed. A few years down the line and this property will shoot way up in value."

Keith paused to digest this.

"Yeah, that's true enough, Vic. I've done okay for myself and ah, now own a few other properties, too. I have no complaints besides the love nest business. But you know, sometimes you just have to go with the flow, know what I mean?"

"Yeah, go with the flow. These days though I wonder where said flow might take me. Should I just let it, or maybe start pumping away on the oars?"

"Only you can answer that question, Vic."

"Yeah, guess so. But I mean, a man's got to have goals, doesn't he? Then, when assets accumulate, well, he knows he's on his way, not going to sit it out, going to go places."

Keith took a drink and shifted about, maybe taking inner inventory.

"Tangible assets, yeah, you're right, keeps gas in the tank and things moving, but there's other things too, not quite so obvious."

"Oh yeah? Like what?"

"Can't quite put it into my own words, Vic, so let me use an example. And hey, look, I'm no philosopher, only read the occasional book, but ah, little lessons are everywhere around us, even in an old movie I watched years ago."

"So what's the story?"

"I really couldn't tell you. Can't even recall the title or the stars, ah, but Jimmy Stewart sticks out. Anyway, it was a late night movie, watched it ages ago. Just one particular scene stuck in my mind."

"Let's hear it."

"Okay. Businessman gets on a plane in, um, let's say Chicago, bound for LA. So he strikes up a conversation with a woman seated beside him. They talk about life in general but then the guy looks out the window, smiles, and clams up for a moment. The woman asks if he's okay. He says he's fine, but as they fly over the Rockies it reminds him of his childhood dream. Curious, she asks him about it. 'Well,' he says, 'it's like this: I always wanted to buy a ranch in Montana, you know, wide open spaces, peace and solitude with those you love. So when I retire, I'm going to buy that ranch, just like I always dreamed.'"

The woman smiles, shares some of her own treasures. Getting late, they both fall asleep. But late that night the plane loses an engine. The fire terrifies all onboard. The pilot struggles for control of the plane. It looks bad, like they're about to crash and burn in the mountains. By some miracle, they make an emergency landing and all survive. You can imagine the feeling. So before the man and the woman part, she takes him by the hand and says, "Buy that ranch. Don't wait another day." So he follows her advice and buys the ranch of his dreams, moves out there, and ah, that's about where my memory of it all fades out."

Vic worked on these images in silence before Keith continued.

"Funny how a thing like that can stick with you, old movie scene. But in most stories there're lessons for us or we wouldn't bother with them. Any story can become a part of our own, at least in part. Yeah, and don't we all live like we've got an endless supply of tomorrows… Sometimes it takes tragedy to wake us up. So, the question here, Vic, is what's your ranch? What's your big dream?"

"Now that you mention it, Keith, I'm not really sure. I mean, I've thought about it but never reached any hard and fast conclusions. Ha, maybe I've been playing it by ear all these years. Just what is the big picture here and how do I fit in? And hey, I'm no kid anymore, should be able to answer that one right off. Lately I've been working on the nuts and bolts—pay the bills angle—but as for the rest, I couldn't really tell you."

"Then that's your homework, Vic. Write an essay on what floats your boat."

"Yeah, what floats my boat…"

That night in bed, Vic's mind churned away. His ranch, what might that be? In Sarnia it had been Alberta, wide open spaces made famous in numerous tunes. It had been an easy dream to love at a shimmering distance, pie in the sky on the prairies. Had that vision faded as he approached, like a mirage on the desert? Well, yes and no. On the one hand, he had in fact embraced that abstract love in the concrete, so much so that it still seeps through his mind in dreams. "Yeah, that love is real enough," he concluded. And he'd had a tangible goal there too, not unlike the one in Keith's film story. But maybe that goal would have always been out of his reach, with him just one working stiff. Even so, it had given him something to shoot for.

Then he'd met Lisa and she became his dream come true, just like in romantic ballads when a guy says he can't live without his gal. "Yeah," he thought, "those songs are beautiful to listen to, and true, too. I mean, we can't live like islands in isolation… Islands, yeah, Gordon Lightfoot… 'Is-land goodbye, is-land goodbye, we've been too longgg together, my is-land and I…' Mmm, love that song, but anyway, if I say to Lisa, darlin', you're my all in all; I live and breathe for you alone. If you walk out on me, I'm sushi. If I say that, maybe I put a burden on her, maybe it makes her feel like a prize to be won instead of her own person and that I can't stand on my own two feet, be strong, lead her on, instead of saying you're my direction… So where do I begin, where does she end? I mean, we can share each other but maybe love can smother, like watering a prized plant too much. I wonder, just don't know…"

And so it goes as day followed day, rain followed sun, sun headed south while at the nearby delta geese took shelter. Now, late November can be gray and bleak, like the day Vic took a walk on Fraser Beach. The layback log shined wet; he plunked down anyway. The scene looked the same as in summer only black and white. He recalled this or that tidbit of conversation with Lisa and the day he wrote *Wet on Red*. Then, out of nowhere, a bolt of white-hot light turned clouds transparent. He headed back home, got pen and paper, and furiously started to write his heart's desire. He wrote it all down in the heat of it all, but the fine tuning proved no easy task. For three weeks after work he labored till late, bringing his brainchild to its fullest perfection.

Finally, at his Saturday night singfest, for his last song Vic performed *I Left 'Cause I Love You*. Well, he started off slow, circled the song, and finding it poured out his heart. Done, an animated crowd applauded in earnest. With high emotion, Darren asked Vic who wrote that curly-twirly piece of music. When he told them all he wrote it, a round of drinks followed, back-slaps and way-to-goes tossed in for good measure.

The ice was broken. Out of freezing water a plump fish plopped right up. Later that week, starving fisherman Vic recalled that his beloved JR FM would soon hold an amateur country-western song contest. A small cash prize involved, the true prize was a chance to sing country for real. So using his maple money, he hired professional backup and cut a CD, even as he worked on two new songs.

The night before the winner was picked Vic tossed and turned. Waking up at 4 a.m., he lit a cigarette, tension and desire exhaled with the smoke. Now, he knew that Lisa often listened to good country music. Likely enough she'd hear the winning song. Then too, they'd play it off and on throughout the week.

At 9 a.m. next morning, with Vic hunched over fried eggs, the winning song was played on his radio. Choking back yolk and emotion, his flatware clanged to the floor. Gulping hard, he washed down the yolk, a brand new world mixing in, with a gulp of black coffee. Looking out the window next, Vic saw a SkyTrain float by. "Yeah," he thought, while slowly absorbing the moment, "I've finally left the station, homeward bound... And thank God for that."